HE'LL BE WAITING

Liz Alterman

HE'LL
BE
WAITING

Between the Lines
PUBLISHING
"An Indie for Indies"

Copyright © 2021 Liz Alterman

Cover Design by Suzanne Johnson
Author image by Gracemarie Photography

Willow River Press
Between the Lines Publishing
410 Caribou Trail
Lutsen, MN 55612
btwnthelines.com

First Published: April 2021

Willow River Press is an imprint of Between the Lines Publishing. The Liminal Books name and logo are trademarks of Between the Lines Publishing.

ISBN: 978-1-950502-38-7 (paperback)
Printed in the United States

For Rich, Sam, Ben, Charlie, and Jag, of course

The Secrets We Keep From Ourselves

December 18

I can handle the broken bones, the bruises, the bald patches—all of it. But there's one thing that's bothering me more than absolutely everything else combined: I can't remember the last time I saw James.

We'd had plans for the night I ended up here, in this hospital bed, in a trauma center, miles from my home in the middle of a snowstorm. Big plans. That was two days ago.

I woke up this afternoon feeling as if I'd been trampled by circus elephants, with no idea where I was and no memory of seeing him. No clue what happened on the night I'd been looking forward to for nearly four months.

It's crazy. And terrifying.

At first, I hoped I was trapped in one of those dreams where you try your hardest to wake up by telling yourself you're still asleep and everything is fine. Everything seemed so bizarre and unfamiliar. I was sure I'd roll over in my bed, James beside me, as I'd planned,

1

plastic glow-in-the-dark stars arranged in madcap constellations on my ceiling. I tried to speak, scream, and jolt myself awake, but I could only gasp.

The moment I lifted my right arm— the one not in a cast—to touch my head, because, honestly, that hurt the absolute worst, Mom shrieked, "Tess, don't!" and rushed over. When she lowered my hand back down to the bed, I felt it, and I had a terrible thought: *I'm not dreaming. This is real.*

I turned from her and toward the window. It was dark outside. I caught a glimpse of myself in the reflection and shut my eyes.

Bandages cover most of my head. I look like a last-minute Halloween zombie costume. Too bad that holiday's long over. It's the week before Christmas and, at seventeen, I'm too old to trick-or-treat anyway. Still, I can't help feeling like I'm starring in my own personal horror show.

When I first opened my eyes, I saw Mom and Dad pacing opposite sides of the hospital bed, a weird, worried march that I assumed was somehow part of my nightmare.

"What is this? What's happening?" I blinked a dozen times as if that would change the scenery.

"Oh, Tess! Thank God you're awake," Mom said after making sure I didn't mess with my bandages. "It's all going to be okay, honey. We're right here."

She squeezed my right hand in hers. I had the oddest reaction. Complete revulsion. If forming each sentence didn't feel as impossible as suddenly speaking fluent

Mandarin, I'd have said, "Leave me alone." Where did that come from?

I tried to move my left leg. Bundled in a giant white plaster cast, it matched my left arm. Even something as simple as attempting to wiggle my toes sent sharp needles shooting through my body.

"You're in the hospital, Tess." She paused and turned toward Dad as if for guidance or confirmation that she should keep talking. He looked at me, his eyes wet and red-rimmed as a basset hound's. Mom kept staring at him as if willing him to speak. He didn't.

"There's been an accident… a bad accident," she said. Deep lines formed a tiny number eleven, creasing the spot between her eyes. "You don't remember?"

I shook my head, causing a throbbing, stabbing pain between my ears.

"What accident? What happened to me?" Panic rose in my chest. I wanted to scream, but my words came out like a whimper as I grew more anxious by the moment.

Dad's eyes finally met Mom's, and I saw a flash of anger in them before he turned back to me.

"We're still piecing it together," he said in the tone he uses when he tries not to lose his patience. After a hint of a sad, lips-together smile, he added, "The main thing is, Tess, in time, you're going to be all right."

"Piecing what together? What happened?" Why were they making me repeat myself when I was already so weak and exhausted from searching my mind for memories, images of what could've landed me here like

Humpty Dumpty after the fall. "Where's James? Is he here, too? What's going on? Just tell me!"

With each passing second, I felt myself spiraling downward, morphing into a madwoman, a feral cat. If I had the strength, I'd try to make a run for it but with a broken leg, how far could I get?

"Ah, I thought I heard some chatting going on in here."

A woman appeared in the doorway wearing a crisp blouse as white as her hair and a red pleated skirt. I don't know how long she'd been standing there. Gold bangle bracelets jingled on each wrist. Their gentle *clink clink clink* grew louder as she walked toward me.

"I'm Lydia, the psychologist assigned to your case." She extended her hand—*clink clink clink*.

I have a case? I stared at her, wishing she'd explain everything without me having to ask.

Again, Mom looked at Dad. She opened and closed her mouth.

"What am I doing here?" I asked, wanting to believe that this woman, a total stranger, might hold the key that would unlock my memory simply because she wore a hospital badge and carried an official-looking folder.

"Well, Tess… May I call you Tess?" She smiled, the corners of her eyes crinkling like her skirt pleats.

I nodded, and the throbbing returned.

"You've suffered an event that's left you with some significant fractures and, from what I just overheard and from what your doctors suspect, you've most likely sustained a traumatic brain injury as well," she continued. "Do you know what that is?"

She stared at me, waiting for my response, her eyes as turquoise as the Caribbean. I pictured my friends and classmates, their vacation photos peppering my Instagram feed. Shots of them leaping into the sea, huge smiles, arms, and legs flung far out like starfish. James' eyes are a much darker blue. Almost navy. Like the ocean, bottomless, with a strong current that pulls you in deeper until you're swimming inside them and never want to be anywhere else.

I thought about James' face. The dimple in his chin. Those eyes, the ones I picture when I can't fall asleep. The left has a tiny black freckle near the very bottom of the blue outer ring. I could hear his voice, the way he smiles and says, "That's funny," but doesn't actually laugh at a joke. I wondered where he was, what he was doing. This has become my default pastime since he left for college. Lost in thought, I didn't realize Lydia was still expecting an answer.

"Tess? Do you know what a traumatic brain injury is?" she repeated. "Can you recall what happened to you?"

No, and no. I shook my head gently to avoid the throbbing.

"Well, sometimes when a situation is particularly jarring or painful, our mind plays a little trick on us by withholding information. It's sort of like a secret your brain decides to keep, to hold back, because it thinks you're not ready to recall it. I believe that's what you may be experiencing."

How is that possible? How could I lose or block out a whole chunk of time? I've been thinking about her words, trying to force them to make sense, for the past few minutes—minutes that crawl by like hours—while she and Mom and Dad stare at me with what? Pity? Concern? Fear? I scroll through the things I can remember, calling up scenes like I'm flicking past photos on my phone's camera roll. Images from both the distant and recent past are still there—birthdays, crabbing with my grandfather during summer vacations, the ending of *The Marvelous Mrs. Maisel*. I know we have a velvety black cat named Daffy, who has a love-hate relationship with our Roomba. All of that's stored as it's always been. It's the events of a single night that I need to get back. That, and I want to know where James is. Did he get home from school okay? Why isn't he here with me?

Lydia—is that her name?—looks at Mom and Dad, then back to me, offering us all another forced smile.

"I know at the moment it's all very frightening, Tess. You've suffered a shock. But I'm sure many, if not all, of your memories will return to you in time when your mind and body are ready. We're going to work together—all of us—to make sense of this."

She places her hand on my good arm, *clink clink clink,* and motions for Mom and Dad to step out into the hallway with her.

"Be right back," Mom says. Her hand shakes as she brings it to her mouth to blow me a kiss.

I watch them from my bed. Heads bent toward one another, necks craning, whispering. What were they saying? Something about me, obviously. I hear my name murmured. What are they keeping from me? And what are the secrets I'm hiding from myself?

"We're going to work together…" That's what Lydia said.

That sounds nice in theory, but the overwhelming feeling I can't seem to shake is that, from here on out, I'm on my own.

Incommunicado

The squiggly black lines in the ceiling tiles begin moving as the cocktail of medication they're giving me kicks in. It's pretty crazy that throughout your entire childhood people tell you not to do drugs, then you break a bunch of bones, and they stuff you full of Oxy like you're a pharmaceutical company's piñata.

Every time I open my eyes now someone is standing there with a small paper cup full of pills asking me to rate my pain on a scale of one to ten. Um, look at me. It's a solid one hundred and eleven, but I only feel it in the lull between when one medication wears off and the next starts swimming through my bloodstream. I'm also flying high on the liquid that slowly *drip-drip-drips* into me through the IV, which I'm told I keep trying to pull out while I sleep. The skin around where it enters my vein looks like a bad tie-dyed t-shirt, an ugly swirl of blue, purple, and yellow. Who knew you could bruise so fast? Normally, this would bother me. I'm squeamish. Just add it to my pile of hideous injuries.

I scan the tiny room for my phone, for the case I'd made, a collage of James and me licking ice cream cones, a selfie of my best friend Izzy and me attempting to kayak, and Daffy, of course, standing defiantly on the keyboard of my laptop.

Mom sits in a recliner at the edge of my bed, hunched over, her face hidden by her hands. The folding chair is empty.

"Where's Dad? Where's my phone?"

When Mom hears my voice, her head whips up as if I've startled her, as if she's forgotten I'm there. She's been like this—distracted, in her own world—a lot over these last few months, pretty much ever since her friend and colleague Mr. Miller died in a freak accident not far from our house.

She rushes over to feel my forehead, first with her fingertips, then with the back of her hand, a move I remember from my childhood each time she'd worry I'd brought home a stomach bug from school.

"I'm sorry, Tess. You're not allowed to look at screens because of your concussion," she says. She's back from her meeting with Lydia. I want to ask what they talked about, but I'm too tired, and I don't know if I can handle any more bad news. "Give your brain a chance to heal."

"I'm totally fine," I lie. Everything aches and my head feels as if someone's hammering at my temples from inside. I run my tongue along my teeth to make sure they're all still there. They are. Thank God. Imagine three years of orthodontia appointments and all that pain for nothing. Izzy got a front tooth knocked out last spring playing lacrosse, and FYI, it's not a good look. She removes it sometimes to freak people out. She's crazy like that.

But this being without a phone, well, that's a whole other level of discomfort. It's like I've lost a limb. That's a messed-up thing to say, but my life is in there. I don't see how a phone could do any more damage. Yes, my body is banged up, and there's a black hole hanging out in my memory bank, but other than that, my mind is still there. At least I think it is. Plus, I'm positive a photo, a text, maybe a single Instagram story would spark something and bring me the smallest bit of clarity about Saturday night.

"Please. I need it. I won't look at the screens. I want to call James and see when he can visit."

Even if something happened with his ride home from Chicago and he got in late or missed our date completely. I'm sure he's visited me here in this ugly, too-bright room that looks like the inside of a refrigerator—where the beeping monitors and buzzing machines create their own never-ending soundtrack, a symphony for the sick. Yet, as hard as I try, I can't play any of it back in my mind, can't picture James standing in this room, can't recall him holding my hand, or brushing the hair away from my face the way he always does.

It's brutally unfair. All the things I wish I could forget—the failed math tests, the days picked last in gym, the way Izzy looked right past me Friday at school. They're all still there.

"Oh, honey, you don't need visitors. You need rest." Mom frowns.

If it weren't for all these drugs making me feel like I'm trying to communicate while trapped inside something sticky and gauzy as cotton candy, I'd have screamed, "James isn't some random 'visitor,' he's my boyfriend!"

Though it's been almost a year, I still get this weird little electric shock-like feeling saying it. Boyfriend. It's a mix of excitement and embarrassment. Like embarrassment over how excited I am to actually have a boyfriend, and that's followed by straight up mortification because there's something so inherently cheesy about saying "my boyfriend" aloud. But then there's the exhilaration again because James is the best. The G.O.A.T (Greatest of All-Time), as Izzy likes to say. Every superlative, he's it. That's why I expect him to rush in at any moment with a caramel macchiato (my favorite), and tell me a great story, filled with gestures and spot-on voice imitations.

James can talk about current affairs or explain poetry without sounding like some try-hard know-it-all. He taught me to use chopsticks and convinced me that black-and-white movies weren't totally lame. Something as basic as standing beside him fills me with pure joy, like when you find money in the pocket of your jeans or you hear your favorite song on the car radio, and suddenly your whole day feels better, brighter. The thought of seeing him, being with him for the holidays, spending every day of his three-week break together; it's the only thing that's gotten me through the past few months of sheer college application hell and the stress of dealing with Mom and Dad.

And I know it makes me seem demanding and selfish and sort of pathetic to wish he would drop everything and sit by my bedside when he's only just gotten home from school, and it's days before Christmas. But, yeah, that's what I want—more than anything.

I don't even care what I look like. No one will give me a mirror until the swelling and the bruising go down, but my reflection in the window is enough to let me know my selfie days are over.

"Oh, honey, your hair!" Mom groaned earlier as a nurse did her best to gently prop me up, revealing where my head had been shaved, before putting the icy cold stethoscope through the opening in the back of my mint chocolate chip-colored hospital gown.

"Don't worry, it'll grow back. Well, not the part where the staples are, but the rest of it," the nurse tried to assure us. "Big breath in, big breath out."

Mom stood over me, hand covering her mouth, the way she looked that time she spotted a mouse in the pantry.

"I've always adored your hair," she said sadly.

That was ironic. Hers had been exactly like mine when she was a teenager. Reddish-brown. The color of rust, I guess you could say. Wavy and long. When she was in her twenties, she cut it to shorter—then to her shoulder, now to a chin-length bob—and dyed it blonde.

What I'm getting at is this: She had it—the exact same hair. If she adored it that much, why did she change it? Chalk it up to the mysteries of Mom, which, over the past few months, have become too many to count.

Normally, I would never want James to see me like this. I'd be too embarrassed that I haven't showered. My

12

teeth feel coated in slime, my tongue thick as if covered in moss from lack of use. I think of Izzy.

"I have the breath of a billy goat," she loves to say after eating a bag of Cool Ranch Doritos or a half-dozen garlic knots.

I know what she means. But I don't care. At all. I suppose when you're lonely and desperate vanity takes a backseat.

I want to ask Mom what she and Lydia talked about in the hallway. Like, why do I need a psychologist? When can I go home? Where's Dad? And, most importantly, why isn't James here?

I can see all the words floating in a field out in front of me. I need to collect them quickly, like a kid filling an Easter basket. There's so much I want to say, but when I open my mouth, the medication wraps me a thick fog, and my thoughts disappear in the mist.

James

"Hey, sleepyhead!"

James strokes the side of my face with his fingers lightly before leaning in to kiss me. A gentle kiss that barely brushes my lips, like I'm breakable.

I knew he'd come.

"Hey," I repeat.

My heart cartwheels inside my chest and a sleeve of goosebumps covers my exposed arm. I feel tingly, alive, for the first time in days. I pull him toward me and bury my face in his neck. I don't care that I look like a monster and probably smell like a dozen old people; he's here. I could cry with relief. He's wearing the navy pea coat I got him for Christmas, but the disappointing thing is, I don't remember giving it to him. Did he love it? Did I tell him I hoped it would keep him warm through the rest of the freezing Chicago winter because I couldn't be there to do it since I'm stuck eight hundred miles away in New Jersey?

I'd saved up my babysitting money, and Izzy's sister, Becca, who works part-time at the Gap, used her discount to get it for me. It was expensive, but totally worth it. He looks amazing in it, like I knew he would.

I try to inhale the clean, crisp scent of him, store it up so I can savor it after he's gone. James usually smells like Irish Spring soap with a hint of vanilla, but this time all I'm getting is the chill of winter, as if the snow followed him in and wove itself deep inside the fibers of his coat.

Looking over his shoulder, I see it's dark outside. Light snowflakes continue to fall. Is it night? I'm thrilled to be alone with James, but where is everyone else? The rest of the floor seems to be asleep. The lights in the hall are dim. No nurses barge in. The beeps and buzzing seem softer, hushed.

"I've missed you so much." Before I can stop myself, I'm crying.

"I've missed you, too," he whispers in my ear.

I pull back to stare at him and drink in the face I've been missing for months. His eyes still totally melt me, but they're less sparkly than usual. Purple half-moons hang beneath them. He looks exhausted. The past two weeks, he's been so busy with finals, papers, wrapping up work at his internship, we've barely spoken. We'd been texting or FaceTiming right before bed. At least, bedtime for me. He was forced to pull a few all-nighters, he'd said, warning me not to be scared if he looked like Jack Nicholson in *The Shining* by the time he made it home.

"It's so good to see you. You're a sight for sore eyes—literally." I hesitate because I always have to stop to think if I'm using "literally" right when I talk to him. Given the state of me and my sore, sore everything, it works.

He smiles, and I want to ask him a thousand questions: Where he's been? Does he know what happened to me? When can I go home? But I'm so tired and happy to have him beside me—finally—nothing else matters.

"I'm sorry I've messed up all our plans," I say as he dabs my salty tears with a tissue before they burn my scraped and scabby cheeks.

We were supposed to take Emmett, James' brother, ice skating on the pond behind their condo. Emmett likes to go in the dark, after dinner, always the same routine. James sets up a Bluetooth speaker and creates a playlist of whatever songs Emmett is into at the moment. We make cool and crazy shadows in the moonlight as we fly around the ice. Free. Like we're the only people on the planet.

James and I had plans to go to New York City, maybe check out the tree at Rockefeller Center, walk the High Line, though we knew we'd freeze from the wind blowing off the Hudson River. We wanted to visit a bookstore near Union Square, get dim sum in Chinatown. No chance of that, now. Though honestly, I didn't really care what we did. I'd be happy to sit in a closet with James. That would be better than being stuck to a hospital bed with broken limbs and a messed-up memory.

"I've ruined everything." I rest my head on his shoulder.

"Shh... Don't, Tess. Save your strength," he says. "Look what I brought you."

He pulls the meal tray toward me. Sunflowers fill a mason jar like a bouquet of smiling faces.

"My favorite!"

"I know," he says. "And, check it out. This, too."

He hands me a warm cappuccino. The scent alone is magical. I take a long sip, hoping a hit of caffeine will help me think more clearly or at least stay awake for longer than ten minutes at a time.

"I had to smuggle it in." He raises his eyebrows, mocking himself. James is a total rule follower, so this is a big deal.

"Thank you!" I can't stop smiling even as my cheeks ache.

"I'm so sorry, Tess, but I have to go—"

"No!" I whine. "You just got here, and I haven't seen you in so long."

"Desperation is more unattractive than spinach in the teeth," Izzy always reminds me. "It's been scientifically proven."

I don't care. I'm lonely and scared. And I haven't seen James since he left for college in late August.

"Can you come back tomorrow? Can you stay all day? I love you," I ramble, whisper-pleading. I'm usually not this needy, but I can't seem to stop myself.

"I was actually here for a while, but you were asleep, and I didn't want to wake you. I'll be back. I promise."

He kisses me goodbye so softly I can barely feel it and gets up to leave. Standing in the doorway, he waves to me. Backlit from the monitors' glow at the nurses' station, he looks taller than I remember. Watching him walk out is by far the worst pain I've felt so far.

Be Still

December 19

"You gave us quite a scare last night, young lady!"

One of the many nurses who stops in to check on me and feed me more pills says this as she shoves a thermometer in my mouth. Phyllis. I read her name on the ID badge dangling from a lanyard that lands on my stomach as she adjusts my pillows.

"Spiked a fever. Saying all sorts of crazy things. 'Come back!' 'Come back!'" She gestures wildly with her hands and rolls her eyes.

I'm too groggy to be annoyed by her impersonation of me. It must be morning. But where is everyone? Her gadget beeps, and she checks my temperature. 99.2 degrees Fahrenheit.

"But *now* look at you! Right as rain. Still, we're going to keep a closer eye on you today," she says.

"Great," I think, "that's exactly what I want. More poking and prodding from strangers."

The room is chilly and smells like medicine. A white-haired woman stands in the doorway. She looks familiar.

Phyllis is about to walk out when I call, "Wait! Where are my flowers?"

"Sorry, darlin'. No flowers allowed in the ICU." She turns on the chunky rubber bottoms of her white work shoes and disappears down the hall. Being a nurse seems hard enough, why make it worse by having to do it in super-ugly footwear?

"Hi Tess." It's the white-haired woman. Sensing my confusion, she steps closer. *Clink clink clink.* "I'm Lydia. Your psychologist? We met yesterday."

"Right," I say. "I remember." I do. Sort of. It's blurry.

"How are you feeling today?" She eyes me cautiously.

"About the same." I was doing a lot better when James was here, but after he left, I started feeling sad and scared. I don't tell her this because it makes me sound weak. And a bit like a sap, which I am when it comes to James—at least that's what Izzy tells me.

"I was hoping you and I could chat for a bit. I have some ideas that I think may be helpful." Lydia's voice is kind yet bossy.

Like I have a choice? I want to say. Being stuck in this bed makes me bitter and defensive because I'm defenseless. I don't want to need anyone's help, but of course I do.

"Sounds good."

I start to gesture toward the empty recliner, forgetting my left arm is in a cast, and cry out from the pain. Lydia winces in sympathy. This broken bone business is new to me. The worst I've ever suffered is a few cuts. I love to cook, so I've had my share of disasters with knives, especially slicing up avocados and pineapples. Still, nothing a couple of Band-Aids couldn't fix.

Lydia sits and opens her laptop.

"Where are my parents?"

She stops what she's doing, looks up, and hesitates, like this question falls outside the boundaries of her job description.

"Your mom said she had to go into work this morning," she says, her light blue eyes returning to her laptop.

Maybe I imagine it, but I think I hear a hint of disgust in her voice, like she's thinking the same thing I am: This woman's teenage daughter nearly died, but wait, duty calls!

Did I nearly die? I'm not sure, because no one will be straight with me.

It shouldn't surprise me that Mom went to work. It's her whole world. Mom's a lawyer. She's always been a bit of a workaholic, but since Mr. Miller's accident she's handling a big case by herself, and it's completely taken over her life.

In her defense, Dad's career stalled majorly about a decade ago, so she's the one who pays most of the bills—something she rarely lets us forget. Dad's a writer. He published a couple of novels. The one he wrote when I was in preschool—a reimagining of the story behind the building of the Brooklyn Bridge, the famous architect, the construction teams, a sweeping love story, everything in one expertly-crafted package—was a bestseller. James said it was "genius." I still haven't read it. I know that's weird, but I've heard so much about it for so long, I already feel like I've read it a dozen times. And what if I don't love it? Awkward.

There was talk of it becoming a movie, but that never happened. Neither did his next book. Now he teaches writing classes at a community college and admires-slash-resents his students who come in with enthusiasm, hope, and fresh ideas. But the past couple of months he's been working on "something new, something big!" He says he's come up with a "heartbreakingly real domestic saga," which he claims could be his "masterwork." I hope for all our sakes he's right. He's been in a much better mood since he began his first draft in October. Until now, that is.

"Your dad is in the cafeteria, grabbing a coffee." Lydia points one of her long, manicured fingers over her shoulder toward the building behind her.

The hospital is U-shaped. From my bed by the window on the fifth floor, I look down and see across into the cafeteria. People carry brown trays to bright yellow tables and cheery orange booths where they sit beneath the glare of blinding lights that never seem to dim. I watched them during the night when I felt too worked up to sleep after James left. Some eat quickly, shoveling in soup, wraps, and muffins as if they've come off a hunger strike. They dump their trash and leave hurriedly. Others sip coffee, wipe their eyes, blow their noses, and linger, all while a green Starbucks sign glows in the window—a beacon promising comfort in the form of caffeine and piping hot familiarity. But its logo, that smiling siren with her wavy goddess hair, taunts me.

Because of my "accident", as Mom called it, and the surgery, the staples, all of it, I'm missing patches, whole swathes of hair. Or is the word swatches? No, that's paint, I think.

I stare at the top of Lydia's tilted head as she types, hunt-and-peck style, into her laptop. I can see her pink scalp through the soft white strands she's woven together. I wonder what my own hair—what's left of it—looks like. Lydia's able to make the most of what she's got. I could learn from her, I think, as I carefully touch the bandages at the base of my skull with my free hand. Right now, that's about the only advice I feel like hearing.

I look down at the Starbucks sign. Where's the coffee James brought me? Did I finish it? I glance over at the empty wastebasket.

"How have things been at home?" Lydia asks.

She cocks her head to the side, reminding me of Daffy when she's hoping for a cat treat. Is Lydia hinting at something? What does she know? It's too hard to think, so I lose myself in the snow swirling silently behind her. Big flakes drift down, and the wind whips them up again, a vicious circle.

"Tess?" Lydia's voice pulls me back. "How have things been at home lately?"

The words that pop into my mind are: it's complicated. I want to say, *Things are great. We've always been close. A tight-knit circle. The Three Musketeers*. I want to rely on clichés to dodge this question. Because, really... Mom, Dad, and me? Lately, we're three sharp points of a triangle, each in our own corner.

Things have been tense, I should say, but why open Pandora's box? What does any of that have to do with how I ended up here anyway?

"Fine," I lie. Anything else feels like a betrayal.

Lydia stares. Her eyes narrow in a forced smile. She's not buying it. I try harder.

"Good. Things are good." She's still looking at me. I blabber on. "I finished all my college applications, so that's a relief. Good timing, too, right?" I gesture toward my head as if to say, "I'd never be able to get it together to do that now."

She studies my face. Seeing she isn't getting anywhere; she shifts the conversation.

"Can you tell me what you remember, Tess?" Her fingers are poised over the keyboard. "From Saturday? The evening, in particular. Anything at all? As time passes, it's common for memories to start to resurface."

"I don't remember much, really." Rage bubbles up in my throat, hot and thick. I want to scream, *we've been over this!* but she looks serious, like she genuinely wants to help. And what if she actually possesses some magic ability to restore my memory? How can I not play along?

"When I try—" I hate how my voice trembles, so I start again. "When I try to think back, I get anxious, but I don't know if it's because of what happened or that I can't remember it."

"That's understandable." Today she's wearing a floral top and lip gloss that matches her plum-colored skirt. I know she's trying to be reassuring, but there's purple lipstick smudged across her front teeth, killing her credibility. Still, I have to try. I close my eyes and think back to Saturday.

"I remember being really excited because James—my boyfriend—was coming home from college."

I get that giddy feeling simply saying his name and "boyfriend" in the same sentence. I want to tell her that he was here last night, but I remember Mom saying, "You don't need visitors, you need rest," so I keep it to myself.

"I was upset because my best friend, Izzy, and I had a fight last week, and we weren't speaking. We're still not, I guess." I feel sick to my stomach when I think about everything with Izzy. I push it out of my mind. "I remember it was snowing. When is it *not* snowing these days, right?"

Lydia stops typing and grins another lipsticky smile. Why am I telling her all this? Like any of it's going to help. But what are my other options? No one else is trying to fix me. Not my parents, who are off doing their own things. Not James. Where did he go in such a rush? Not Izzy. Though, if I'm honest, I know it's my fault she's not visiting me.

"I see fragments, like flashes of images, and with them comes this intense rush of fear, mostly. But then it fades, and I don't know what's real."

I sound crazy, but it's like a kaleidoscope in my mind's eye. Things come together inside my head, and I panic and push them apart. It leaves me dizzy and breathless, like when we're forced to run a mile in gym class, and I'm convinced I'm going to die.

"I'm not seeing a complete picture, and I can't figure out the order of things," I tell her.

Lydia nods and reaches into a bag beside her shiny, black heels. She pulls out a book. Oh, Lord, don't let it be some Dr. Phil self-help crap, is what I think as she says, "In situations like yours, Tess, sometimes people find it can be helpful to keep a journal."

She hands me what looks like a diary. On the cover, pink and blue hydrangeas ring the words: Be Still. I frown, like, *Way to be subtle, Lydia!* and place the book—clearly a Hallmark store special—face down on my meal tray. My breakfast waits under a brown plastic dome that reminds me of a poop emoji.

"When you're feeling up to it, walk, or, in this case, write, your way through the last moments you remember," she advises, speaking slowly, deliberately. "Take your time. Linger over each thought. Leave nothing out. I'm certain you'll find that you recall more than you think you can. Trust in the power of the mind."

She makes it sound so simple. Pick up a pen, put it to paper, and *voila!* Watch as the whole episode unfolds as if I'm queuing up a Netflix series. What I'd really like to do is fast forward to the ending.

"Or, we could drop all this, and you could tell me what happened!" The words fly out before I can stop myself. I sound like an obnoxious bitch, but I don't care. My pain medication is wearing off, and I've had it with this whole See What You Can Remember bullshit.

"Well, Tess," Lydia shifts in her seat, hesitating as if she's weighing her words. "I'm going to be honest with you. Your parents, your doctors, the police, and I—none of us are certain about exactly what took place. Unfortunately, this is one of those cases where there are more questions than answers. So, you might say we're as eager for your memory to return as you are."

The police? A lump swells in my throat, and my pulse throbs in my neck. The thought that the answers to this are buried deep in my brain makes me scared and sick to my stomach—like barfing-after-a-thrill-ride ill.

For the first time since I woke up here yesterday afternoon, I find myself actively trying *not* to remember as another eerie thought crosses my mind: What if I'm better off never knowing what happened?

Circling the Drain

Lydia's gone. I'm alone, yet the room feels more cramped and airless than ever. This news—the fact that people are waiting for me to remember critical information—is suffocating. The walls are closing in. Sweat slides down my stomach beneath the thin hospital gown. My fever must be back.

Dad appears in the doorway. He raises the coffee cup in his hand when he sees that my eyes are open—a one-man toast.

"Tess! You're awake!" His hair, wiry as a toilet brush, points in all directions. He looks like a deranged Statue of Liberty. "Sorry to leave you by yourself. I really needed this. Rough night in the old recliner."

"You slept here? The whole night?"

I don't remember seeing him. Was he there asleep at the foot of my bed when James was here? It's beyond embarrassing to think that he heard me begging James not to leave. Hopefully, he was off getting dinner or talking with the nurses. I've lost all track of what day and time it is—kind of like summer, only this is the polar opposite of a relaxing, good time.

"Yes, Tess, of course, I was here."

He sits on the edge of my bed, and I have a sudden flash of him pleading, "C'mon, Tessie! C'mon, girl! Come back to us!" Repeating it over and over as if he were encouraging a retriever to bound out of a river. Where were we when he said this? Not here. With the memory of his voice comes the taste of blood in my mouth and an icy wind whipping across my face. I hear a whirring sound overhead *whop whop whop*. Faint sirens growing closer. It's all so real, I feel dizzy, ill.

"Tess? Tess, are you all right? You're as pale as the sheet. Do you want me to get the nurse?" Dad's eyes bug out with panic.

"No, no, I'm okay."

I'm anything but okay. How can I not remember seeing him here last night, yet I can recall his voice clearly in a memory I can't place? I'm starting to lose it.

"Can't you please, please, tell me what happened? What's going on?" My attempt to stay strong fails fast, and I'm crying, long, ugly sobs, like some brokenhearted contestant on *The Bachelor*.

"I wish I could, Tess. The doctors, the specialists, Lydia… *everyone* agrees it'll be better if you come around to remember things on your own. There are certain parts, details, I guess, that no one can account for. Some people are afraid that if we tell you things, it'll mess with your memory. Influence it, I guess, is more the right word."

His tone is compassionate, like on some level he's thinking the same thing I am. Who withholds crucial information from someone who's already pretty badly shaken up? Why add to the torment?

I'm devastated that all these people are keeping things from me, but I sort of get what he means. When someone gives you a few small details, your mind begins creating a whole story, filling in the blanks. Nearly all of my childhood memories are based on photos, either the ones in frames displayed around the house or arranged in albums. With each picture, I think I remember that moment as well as what happened before and after. But really, that's only because it's what's captured there, and Mom or Dad told me the rest. None of those memories are legitimately my own.

"What 'people?' The police? Lydia mentioned the police. Am I in danger?"

He stops blowing on his coffee and places his hand on my knee.

"I know this is an absolute nightmare, Tess, but in time, you'll remember everything, I'm sure. For better or worse."

He mumbles this last bit to himself. But I hear it. And he hasn't answered my question. After putting his coffee cup down on the meal tray, Dad picks up my hand and holds it. He doesn't notice it's clammy with fear.

"Listen, while we're alone, while we have a few minutes, I want to say I'm sorry, Tess. I know I haven't always been as present as I should be. Even though I've been right there in the house with you, I've been distracted. I know I've put myself, my writing, my career—which, let's be honest, has been circling the drain for years now—above you. And your mother. And, I'm so, so sorry."

Words pour out of him. I want to believe they're genuine, heartfelt, but with Dad sometimes I can't help wondering if everything is a scene to him, like he's trying out dialogue for a story he hopes will be his next big thing. It never is. Instead of acknowledging his little speech or feeling sorry for him, a wave of disgust washes over me. I pull my hand out of his grasp.

"Your father is a loser. A pathetic has-been." I hear a man's voice, one I don't recognize, saying it so clearly, I'd swear he's in the room with us. I look around. Nurses stride past the doorway, pills, and bedpans in hand—no one else in sight. I feel sick again. It's a struggle to form a sentence, but I have to try.

"What you just said, does it have something to do with my accident, with what happened to me?"

Before he can answer, Mom appears.

"How are you feeling, honey?" She stands with one foot in the room, the other in the hallway. Dad doesn't turn around.

How have things been at home lately? Lydia's words echo in my ears. She's offering me a clue—if my mind allows me to follow it.

First Person, Present Tense

Mom went back to work after making sure I ate my breakfast—cold oatmeal and warm yogurt. Dad left to go home and shower minutes after she arrived. Things were hardly perfect before my accident, but it was nothing like this. I'd need a chainsaw to slice through the tension between them now.

I stare out the window and hope James comes back soon. Winter hasn't officially begun, and already I wish it were over. Snow continues to fall, lovely and delicate as it drifts toward the earth. Too bad after a few seconds in the street, it'll turn into filthy gray slush that sits there waiting to disappear. How can something that starts out seeming so magical end up so ruined? Again, my mind drifts back to Saturday. I'd been beyond excited to see James and now look where I am—another thing that started off seeming perfect and then turned out so ugly. But where did it go wrong?

I glance at the diary Lydia gave me. There's a pen placed inside the wires that bind it together. It looks like a Gerbera daisy. Purple petals and a cheery yellow center decorate the top. I pick it up. The weight of it surprises me. I've done nothing but sleep and rest for the past few days, so I guess it's no wonder I can barely lift two ounces. When will my strength return? When will I be able to walk again? That comes second now. My memories of Saturday night are what I really need.

Opening the book, I stare down at the blank page.

"Every writer's best friend and mortal enemy," James would say. Editor of our high school newspaper, pursuing a journalism degree, always using the perfect words, getting the details right. I admire that. I admire him. I love him. I miss him. Where is he now? What's he doing?

How do I start this? I want to be a chef, not a writer.

"Write it in the third person, if that's easier," Lydia suggested. "Taking an aerial view can help you gain some perspective. Imagine you're telling the story to a stranger, someone who doesn't know you well. This way you'll find yourself paying closer attention to each moment. Remember, leave nothing out."

I know what she's getting at. "The devil is in the details," Mom always reminds me when she's working on a tricky defense.

But in this case, who's the devil? And am I ready to face him?

"Start whenever you feel up to it," Lydia advised.

Will I ever feel up to it, Lydia? I wonder. Still, I can't hang out in this fog indefinitely. I need to know what happened Saturday night. The early afternoon is so clear. That's not a problem. It's what happened after that scares me—terrifies me, actually, to think that my mind may be blocking whatever took place. But if I can hear Dad's voice in that odd memory telling me to "come back," doesn't that mean there's more in there, waiting, trapped behind a trap door only I can open?

The emptiness of the journal's white pages mirrors my memory of that night. I haven't kept a diary since second grade. I'd been given one as a present on my eighth birthday. It had a lock. I thought it was the coolest thing ever. I wrote in it before bed for months until I lost the key. How many afternoons did I waste trying to pick the lock with bobby pins? When I was in middle school, I found the tiny key tucked beneath a Rainbow Loom bracelet at the bottom of a shoebox. I couldn't wait to crack the diary open. But instead of being even remotely interesting, it was super-cringeworthy. I'd numbered every entry though they were nearly identical.

My life had to be literally the dullest on the planet: "Tonight I had spaghetti for dinner. I hate meatballs." "I wish I had a dog." "When I grow up, I want a job where I get to use a walkie-talkie." "I suck at hula-hooping." "Today, I learned to French braid." What a loser. What an unremarkable existence. Not much has changed, really. Well, that's not entirely true. Aside from this bizarre accident, one extraordinary thing happened to me. Two actually. But one led to the other. So does that count as one or two? I'm too tired to figure it out.

I hate the idea of starting another diary. What if I find it in ten years and realize I'm still living the most boring, uninspired life ever? But if Lydia thinks there's a chance it'll help, how can I not try? This business about referring to yourself in the third person, though? That's batshit crazy in conversation. Imagine writing that way.

"Tess Porter, immobilized in her hospital bed, assumes the role of omniscient narrator to tackle the task of recalling one mysterious night by writing about it in a journal given to her by a woman still struggling to master the art of applying lipstick."

No. Not happening. I was there. I lived it. I survived it. Whatever "it" might be. So if I'm going to try to go back, I'm doing it as myself. My way. In the first person. I. I. I. Present tense.

I glance down at the creamy white paper.

What have I got to lose?

Diary

Tuesday, December 19

If I'm going to do this—make a real stab at getting my memory back through this journal—by sharing what I can recall with an imaginary audience of strangers as Lydia suggests, well, then I should introduce myself properly. My name is Tess —short for Theresa, named for a great-grandmother I never met—Tess Porter. I'm seventeen, eighteen in April. I'm Aries. So if you believe in that stuff, I'm unstoppable but also reckless. Don't say I didn't warn you.

I'm 5'8", which I used to hate, but now accept. Mom says I'll appreciate it later in life.

"When your metabolism slows down, you'll be glad to be so long and lean," she's told me repeatedly. "No one wants a pear-shaped wife."

"Great, Mom, thanks. Like that's not a highway to Eating Disorder City. And it's the twenty-first century. Did you ever think 'wife' isn't my only option, even if I'm not as smart as you are?" I've wanted to tell her, not that it would do any good.

Yes, it bothered me that I'd been the tallest in my grade all through elementary school.

"Look, it's a giraffe! No, it's a flamingo! I think I saw her on NatGeo last night!" Boys at my bus stop would snicker behind my back. Tiny boys, in mind and body.

But I could deal with it. What I couldn't stand were the teachers, coaches, relatives asking me which sports I played, always shoving a basketball toward my unskilled palms.

"I only dribble when I'm drinking," I'd reply, rolling my eyes like a drunk and making a chugging gesture with my left hand.

It was Izzy who told me to say that.

"Act like Homer Simpson," she advised. "A kid talking about alcohol and getting annihilated, that'll shut 'em up."

She'd been right. It had worked like a dream until Mr. Falzo, an eager new science teacher and lacrosse coach, told my guidance counselor I may be "at risk." I was forced to attend three one-hour after-school meetings on the hazards of drugs and alcohol, which, honestly, made them seem that much more appealing, you know, that whole wanting-what-you're-not-supposed-to-have thing.

Anyway, I have hazel eyes. I'm a solid B student. By all counts, I'm incredibly average. Or, I was until I became the victim of an accident I can't remember.

And that brings me to my next point, dear reader, whoever you are. I should warn you now, this probably won't be linear. I will also endeavor to use the best words I know because a) I spent months last year studying for the SATs and ACTs, and though my scores still ended up fairly average, my vocabulary is stellar (that means excellent, btw). And b) because "One's vocabulary needs constant fertilizing or it will die."

37

James taught me that. It's Evelyn Waugh, an English novelist, journalist, and all-around prose god, according to some.

Waugh also wrote, "Punctuality is the virtue of the bored." That one's my favorite because I'm always late.

But here I go, already getting off track. I have a tendency to procrastinate.

Shall we begin?

Saturday, December 16, mid-afternoon

"The forecast is ominous," Mom says, slipping her arms inside the sleeves of the coat Dad holds out for her. "Promise me you won't go anywhere. The roads will be treacherous."

"What if I run out of beer or biscotti?" I ask without turning around to see her reaction.

I'm watching The Great British Baking Show and wishing they'd leave already. My heart beats so hard and fast with anticipation, I'm surprised they can't hear it above the television and the snowplows, which seem to scrape the street every thirty seconds making that irritating krrrrrrr, krrrrrr, krrrrrrr sound. But nothing can bother me today—and I need those roads clear, or at least passable.

James should be here by seven—eight o'clock at the latest. I have a ton to do between now and then. It's already 3 p.m. the clock on the mantel tells me. I've waited for this day for months, each minute stretching out like a decade. But now that it's here, everything seems sped up, and I want more time to get ready.

"I'm serious, Tess. If your father hadn't bought these tickets for I-don't-want-to-know-how-much money, I'd be right there curled up on the couch with you," she says, knotting the belt of her coat.

No doubt with a glass of wine in your hand, I want to say, but I've been snarky enough lately, so I keep this one to myself.

"Tess, listen to your mother," Dad adds, like the puppet he's become over the last few months. He'll say and do anything in an attempt to raise her spirits, make her normal again—if such a state still exists for her. "We're taking the train in and leaving the car at the station."

"We're having an early dinner somewhere on the Upper West Side," Mom says as if I haven't heard this information ten times already this week.

"It's a surprise!" Dad raises his eyebrows and puts on his coat with an exaggerated flourish like he's a master magician and not a middle-aged man with a dinner reservation and hopefully-not-fake Hamilton tickets.

"Our cell phones will be on the whole time, or at least until the show starts at eight," Mom says. "Then we'll be at the hotel after that if you need us. Call us—Tess, are you listening? Call us if you need anything."

"She'll be fine, Carolyn."

Dad lifts their overnight bags. I know without turning around that Mom's is twice the size of his.

Since Mr. Miller's accident back in September, Dad will do anything—including buying overpriced seats to a Broadway musical on some third-party vendor site—to make Mom smile. He's trying so hard. If there were an Olympic event dedicated to willing someone else to be happy, he'd medal in it. I don't have the heart to tell him it's a lost cause.

"What time is Izzy coming over?" Mom asks. "I hate to think of you sitting here all alone."

"I think she said around four o'clock," I lie. Izzy isn't coming. She's been my best friend since fourth grade, but we've barely spoken this week. It's Izzy's birthday. Not that Mom, in her distracted state, will remember.

"The temperature is supposed to keep dropping, so turn up the heat if you get chilly. And, please, Tess, don't fool around with the fireplace. You know what happened last time," Mom says. Her tone has lost all its old playfulness. She's forty percent stress and sixty percent worry now. Twenty-four-seven.

And, okay, I'll admit it. There was a small "episode" last month when Izzy and I tried to make s'mores in the fireplace, and I forgot to open the flue. Smoke filled the entire downstairs and scared the crap out of Mom, who came home to the fire alarms shrieking. She'd been out for one of her "walks" again. The smell's nearly gone, but it's taken weeks.

"Yeah, yeah, I know. I won't touch it," I lie again. I'm totally starting a fire. I sound like a total sap, but, honestly, is there anything more romantic than a roaring fire?

"We love you," Dad says, kissing the top of my head.

"Can I get a hug?" Mom asks. Her neediness is spectacularly unattractive, but I know she won't leave until I get up and give her one. I uncross my legs, stretch, and yawn. I want them to think I've got no plans other than to spend a lazy day in the living room binge-watching Netflix with Izzy.

"'Bye, have fun," I say, wrapping my arms around Mom.

It's awkward now because we're the same height, and she's gotten eerily thin. I feel like I'm holding a mannequin. I focus on the softness of her camel hair coat, breathe in her perfume. At least that's the same as it's always been.

"Love you," Mom says, squeezing me tight.

41

She wasn't always like this and I'm afraid if it keeps up, she'll insist I pick a local school rather than go away to college. Despite being a mediocre student, there's nothing I want more than to leave this town behind, get a taste of freedom.

"Love you, too." I pry myself out of her embrace.

"C'mon, Carolyn. We need to catch the three-eighteen express. I still have to brush off the car," Dad says.

"Okay, okay." Mom walks toward the door. "If you need anything..."

"Mom! I know!" I interrupt, losing my patience. "Have a good time. I hope the show is amazing, and your tickets aren't counterfeit."

"Don't even joke!" Dad calls from the walkway, making fresh tracks in the pristine snow.

It's coming down harder. I shoveled the steps an hour ago, but you'd never know it now. Locking the door behind them, I move to the picture window and watch the trusty old Volvo slide out the driveway and disappear down the street. It looks as if the whole neighborhood's trapped inside a snow globe. With Mom and Dad on their way, the day takes on a magical vibe. Like it's incredibly calm but vibrating beneath the surface. I let out my breath; I hadn't realized I'd been holding it. They're gone. Finally.

I run to the kitchen. Daffy, the cat we adopted when I was in fifth grade, chases me, nipping at my heels.

"Sorry, Daff, you've got at least three hours to go until dinner."

Dog-like, Daffy cocks her head to one side, expressing her disappointment that it isn't closer to feeding time. I'm convinced once again that this cat understands me better than my parents ever will.

When we picked her up from the shelter, Dad and I agreed she looked a bit like Daffy Duck with her abundance of black fur, her curious expression, and the little smudge of orange on her nose.

"We can call her Daffy, but let's give her a more formal name," Mom suggested. "How about Daffodil? Remember, Tess? That's the word that knocked you out of the third-grade spelling bee. Maybe if you have a pet with that name, it'll help you remember how to spell it."

That's Mom. Sucking the joy out of the room by focusing on all the ways someone doesn't measure up. That was years ago. I'd hoped she'd ease up once I got to high school. I didn't realize how the older someone gets, the more certain traits become exaggerated. She's been better lately, but she's been preoccupied with work and Mr. Miller's sudden passing.

As I pull out all the ingredients, moving between the fridge and the pantry, and place them on the island, Daffy follows me back and forth. My furry little bodyguard.

"Cats don't eat lasagna," I tell her.

I'm preparing James' favorite meal. After a steady diet of college cafeteria food and take-out, I want his first dinner back to be homemade perfection. I've learned it's best to line up everything you need before you begin. Too many times I've been halfway through a recipe only to realize we're out of eggs or sugar. I have a tendency to charge ahead without thinking things all the way through. Not my best quality.

I grab dried spices from the cupboard. Oregano, basil, parsley—things I tried to grow in the windowsill but killed.

Fishing out a rubber band from our junk drawer, I twist my hair up into a bun. Finding a hair in your food—or worse, your mouth—is the grossest thing ever. I want nothing to ruin this dinner.

As I fill a stockpot with water, Daffy weaves between my ankles. Usually, I'd turn on some music. Florence and the Machine, Leon Bridges. Singing along when no one else can hear you is the best. But today the house—the whole world—feels delightfully still. Aside from the gentle chink, chink, chink of snowflakes hitting the windowpanes, the only sound I hear comes from Samira, my neighbor. Looking out the window above the sink, I see her at her music stand, clarinet in her capable hands, slender fingers playing from memory. I admire her dedication. There are days when it seems no matter what time I look through the French doors that lead to our patio, there she is, on the other side of her patio, beyond her French doors. Steady as a weathervane on an airless August afternoon. She's practicing a piece I don't recognize. When she thinks her parents aren't listening, she sneaks in a few bars of Bruno Mars' "Uptown Funk" and then gets right back to work.

I'm a senior, and she's a junior. On paper, we have very little in common, but we've formed an unlikely friendship, she and I, envying one another for the traits we lack.

I like to listen to her play, though I know she hates it after years of practicing. We've really only gotten to know each other over the last few months, though she and her family moved here from Mumbai the summer before her freshman year.

We'd been standing at the bus stop this past March when Trey Larkin, a complete waste of blood and bones, started in on her.

"So Samira, you like sticking that reed in your mouth? I got something you could put in there."

44

I'd taken out my earbuds to untangle the wires and watched as her shoulders slumped a little lower, her small frame buckling under the weight of her enormous backpack, the clarinet in its case always pulling her closer to the ground.

"You know what, Samira? You might like the taste a whole lot better too—"

"That's enough, Trey," I'd said.

"Oh, now look who it is. Tess, how nice of you to join us again. What? No ride from Clark Kent today?"

James had started driving me to school, saving me from the pure hell that was the ten-minute bus ride, but that day he was going in late so he could help his mom take his brother to the dentist.

"So, Samira, at first your mouth might not be big enough to handle it, but you'll get used to—"

"Actually, Trey, I heard what you're packing isn't enough to fill your own tiny hands." The sound of my voice startled me. I hadn't planned to say a word. Definitely not those words.

"Gee, Tess, what makes you say that? Was your boyfriend checking me out at the urinal? That's pretty fucking creepy."

Gasps and giggles erupted from the group of kids waiting with us at the corner. Their reaction made me bold.

"I got my info from a reliable source. You remember Lena, the disappointed freshman you hooked up with when you checked out Rutgers last month? Apparently, she'd never seen anything so small. It's crazy how far and how fast stuff like this spreads."

As soon as I said "Lena," the blood drained from Trey's face. I couldn't believe I'd remembered that story in such

45

a clutch moment. It seemed almost too far-fetched to be believed, but in one of those six-degrees-of-separation coincidences, Becca, Izzy's older sister, went to Rutgers and was friends with Lena's roommate. Obviously, I had no idea if what she told us about Trey was true, but it was enough.

I stopped short of blurting out the other thing Becca had mentioned—the thing that made Sprite come out of Izzy's nose she'd laughed so hard—Trey has a massive case of butt acne. Revealing that was on the tip of my tongue, but I didn't. I might be mean, but I'm not a monster.

"Screw you, Tess, I'm walking."

"Suit yourself, Trey."

"Thank you," Samira whispered, her soft voice exotic and intriguing, as she looked up at me from behind sweeping black eyelashes.

"Happy to help," I'd said and quickly replaced my earbuds to drown out the sound of my beating heart echoing throughout my body.

I wasn't trying to do the whole "be an upstander, not a bystander!" thing, like they tell you to be in all those unbearable bullying assemblies. And maybe, in this case, you could argue that I was the bully. I'd had a fight with Mom right before I'd left the house. My SAT scores hadn't increased after the countless hours of tutoring she'd paid for.

"You don't seem to care, do you, Tess? Ever since you've met James, you're off in la-la-land. He's going to college, Tess. A good one. Where are you going?" Her words echoed in my head long after I'd shoved my ears buds in and blinked away the tears that sprung to my eyes against my will.

I'd slammed the door then ran down the street to get away from her. It was still months before James left for school, but the thought made me dizzy with loss. I'd only just found him.

So, you could say Trey was the victim of some misdirected anger—not that he didn't deserve it.

I typically avoided confrontation. But as a tall, skinny, and awkward kid, I'd been mocked at the bus stop. It's an awful way to start your day.

The stockpot full, I start to lift it from the sink to place it on the stovetop when I see Samira wave to me between changing reeds. I wave back as her dad comes into view. He's eyeing her sheet music, giving her some advice, though all he can play is the radio, she says.

Seeing him reminds me to treasure every second of having the house parent-free and all to myself for the next few hours. Then James will be here. My heart and stomach somersault thinking about him. I pull my phone out of my back pocket and place it on the counter. It's been off for a few hours, so Mom and Dad wouldn't hear the pinging of texts and notifications while I was watching TV.

"One screen or the other, Tess, not two," Dad always says.

"Do you know when we were your age we had only three channels? Three channels! That was it. You have too many choices now," Mom likes to add.

"Do you two ever shut up?" The words lurk on the tip of my tongue lately. This is why I wish I had a sibling to take the spotlight off me for a while. Like, go bother someone else for a few minutes, please. I love them, of course. They're my parents. But their hovering makes me want to leave for college now. Of course, I have to be accepted somewhere first.

He'll Be Waiting

I push the button and wait for my phone to glow back to life. A text message catches my eye. It's from James. "Hey, I may need a favor."

My New Bestie

"Hey, Tess! I'm Michelle, your occupational therapist. I'm not sure if you remember me, I was here yesterday. Anyway, don't worry if you don't, we're going to be spending lots of time together. In fact, we're going to become besties."

Ugh. Not this one again. I have a vague memory of her über-perky voice—and the strong desire to not hear it again. Ever. But here she is. I must've fallen asleep. The journal is in my lap. I slip it under the sheet before my new "bestie" asks me about it.

It's not that I don't appreciate her enthusiasm. I can see she's making an effort by attempting to use what she thinks is the latest teen slang. But I want to tell her not to bother. I already have my ride-or-die friend. Or, at least I did. Izzy hasn't been to visit me—not that I blame her after the way I ditched her.

"So, we're still a little way away from really working together, but I was passing by and wanted to come in and say hi and ask how you're doing. So, hi! How *are* you doing?" Michelle giggles and tilts her head to the side, reminding me of Daffy. It makes me not want to disappoint her.

49

"Better. Stronger," I lie.

Saying it seems like it could improve my odds of getting out of here, so I nod at her even though that makes my head throb. Also, it's hard to be totally negative when someone looks at you so expectantly. But her slight frown tells me she's not buying it. She's right. I'm not better. I'm sad. Miserable, really. Waking up alone in the hospital is majorly disorienting. I'd hoped James would be here this afternoon. He isn't.

"What I like to tell patients is to focus on something they're looking forward to doing when they're well again. It can really keep those spirits up." She's busy re-fluffing my sheet and blanket. "You know, help you stay positive!"

I listen as the little cuff around my right ankle puffs up, and then sighs. It's supposed to help prevent blood clots. How do people think of these things?

"Tess, honey? I asked what you're looking forward to doing when you're back on your feet again?" Michelle's head tilts to the other side now, but her smile is the same. "What's something you enjoy doing? Maybe I can bring you pictures from a magazine and put them up around the room so you can look at them. Would you like that? Some patients find it very motivating!"

After just waking up, thinking feels like too much work. Thoughts come and go like quick-moving clouds, and I can't catch them. Still, I want to be a good patient. I need them to release me so I can get out of here and go home as soon as possible.

"Ice skating. I like to go ice skating."

50

"Super fun!" she says.

I get the feeling that even if I'd said something like "clipping coupons" or "shooting squirrels," she'd still have said "Super fun!" with the same inflection. She stares, waiting for me to continue.

"I usually skate with James and Emmett," I say. "My boyfriend and his younger brother."

"Boyfriend?" Her mouth forms an "O."

Maybe she thinks I'm too young to have a boyfriend. Without any makeup, I look like I'm twelve. She recovers from her surprise and continues. "Well, I just married my boyfriend!" She wiggles her ring finger. "Two weeks ago! Thankfully, the snow held off. What a day! But we met in a snowstorm, actually. We were at the grocery store. We reached for the last loaf of bread at the same time. He let me have it, so what else could I do? Patient, I married him!"

Her nervous energy should be infectious, but instead, it exhausts me.

"I have to scoot," she says, bouncing on her toes. "Get some rest!"

"I will."

Gently, I place my head on the pillow. Maybe the next time I see Michelle, I'll prove I'm feeling better by sharing how James and I met. It's a silly story, but I still love to tell it.

A Life-saver

Remember when I said that aside from this accident one or two extraordinary things happened to me? Here we go.

It's early December 2016, and Izzy and I sit on my bedroom floor, chewing our way through a bag of Starbursts. A mountain of pink and red wrappers piles up between us.

"You should totally do it!" Izzy says.

"I don't know," I tell her. "Don't you think it's sort of embarrassing, like, 'Look at me! Look at me!'"

"Tess, c'mon! You saved a kid's life. People should know about you. You're a hero. No! You're a shero!" she shouts, clapping and laughing.

Izzy can make me do things I wouldn't otherwise consider – jump off high-dives, wear big, funky earrings, be a braver, bolder version of myself. I love and hate this about her.

We're staring at my laptop, reading an email from some guy, a senior named James Potter, who says he's the editor of the school newspaper.

"Besides, did you even know we have a school newspaper? Nobody reads it. Do it!" Izzy commands.

"I don't know. It feels like I'd be bragging about myself. And then what if they want a photo and I've got this chronic acne?"

"You've got like one zit on your chin, Tess! Besides, it's 2016. He can Photoshop you. You're gorgeous. Do it."

"If I agree to this interview, you have to come with me, okay?"

"I wouldn't miss it." Her blue eyes twinkle mischievously.

We bump our red Starbursts together, a toast to a new and brighter future in which I'm a shero and not a girl with mediocre grades and a cooking show addiction.

When Izzy and I walk into the school library—a place I'd spent years avoiding—James Potter is there waiting for us.

"Tess?" he says. "James Potter. Thanks for coming."

"Thanks for asking." I try to act cool and normal but it's hard because he's cuter than his yearbook picture. "Nice to meet you."

"Actually, we had a photography class together my sophomore, your freshman year. You sat in front of me. You know, Porter, Potter, alphabetical order and all."

I stare, confused and surprised that he remembers me.

"I'm sorry, I…" I stammer, praying I'm not sprouting a sweat mustache caused by the anxiety of the instant crush blooming in my beating heart.

"Don't worry about it, I grew six inches since then." His warm smile melts me.

"This is my friend, Izzy." I gesture in her direction.

"Oh, I know Izzy." He laughs and rolls his eyes a little as if he already gets how funny and special my friend is. "We're in AP French together. She's the one who gave me the scoop."

Izzy winks at me, and I mouth the words, "I'm going to kill you!" as we sit down at a round table in the corner of the library.

"Okay, so you'd taken this lifesaving class at the Red Cross, but you never imagined you'd actually use the skills you learned and then..." He's got his laptop out, fingers over keys.

It's dumb, but I'd been dreading the whole idea of talking about myself to some guy I didn't know, so I purposely scheduled the interview so that there'd be fifteens minutes left in our lunch period—a hard stop. But now, sitting across from him, looking into his open, handsome face, I notice the tiniest black freckle dotting the dark blue of his left eye. Suddenly, I wish I could spend all afternoon with him, holding his gaze, capturing his attention.

"Right, so, yeah." I need to pull it together and sound coherent, but I'm hypnotized by his eyes and devolving into a babbling idiot.

"Deep breath." Izzy squeezes my hand.

"Right, sorry. So I babysit for Evie Walters every Wednesday afternoon. She's four. Completely adorable. Last week, I was leaving, walking out the door, and her mom had given her a bowl of grapes and set her up on her iPad to watch *Peppa Pig* in the playroom while she made dinner. I was halfway down the driveway when I realized I'd left my physics textbook behind. I had a test coming up, and I've got a C, maybe a D+ average right now—sorry, maybe don't include that. I'm trying to get that grade up, but physics is tough."

"Stay focused, Tess. Time's a-wastin'.'" Izzy nudges me.

"Right. So I ran back, and when I walked into the playroom, Evie turned and looked up at me, and her eyes were huge, like, totally wild with fear. She was pointing to her throat and turning blue. I ran to her and did the Heimlich maneuver. A whole grape shot across the room. It actually hit this framed photo of Evie's parents standing in the middle of a vineyard, which is, like, a totally random coincidence, right? Grapes and wine? So ironic."

James smiles like either he gets it, or he thinks I'm completely bananas.

"I talked to Evie's mom, Mrs. Walters, you know, to ask if it would be okay to share the story and get her comments." He looks up from his keyboard, our eyes meet, and I hope I don't have cartoon hearts in mine like I think I might. "She said, 'If it weren't for you…' Well, she started crying on the phone just thinking about it."

"I was in the right place at the right time," I say, and immediately hate myself. Like, way to be original, Tess.

"She's so modest," Izzy says. "Can you imagine thinking on your feet like that?"

"That's the thing—I didn't think at all. I rushed in, and all the stuff I learned at that lifesaving class came flooding back," I say, suddenly hot and shaky remembering Evie's face, the terror in her huge brown eyes.

James looks up from his laptop again and smiles. "Sounds like you're a pretty good student after all." There's a dimple in his chin.

"Can you call my parents and tell them that?" I laugh.

"So, Tess, when you aren't saving lives, what do you like to do?"

"Well, right now I'm really into making fudge."

James looks confused while Izzy puts a hand over her mouth to mute her laughter.

"Shut up, Izzy, you're my number one taste-tester." I slap her arm. "I've been experimenting with caramel sea salt, peanut butter, maple walnut. I want to be a chef or a baker. I go back and forth. I can't decide."

"Cool," James says as the bell rings. "Hey, before you go, can I get your phone number so I can text you if I have any questions as I'm putting this together."

"Of course." My heart leaps into my esophagus.

His hands are busy, putting his laptop in its sleeve, hoisting his backpack onto his shoulder, gathering his books and pens.

"If you give me your phone, I'll enter my contact info," I tell him. When am I ever this bold?

"Of course, good thinking." He hands me an outdated iPhone. A crack divides a photo of James with his arm around someone.

"It's locked. Sorry," I say, handing it back.

"Whoops." He takes it but not before he catches me staring. "That's me and my brother, Emmett. He has autism."

"Oh," I say, surprised by his openness. I almost add, "I'm sorry," but that doesn't seem right.

"Those are noise-canceling headphones he's wearing. He's not a DJ or anything," he says with a smile.

"Not yet, maybe someday." I smile back and add my contact info.

"Time to go, Tess. You're one 'late' away from detention, remember?" Izzy chimes in.

"Who's the babysitter now?" James grins and motions for us to pass through the library's turnstile ahead of him.

When Izzy and I are alone heading down the east wing toward class, she turns to me and says, "He's beyond, am I right?"

"Wait, what?" I ask, confused.

"I mean, I don't even like boys, but he's like, I don't know, a catch. Those blue eyes, it's like he's looking into your soul. He was hanging on your every word. That's pretty rare."

"Why?" I laugh. "Am I that dull?"

"No, I mean he seems sweet and kind of mature. And you know how I feel. Being earnest is usually something I despise in a person. But I don't know, I get good vibes from him."

She's right. I sense it too. I also suddenly get the feeling that I've been set up.

"Yeah, well, he was interviewing me," I say. "It would be weird if he showed up, asked me questions, and then didn't pay attention to the answers."

"I'm telling you, you're going to hear from him. Soon. And it isn't going to be about Evie Walters or the Heimlich maneuver."

We arrive at the point where the hallway comes to a T. Izzy will turn right for Modern British Lit, and I'll go left for Pre-Calc, which I'm barely passing.

"One thing, though," she grimaces, "when you say 'I like to make fudge' it kinda sounds like you enjoy shitting yourself. Just an FYI."

The second bell rings, and I stare at her, regret making my scalp tingle. Had I said that? I'd already forgotten everything, everything but that freckle in James' eye.

Months later, because of James' article, I was honored at a town council meeting. Mrs. Walters gave a short speech. People from the Red Cross showed up. Who could blame them? Free publicity and all. Only Izzy knew I'd taken that class because I wanted more cash. I'd been told I could charge at least two dollars more per hour for babysitting if I were CPR-certified. I received a certificate, a plaque, a small bouquet of daisies. But even with all that, I've always thought of James as my real reward. The way I see it, two girls were saved that day.

James

James sits in the recliner. I have no idea how long I've been asleep. He smiles when he sees I'm awake.

"Hey, you're here." I can't stop myself from grinning even though it makes my face hurt. I want to jump up and down like someone who won a car on a game show, except I can barely move. But when I see James all my pain disappears. "You're so far away. C'mere."

He sits lightly on the edge of the bed, careful not to jostle my leg. My toes, with their chipped blue polish, peek out of the cast. I wish I'd gotten a pedicure, but the rest of me is such a mess, it hardly matters.

"Don't let me sleep when you're here. I don't want to miss a minute with you," I say, needy as a grandmother. "How's Emmett? What have you been doing since you've been home? Have you seen your dad? I wish you could spend more time here."

"So many questions. That's a good sign." James smiles and holds my hand. "But you've got to rest, Tess. You've been through a lot." He looks at me with what he probably thinks is compassion but feels more like pity.

Have I? Have I been through a lot? For the first time ever, I feel angry with James. Really angry. On nights

59

when his phone would go straight to voicemail, and I'd have no idea if he was asleep, in the library, or hooking up with some girl who actually understands Shakespeare, my mind would spin out of control with visions of him breaking my heart. Even then, I never felt the rage I do right now.

You've been through a lot.

My head is an echo chamber where that sentence repeats, fueling my fury. James knows everything. I know nothing. The imbalance rocks me. I yank my hand away from his and lash out.

"Really, James? What exactly have I been through? Why don't you tell me since no one else will?"

His expression shifts from sympathy to sadness to something that looks like anger. He pulls back, makes a fist, and punches it into his open palm before resting his face on his white knuckles.

"I'm sorry, Tess. I don't really know much either. I wasn't there for all of it. I do know that I'm part of the reason you're here, in the middle of this totally messed up situation. I got you into it, and then I didn't do enough to protect you, and I'm so sorry. I never should've asked you to go get him. And you should've told me it was a goddamn blizzard here. You could've been killed."

I can't recall ever seeing James this upset, and that includes all the times his dad has let him and Emmett down. I start to cry. I didn't mean to start this. We have so little time together; I don't want to ruin it. I know he'd never hurt me—not intentionally. If he knew everything, if he had all the answers, I'm sure he'd tell me.

"I'm sorry. I feel so lost and scared." I want him to hold me, but he's deep in his own thoughts. I try to focus on what he said: a blizzard, me going out to get someone. It's like figuring out a riddle in a foreign language.

"So, was I in a car accident?" I'm about to ask when he begins rambling.

"Why didn't I let him deal with it? It was his own fault. He's the one who fell asleep and had all his stuff stolen. That's what started this, set the wheels in motion. You should've stayed home. Kept all the doors locked. I know that's only a part of this insane puzzle, but it's the first piece. It opened the gates to everything that came next. If I could go back in time, Tess, I want you to know I'd do everything differently. I'd never have taken his call. Never have asked you to help. I'd have gotten back home faster."

"What are you talking about?" I try to sit up and focus, but it's so hard with the medication weighing me down. Still, I'm desperate, hungry for more information. "Who asked for your help? I don't understand."

"You really don't remember, do you?" James shakes his head, his anger and frustration building. He stands and paces the tiny room like a mountain lion confined to a cat carrier.

My anger bubbles back up. Does he think I'm faking it? Pretending not to remember? For what? Sympathy? Attention? I push my rage aside because it feels like he's going to tell me everything. Finally, it'll all make sense.

"No. I don't remember going anywhere or getting anyone. Who are you talking about?" Drowning in a sea of unknowns, I reach for his hand.

"Nick," he says. "I asked you to go get Nick."

At the mention of that name, the room tilts. Everything goes black.

Nick

December 20

When I wake up James is gone. Mom's asleep in the recliner, covered by a vomit-colored blanket. The sun, rising in the distance, peeks through the blinds. Mom's frowning in her sleep. I have a pounding headache, and my stomach growls. I haven't eaten or had anything to drink in what feels like days. I'm sweating and my bones hurt. I think about ringing for the nurse, asking for crackers, tea, more pain medication. Anything. But all I want to do is say the name.

Nick. Nick. Nick.

A meditation. I say it aloud, turning it over in my mouth. An incantation. Casting a spell. Each time I whisper "Nick," a ripple of fear creeps up the notches of my spine. I want to say it as many times as it takes for it to lose its power over me.

Izzy would help me figure this out. I miss her more than ever. I need to talk to her. How could I lose her? Especially now. Of all the times to destroy a friendship, this has to be the worst. I suppose that's how she felt about me when I wasn't there for her.

I pull the diary from beneath the cast on my leg where I've hidden it and wonder if I can force my mind to focus on the questions that won't go away: Who is Nick? What does he have to do with this? The possible answers scare me, but I'll choose fear over uncertainty any day.

Saturday, December 16, mid-afternoon

"Hey. I may need a favor."

I reread James' text and hope he's about to make a joke, like "Spend every minute with me while I'm home for the next three weeks."

Maybe he's going to ask for something easy like, "Can you whip up a box of caramel sea salt fudge for the guy driving me home from Chicago? I owe him big time."

"Of course. U know I'll do anything for u."

I'm not supposed to talk like that. It makes me sound weak. I would be kicked out of the feminist club for even thinking it let alone putting it in writing. But I would and will do anything for him. And deep down, I know he feels the same way about me.

I watch as the dots bounce inside the gray bubble, meaning he's there, on the other side of the phone, on his way home to me. I'm hit with a rush of heat that I initially think is excitement at the thought of seeing him again, but then realize I'm so distracted, I'm standing too close to the flame under the stockpot.

"How are you going to be a chef if you don't understand the inherent danger of fire?" Mom always asks when I'm working in the kitchen. Of course, she doesn't want me to be a chef. It's not enough for her. "If you can read, you can cook, Tess. Make it a hobby, not a career."

I step away from the stove and watch as the dots disappear. The bubble is gone.

Then it's back.

"Sorry, it might be easier to explain if I call."

I type OK but the phone, with a mind of its own, sends back a thumbs-up emoji. I'm staring at it when it starts playing Kool & the Gang's "Let's Groove," the song that blared through speakers hung in every corner of the room, as we swayed into each other and kissed at a New Year's Eve party almost a year ago.

The day before the party, James had texted me to ask if I'd be there—at "Fix" Kelly's house. His name isn't really Fix. It's Brendon, but he's earned his nickname by hacking into the school's database and "fixing" a grade here or there in exchange for weed or edibles. Neither Izzy nor I really knew Fix or had sought out his "services"—not that I couldn't have used his help. From Science to Spanish, my marks were pretty disappointing, but unless he would accept peppermint fudge—my flavor of the month—as payment, he'd never make a single keystroke on my behalf.

Izzy and I hadn't even known about the party until I got James' text, which ended with:

"You should go, in case anyone starts choking. I'd feel a lot safer if you were there…and it'd be great to see you again."

That last part made me almost drop my phone in the toilet. I'd been brushing my teeth before bed when that text came in, and I started freaking out in the bathroom—worse than if I'd spotted a hairy tarantula.

I couldn't answer him right away. What if I said the wrong thing? What if it was a prank? I was losing it. I FaceTimed Izzy, expecting her to spaz out like I was doing, but she got all smug and smirky.

"See! I knew it! I told you you'd hear from him!" She was in her kitchen, scooping herself a bowl of ice cream.

"Please, please, will you go to this party with me? I know we were going to rewatch "Gilmore Girls" and make fun of Ryan Seacrest and the whole ball-dropping thing, but please, I really want to see him again."

"You don't need me now. My work here is done."

This was how Izzy got sometimes. She liked to be begged.

"Pleeease, let's go!"

Silence. She'd placed her phone on the kitchen counter, leaving me with a view of her ceiling while she put her beloved mint chocolate chip back in the freezer.

"That's at least three 'pleases,' Iz, c'mon. You started this! You owe it to me to—"

"How great would it be if you two get married?" She reappeared, licking her spoon with a devilish grin. "You'd be Tess Porter-Potter. Like Port-a-Potty." She was in her room and nearly rolled off her bed, laughing at her own joke. "Okay, okay, I'll go, but only because I'm going to do everything to make that happen. Promise me you'll name your first child John. John Porter-Potter."

More maniacal laughing.

I didn't mind. I got what I wanted.

Fix lived two blocks from Izzy's, so we didn't need a ride. The theme was "Decades." Becca helped us get ready, digging their mom's old costumes and clothes out of the attic. We found bell bottoms and an orangey suede fringe vest for Izzy and a black flapper dress for me. Though it was mid-way through our sophomore year, this was our first high school party, and we were both sort of terrified we'd end up standing in the corner like a couple of losers. But, of course, Izzy did fine, dominating the beer pong

67

table. I stayed by her side until James, dressed as Jay Gatsby and looking even better than that afternoon in the library, found me.

"See! You're perfect together!" Izzy whispered. "Go get him, Daisy!"

Normally, I'd have had no idea what she was talking about, but we'd just finished 'The Great Gatsby' in American Lit the week before the holiday break.

James and I danced to 1970s music, ABBA's 'Dancing Queen' drowning out all attempts at conversation, the vodka and blackberry drink in my red Solo cup giving me courage and moves I never knew I had. We were full-on making out by the 1980s.

Now, listening to Kool & the Gang makes my knees wobble with desire, as cheesy as that sounds. Sometimes I let the song play a few extra bars before I answer the phone to swim in the sweetness of that memory. But now I want to hear James' voice.

"Hey!" I say. "How are you? Where are you?"

"Good, we're somewhere in PA. Getting closer to you with every mile."

Normally, guys our age would never talk like this at all, let alone, in front of a guy friend. But it's like James never got that info. He's always comfortable with himself.

"Listen, Tess, about this favor, please feel free to say no, but my friend—this guy from my dorm—he's totally desperate. He landed at Newark airport, and he's got nothing. No wallet, no phone, no house keys."

"How did he get on the plane?" I interrupt. I have a bad habit of doing that. "Where are all those TSA agents? It's the holiday season. That's crazy."

"No, no. He fell asleep at the gate at O'Hare. He'd put everything inside his bag, except his boarding pass. Someone must've been watching him. Everything's gone. He just landed, and he's got nothing except an empty duffle bag. He had to borrow a phone to call me. He knows I live fifteen minutes from the airport. He called my mom to get my cell number—"

"Wait, your mom doesn't know that you're coming home a day early, does she?" Massively selfish, I know, but after not seeing James for months, I want one night of having him all to myself. If his mom knew he was back in town, she'd come dashing over with Emmett to pick him up and bring him straight home.

"No, no, don't worry. I'm definitely staying over. Anyway, I feel bad for the guy. His parents drove up to Syracuse to bring his sister home. They won't be back until tomorrow. It's not snowing there yet, is it?"

I look outside. I can no longer see our patio furniture. My eyes dart to the roof of our shed, there must be six inches of snow and counting. I hesitate. I'm not the greatest driver, and since Mr. Miller's accident—he was killed when his car got trapped between the gates of the railroad crossing not a mile from our house—Mom hardly lets me drive at all.

"Nope, not snowing too hard yet," I lie. I never lie to James. But is it a bad thing if you're doing it to help someone?

"So I was thinking maybe, if it's not too much trouble, you could pick him up, and he could stay over. Don't worry, we can stick him in your mom's office. We won't even know he's there." He pauses, expecting me to object. When I don't, he continues, "You don't mind? You'll get him?"

"Sure," I say, wondering if I'll really be able to pull off driving on multiple highways in a snowstorm. "Text me a photo of him so I know who I'm looking for. Is he tagged in any of your Insta pics?"

Silence.

"Shit." James never curses. He says he doesn't want Emmett to imitate him, plus he considers it a challenge to think of other, better words to express frustration.

"What's wrong?"

"I don't think you're going to find any photos of him. His profile pics on all his social media accounts are shots of his family's bulldog, Rosalita."

"What?" I laugh.

"Yeah, I don't know if it's the whole being-from-New-Jersey thing, but he and his family are huge Springsteen fans. He came stumbling into the dorm last night drunk, singing, 'Rosalita,' and woke up the entire floor. He's obsessed with this dog. Seriously obsessed. He's got standing FaceTime dates with her on Wednesdays and Sundays."

For a second, I forget all about the fact that I've agreed to drive to an airport in a blizzard. It's so nice to hear his voice again. I still can't believe I'll see him in a few hours.

"He's actually an interesting guy, kind of quirky. But I don't know if you'll find any pictures of him. He's not really the selfie type."

"Isn't there a saying, 'If you can't be found by a Google search, do you even exist?'" I joke.

"So, listen, my battery's dying, but he's about my height, brown hair, brown eyes."

"You described probably a fifth of the people at Newark airport right now," I say.

"Wait! He'll recognize you. I have a bunch of photos of us in my dorm room."

70

I smile. Izzy, who usually tells me to play it cool, suggested I print out enough photos of James and me together to wallpaper his side of the room.

"Keep the ladies at bay," she'd said.

"I don't think it works like that. If anything, that makes him even more attractive. Like, here's a guy who's willing to go peach picking? Ding! Ding! Ding! Total catch."

After skimming Pinterest, she suggested I take a strand of twine, wrap white lights around it, and hang a dozen pictures of us on it with clothespins.

"Geez, Iz, what's next, send him flowers every Friday?"

Still, I put our prom picture and another of him and Emmett skating together in frames he could keep on his desk. If he had plenty of pictures of us around his room, it was because he'd put them there. And that made it so much sweeter.

"Okay, I'll check online anyway, just in case," I say.

"Tess, I really appreciate this. I know it's last minute and totally screws up our night. But I'll make it up to you. I promise. Anyway, he's a good guy. You'll like him."

"I hope so." I try to hide that I'm mildly heartbroken our romantic dinner for two has been ruined.

"Thanks. I'll call him now and then text you the details. Leave whenever it's good for you. He'll be waiting."

"Wait, James!" I shout, afraid he's already hung up. "You never told me his name."

"Right, sorry. It's Nick. Nick Lawrence."

This Is How It Ends

"Tess! Tess!' Mom pats my right arm gently. "Honey, wake up, you're having a bad dream."

I stare at her, confused. It was so real. I'd been tumbling, falling down beside a flat cement wall. I'd tried to stop myself, but there was nothing to grab on to, no banister or ledge. All I could smell was damp, wet earth. A man stood above me. I couldn't see his face and had no idea who he was. But one thing was clear: He'd come to hurt me. Me specifically.

In my nightmare and in real life, my mouth is dry, my tongue as sandpapery as Daffy's. I can't speak. My heart gallops, thumping hoofbeats pound in my ears.

"This is how it ends!" he shouted in the dream, his voice echoing as I plunged into total darkness and struggled to crawl out of sight. I couldn't move. My legs wouldn't work.

I want to tell Mom everything, but I can't catch my breath. Was it only a dream or does it have something to do with my accident? What if it's one of the flashes Lydia talked about? Memories attempting to resurface? Is the man in the dream Nick? My head hurts thinking about it. For once, I'm actually grateful to be in this hospital bed. Safe.

I must've fallen asleep. The focus that comes with trying to piece together Saturday night exhausts me. Or maybe I blacked out after remembering James saying, "Nick. Nick Lawrence."

Mom rubs my good arm. It's prickly with goosebumps. "You're okay, Tess. I'm here."

For now, I think, but don't say it. Running off somewhere is her typical MO. Her go-to spot is her office—the one in Manhattan or the one in our house. Either will do.

Lately, she's been taking these long walks in the late afternoon on the days she works from home. She's gone for hours. She comes back pale and tired. Ravaged. Run-off mascara outlines the bags beneath her eyes. It's not a good look.

One day Izzy and I followed her (Izzy's idea). We were dying to know what she was up to. Of course, we could track her thanks to the Find Friends app she made me put on my phone. So, technically, I knew where she was, but not what she was doing there.

Izzy and I let her get a head start and then crept behind. Crisp leaves crunched beneath our feet with every step, threatening to give us away. We had to stop ourselves from laughing at what awful detectives we'd make.

When we caught up to Mom, we peeked out from behind the crumbling brick train station and watched. She sat on a bench, facing the railroad crossing where Mr.

Miller was killed. From the way her shoulders shook, it was obvious she was crying, and I instantly regretted following her.

Mom and Mr. Miller had been more than colleagues. They were old friends. They'd met in law school and started their careers together at the same firm in Manhattan more than twenty years ago. They'd been at a bar in Midtown celebrating winning some never-ending case with a bunch of other lawyers and paralegals the night Mom and Dad met.

Dad had been tending bar to keep his days free to write. He was in a good mood, too, that night. He'd signed with the agent who, the following year, would sell his first novel. The way Dad tells it, he'd spotted Mom across the bar. He said he took one look at her and knew: There she was. He always follows it up by saying, "After years of waiting for things to happen, my whole life changed in one perfect day."

Whenever he told that story, I'd think, "Whatever. Dad is such a goofball." But after I first met James, I understood what he meant. Sometimes all it takes is one look, and you know. Three months later, they were engaged. Right before Mom and Dad got married, Mr. Miller left the firm and moved to Cleveland, telling Mom he didn't want to be a "small fish in a big pond," any longer. He got married, too, and had a daughter, Danielle, and a son, Luke.

For years, our families exchanged Christmas cards. In the photo on the front, Danielle always smiled—even the year her two front teeth were missing—but Luke's eyes never looked toward the camera, making it clear he wasn't a fan of the annual photo shoot. Mostly, I focused on their St. Bernard, Louie. Each December when their card arrived, I'd beg Mom and Dad for a puppy. Mrs. Miller—Sarah was her name—used to write these little holiday-inspired poems inside. They were sweet but kind of corny, and, as Dad liked to point out, the rhymes felt totally forced.

"I'm sorry, but, 'Season's greetings from the Heartland where we're busy stringing garland!' that's a bit of a stretch." He mocked them a bit more each year.

"Stop, Jack. I'm sure she doesn't fancy herself the next Maya Angelou. She's having fun and, hey, at least she's trying to be creative," Mom said in Mrs. Miller's defense.

I don't think Mom meant it as a dig— like Mrs. Miller was actually writing something while Dad was stuck in yet another one of his blocked periods—but that's how he took it. He retreated to his office and barely spoke to Mom for days.

After that, I started hiding the Millers' cards as soon as they came. Mom, eternally busy with work, had a policy: Send a card only after one came in. Because she never got the cards from the Millers, they stopped getting one from us, and Mom and Mr. Miller lost touch for about a decade.

Then, two years ago, Mom bumped into him, literally, on the street in Manhattan. He'd moved back to the area because his wife had been diagnosed with an aggressive form of breast cancer at the same time their daughter had enrolled in an art school in the city. By moving, he thought he could find the best care for his wife and still keep the family together. But his job wasn't a good fit, and even the best care wasn't enough. Mrs. Miller died last fall right before Thanksgiving. Mom went to the funeral. It turned out they lived a few towns away from us. Then she helped Mr. Miller get a job at the firm she joined when I was in kindergarten, hoping a fresh start might help.

"Oh Jesus, that's so freakin' sad," Izzy said as we watched Mom alone on the bench, oblivious to the chilly autumn breeze. "Do you think your mom feels guilty, like she gave him so much work he fell asleep while driving?"

Normally, this would've made me feel upset or even angry because it sounded like Izzy blamed Mom for Mr. Miller's tragic fate. And while I could and sometimes did say all sorts of bad things about Mom, I didn't want anyone else to. But it's not like that with Izzy. Izzy's family.

"I never thought of it that way." I hadn't. But I had wondered why Mr. Miller was so close to our house. Was he dropping something off or picking up Mom so they could go into the city together? Did he stop on the tracks to answer a call, reply to a text? I didn't want to ask when it was so raw, and then, as more time passed, it would've been too weird to bring it up.

"He'd lost his wife. My mom said she thought keeping busy would be good for him. I think it was just a bizarre, freak thing."

"I guess," Izzy shrugged. "Wanna go to Five Guys?"

We turned and walked off, hungry for salt, grease, and the ticklish fizz of fountain soda, leaving my mother alone with her grief.

I turn away from the window and look at Mom now, really look, and notice how sad and tired she seems. She's rubbing my arm. My goosebumps are gone, but the uneasy, anxious feeling I woke up with remains. I picture it growing and shifting inside my stomach like those blobs of goo inside a lava lamp.

"I'm going to run downstairs and pick up a salad for lunch," Mom says. "Can I get you anything? Frozen yogurt? The nurses told me you haven't really been eating."

"No, thanks." I stare out the window and down toward the cafeteria. The Starbucks goddess stares back, a smirk on her lips as if she, too, knew that Mom wouldn't be staying with me very long. "Where's Dad? Is he down there now?"

"No." Mom's face betrays nothing.

This is a skill she's worked hard to perfect for her job. People say all sorts of things to rattle her in court, and even if it gets to her, she can't let it show.

"He's at home. We're taking shifts since sleeping here in the recliner isn't all that comfortable."

My reaction splits into three parts: 1) Gee, sorry, I'd love to order you up a freakin' king-sized mattress where you could catch up on your beauty rest; 2) You're uncomfortable? I'm the one with broken bones and stitches in her head; 3) Shifts. Shifts?

I'm their only child, and Daffy, being a middle-aged house cat, is pretty self-sufficient. They can't suck it up and stay here together with me? The word "shifts" has a bad association for me. James' parents are divorced. Everything in their fractured family happens in shifts. On Christmas Day, James and Emmett wake up in their mom's condo, eat breakfast, and open presents. Then they spend the rest of the day with their dad—unless he forgets or gets a better invitation. It's the same for Easter, Thanksgiving, birthdays. "On to the second shift," James usually says when he calls from the car, shuttling back and forth. Emmett repeats him, a sad echo. If there's an event at school, the Potters take turns attending it. They made an exception for James' high school graduation. But other than that, they never deviate, which James says is probably good because if they were more flexible, it might confuse Emmett.

After we'd been together for a few months, I asked James how things got so bad.

"So, check this out: I'm nine, Emmett is five. My dad tells us he's going on a business trip, which isn't uncommon. But, it turns out, he's actually across town, setting up his new apartment for his new life. He comes back, a day late—probably got stuck waiting for the cable guy," James sarcastically interrupted himself. "And, like it's no big deal, tells my mom, 'I can't do this anymore.' As if that were an option—not doing 'this' anymore."

That was about two years after Emmett was diagnosed with autism. James says the stats on couples getting divorced when their child has special needs are pretty high, but it's one of those times when being part of the majority isn't exactly comforting.

James' mom was blindsided, but there were clues, he said. After he'd gone to bed, he'd hear his parents fighting about money, the best school for Emmett, why therapy and special, expensive diets weren't helping, his dad's frequent work trips. Soon, they barely communicated beyond grunts. Then they stopped looking at each other.

I pictured Mom and Dad now. Is this the end of my parents' marriage too?

"This is how it ends." the man in my nightmare says as he yells at me.

I shake my head as if that will make it stop, and look up just in time to see Mom walking toward the door on her way to the cafeteria.

"Wait, Mom? Who's Nick?" I ask. "Who's Nick Lawrence?"

She turns. For once, her mask disappears. She looks genuinely stunned.

"We don't know, Tess. We're hoping you'll tell us."

He'll Be Waiting

Saturday, December 16, late afternoon

Love makes you do some pretty dumb things, right? Not like that isn't totally obvious. How many movies and pop songs are based on the way love can cause you to lose all common sense?

I know driving to the airport in the middle of a snowstorm to pick up some guy I don't even know—a guy's who's kind of "quirky"—has flaming red flags all over it. Like if this were a movie, half the people would be screaming, "Don't go! Don't do it!" The other half would be mumbling, "This chick is nuts." I get it. But I don't want to let James down. Plus, he has no idea it's a blizzard here or I'm sure he'd never have asked.

I wish I could send an Uber for his friend, Nick, but I don't have the app, and I don't have a credit card. Izzy has it on her phone because even though she's had her license for a year, she rarely has access to a car. Her parents pay for it as a sort of consolation prize. She's the second of five kids. Her mom jokes that she should've invented ride-sharing because she's been driving people—mainly Izzy, her grandmother, her brothers, and their friends—around for years. The family's Suburban feels like a playroom on wheels. Izzy says that the car, like her house, is bursting at the seams. Her grandmother, aka Grams, moved in after Izzy's grandfather passed away.

Becca, her older sister, always has a new boyfriend, and their three younger brothers give off enough energy to make the house feel like it's levitating. But, to me, it's the perfect amount of full.

When we first became friends, Izzy loved coming over to my house after school because Mom was in Manhattan and Dad hid out upstairs in his office. So really, it was like no one was here. Our home is tiny. You walk in the front door, and you're pretty much in the living room. The staircase that leads to the bedrooms is on your right. You can see the kitchen straight ahead, and off to the left is the dining area. When Mom made partner, she hired a contractor to knock down a wall, so it's more like an eat-in kitchen with an island in the middle where the wall used to be. She added a home office, too. As a surprise for me, they put in the pool, which sounds great, but when you live in New Jersey, you only get to use it maybe three months out of the year. Still, it's nice to have. Dad wanted some massive second-story addition, but Mom vetoed it.

"It's just the three of us," she'd said, annoyed. "How much space do we need?"

"You're never here, anyway," I wanted to add but didn't.

With Mom and Dad busy working, I'd tip up a planter on our porch, pull out our hidden house key, let myself in, and do whatever I wanted.

"Hear that?" Izzy would say, standing in the living room, spinning in a circle.

"No, what?" I'd ask.

"Exactly," she'd laugh. "The heavenly sound of nothing."

I wish I could ask her to send an Uber for Nick, but she's still not speaking to me. I check my messages again. No response to the text I sent her this morning. I made her a quick video like I do every year for her birthday, of

81

me, my hair up in a high ponytail, singing into my hairbrush, pretending to be Ariana Grande.

When it's my birthday, she spikes up her black hair and pretends to be Joan Jett. It's this dumb tradition we started, like, five years ago, and even though we're in a fight, I can't be the one to break it. I knew when she didn't reply right away—not even a "nice one!" or a thumbs up emoji—that she's still furious with me. But I'll be the first to admit, my video was pretty lame. My heart wasn't in it. My mind was preoccupied with thoughts of James.

I turn off the flame under the stockpot. The lasagna will have to wait. Daffy circles the kitchen island. I wish cats could be more like dogs and embrace the whole riding-in-a-car thing because I'd love some company.

"Sorry, Daff. I have to go out now. You're in charge of the house."

When I talk to her, my voice registers a dozen octaves higher. Samira once heard me talking to Daffy in the backyard and called over the low picket fence that divides our properties, "You know that's a cat, right? Not a baby."

But to me, Daffy's so person-like, I can't help myself. Like right now, she's looking out the French doors and then back at me, like, "Are you crazy? Go out in this? Remember what Mom said? 'The roads will be treacherous!'"

"I know, Daffy, but don't worry, I'll take the old car just in case I slide into a guard rail." Saying it out loud makes it seem like it can't possibly happen. Like, I said it first, so if the universe followed up on it, how unoriginal, right? I do this all the time, tempt fate, and then acknowledge the stupid thing I'm about to do by describing it as if I'm daring the universe. I'm aware that one of these days this trick—flirting with disaster—could backfire. I'm crazy, not stupid.

82

Walking out of the kitchen, I hope to find the car keys in the hand-shaped ceramic bowl I made in kindergarten that rests on the table beside the front door. Looking at my five-year-old open palm sitting there empty, I remember that Dad drove the car to the train station, which means I have to walk up and get it. I groan thinking about adding one more annoying hurdle to this already bad idea of a trip, which has derailed my plans for a magical afternoon of cooking, baking, and getting ready for James. I need time to paint my nails, fix my eyebrows, straighten my hair. After not seeing him for four months, I want to look perfect. I'd begged to fly out to visit him during the early November school break, but Mom and Dad said no way.

"A young woman flying alone to spend a long weekend with her boyfriend in a dorm in the middle of Chicago? You've got to be kidding!" They'd laughed as if I were requesting a one-way ticket to Mars.

"Jeez, what's wrong with them? Why are they so overprotective?" Izzy had rolled her eyes when I told her they'd said no—and that was even after I'd volunteered to buy my own ticket with my babysitting money. "My parents would drop me in the middle of Afghanistan if it meant one less kid in the house for a few days."

I knew that wasn't true, but Izzy's twisted take on things always coaxed me out of a bad mood.

Looking in the driveway, the tracks Dad made backing out are already covered with freshly fallen snow. The midlife-crisis convertible Mom bought herself for her forty-fifth birthday in November has all but disappeared under a thick blanket of white. Not only do I not want to dig it out, but I also can't risk anything happening to that car.

I find the spare set of keys in the table drawer. As I'm wondering if there's some way I can get out of doing James this "favor," the wind picks up, slamming the storm door into the rocking chair on the porch. I jump. The shock of the sudden thud sends a rush of adrenaline up my spine and a message to my brain: Go before the storm gets worse! I open the hall closet and stare at my jacket. It's fairly short and made of wool—no match for this weather. I realize now it's pretty much useless, but I bought it because Becca convinced me its olive color made my eyes "pop."

I study my other options and pull out a long, down coat. It's Mom's, the one she wears to work. It's kind of homely. Picture someone wrapped in a shapeless black comforter, and you get the visual, but it's probably the warmest thing either of us owns. It has a hood, that will simultaneously flatten and frizz up my hair, but it's better than a hat.

"Why did I agree to this?" I ask Daffy as she noses around a pile of scarves while I tug on my boots. Fishing through a basket of gloves and mittens at the bottom of the closet, I keep finding mismatched sets. An odd leather glove, a lone wool mitten. I shrug on Mom's coat and shove my hands into the pockets hoping my mother, with her love for being prepared, will have the perfect pair of gloves tucked neatly inside. I wiggle my fingers in deep but feel nothing other than a hole and a folded slip of paper, probably an ATM or grocery store receipt. I don't know what makes me remove it, but when I do, I see that it's neither. It's a note. I'm holding it upside down. When I turn it around, the message surprises me and causes my already-racing heart to beat faster.

"I'm counting the minutes until we're together again. I'm hoping you're doing the same."

I stare down at it dumbly, confused. The coat, pretty much all feathers, is light but feels weighted down on one side. The left. The same side as the note. I should be walking toward the train station. I'm wasting precious minutes. I think about James and Nick. I hear James' voice in my head. "He'll be waiting."

But why is the coat heavier, almost pulling toward the floor on the left? Something must've fallen through the hole in the pocket. Bending over, I run my hand along the hem. Bingo. I feel a round item, like a circle with a peg on its side. I crouch down, easing it up from the bottom and through the hole in the lining.

In my hand is a beautiful silver pocket watch on a long, delicate chain. It looks antique, but it's been polished and shined to appear almost new again. 5:05 it reads. How can it be that late already? I glance at the clock on the mantle. 4:05. It's been in there since before Daylight Saving Time ended in early November. But how did it get there? Who gave it to Mom? It's ticking in my hand. A truth bomb.

I read the note once more.

"I'm counting the minutes until we're together again. I'm hoping you're doing the same."

I study it. No loops or swirls. This isn't a woman's script. Aside from the fact that someone is pretty eager to see Mom again, what does this mean? I haven't a clue, but I do know this: That is not my father's handwriting.

A Fresh Start

"Hey, Tess! Remember me? Michelle? I know there are so many of us coming in and out all the time, it's hard to keep track. Plus, I know you're…" She rolls her eyes and bonks herself on the head while chuckling as if she's absolving me of forgetting her because of my head injury.

"Right, no, I remember you," I say, smiling.

I don't want to encourage conversation. I want her out of my room as fast as possible. Sliding the diary under the sheet, I don't break eye contact hoping she won't notice and ask about it. I need to get back to picturing Saturday, while the video camera in my mind is at full battery, running me through scenes, moments of my life, I never thought I'd get back. The note, the pocket watch, a possible betrayal. I'm so confused and upset, but at the same time, shocked and excited that Lydia's idea of trying to recreate that day is working.

Or is it?

Can I trust these memories? What if my mind is simply pulling up fragments and then filling in the blanks on its own? I want to tell Lydia about the things I've recalled because of her exercise, but I'm scared.

She'll obviously want to know what I've remembered. How can I say, "Well, my boyfriend asked me to pick up a stranger at the airport and apparently I did it. I also think my mom may be having an affair..." Like, where do I go from there?

I wish James were here. Or Izzy. I'm dying to talk this through with someone I trust. How I can contact them?

"Awesome!" Michelle says, though I have no clue why.

I wonder if she's always this peppy—and if it drives her new husband bonkers.

She's looking at my arm, checking out my cast. It's so weird, when I was a kid I was always jealous of classmates who broke a leg skiing or fractured an arm falling off a jungle gym. They got so much sympathy. So much attention. Everyone rushing to sign their names to those white plaster bandages. And slings? Forget about it. I was green with envy. Now I just want to get the hell out of here and have everything return to normal.

I think about the note I found again and wonder if that's possible—things going back to normal. What will I remember next? I wish Michelle would leave so I could close my eyes and try to recreate the day I've lost that's slowly returning to me.

"So, has anyone come in and talked to you about rehab yet?" Michelle asks.

Rehab? My first thought is, that's for celebrities, then I realize what she means.

"No, not yet," I say. "Or, if they did, I don't remember."

"Well, your PT? Kate? Remember her?" she asks.

I don't, but I don't say that.

"She and I have been talking with your doctors about when you'll be ready to make the move. But, boy, this snow complicates things!"

I look out the window. Fat snowflakes the size of packing peanuts pour from the sky.

"How long would I be there? In rehab?" I brace for the answer. I'd thought I'd be going home. I'd fantasized about spending my days on the living room couch, resting my broken leg across James' lap while we binge-watched an entire series together. Comedy, drama, even reality shows about cabin builders, I don't care. Just not more time being alone in this ugly, off-white hospital room.

"That depends," Michelle says. "One, maybe two weeks."

My heart sinks. James is only home until January seventh.

Michelle pipes up, cheery as ever, "I know it's hard to hear that you're not heading home just yet, Tess, but try to think of it not as a setback but as a fresh start!"

You try being stuck in a small room, in pain, with all sorts of people invading your privacy and personal space, and then let's see if you're able to always look on the bright side, bitch.

Without my phone, a laptop, or even a television, I'm completely cut off from the outside world. I might as well be on a desert island. Some people would probably find it refreshing. A nice break from the insanity of politics, celebrity gossip, and news of constant school shootings. Plus, I have the ultimate excuse not to return texts or 'like' anyone's posts. No more FOMO if I can't see photos of all the ideal dinners, vacations, clothes, and holiday gifts without social media. But I miss it. I want to get back to my life.

Emmett and I had a ninety-eight-day Snapchat streak going. His teacher taught him how to use the app to send Snaps to James while he was away at school. Now every night around eight-thirty Emmett sends me a message saying, "G'night, Tess. See you soon."

I play it over and over, his innocent sweetness never gets old. I hate that I've ruined our streak. I hope James told him I'm not allowed to have my phone.

Michelle keeps talking as my eyes threaten to close when I spot the outline of a phone in her pocket. I want to ask her to loan it to me for a sec so I can call James. She'd probably refuse. Everyone here is so tragically serious.

"Kate and I will go over all the logistics with you later in the week. It's all gonna work out great, 'K?" Michelle's so bubbly. To hear her spin it, it's as if she and this Kate person are sending me to a resort in Cabo.

Maybe I'll at least get my phone back in rehab. At this point, I'd settle for one of those cheap-ass burner phones drug dealers use on TV. Remembering something, I turn my head quickly. The throbbing starts again, but it's worth it. I see what I'm looking for.

Michelle turns to walk out.

"Wait!" I call. "There's a phone jack on the wall."

She stares, and I realize I must be speaking in slow motion from the medication. My mouth can't keep up with my mind. I have to talk faster if I'm going to stop her from darting off to her next patient.

"There's a phone jack on the wall. But there's no phone. Can I get one? Can someone please bring me a phone?" I ask as quickly and politely as I can.

If she grants what is suddenly the greatest wish of my life, I can call James. I could even try Izzy. Apologize. Beg her forgiveness. Plead with them both to visit me. Whatever it takes. I'm tired of being alone, trapped in this stupid bed, wrestling with my memory to figure out what got me here in the first place.

Michelle stares at me with what I hope is compassion. This is the first time I've seen her at a loss for words. She looks down, opens my chart, frowns, and nods as if confirming something she knew.

"I'm sorry, Tess. Your parents put in a request to have it removed. You'll have to ask them about it. But if it makes you feel better, your dad called. He said to tell you he loves you and that he'll try to be here soon for his shift."

The bruises on my face sting as the blood rushes to my head. What the hell? I'm not even allowed a landline phone? And now more of this "shift" talk —like I'm some pain-in-the-ass part-time job.

I think about the watch and the note in Mom's pocket and I feel the overwhelming need to observe my parents together, see how they interact. Since I woke up yesterday, they've barely been here at the same time.

When they were, they stayed on opposite sides of the room. They talk to me, but never to each other. How much does Dad know? He sat by my bedside, head in his hands, rubbing his chin, as if he were trying to decide if he needs to shave. (He does.) This whole time I've believed I was the sole source of his worry. I'm no longer so sure.

And Mom. Her ability to maintain that poker face is slipping. What I thought was her concern for my health may be fear as she tries to figure out what I know.

Something tells me I might not be the only one on the verge of being forced to make a fresh start.

Saturday, December 16, Late Afternoon

Cold. I ball my hands into fists and punch them inside the pockets of Mom's coat. It doesn't help. My fingers freeze before I even turn the corner to walk up the hill toward the train station. I forgot to change, so I'm still wearing my most comfortable pair of jeans, the ones with holes in both knees. Even though Mom's coat is long, the wind gets in, turning my thighs to blocks of ice. Snow flies into my face in frosty little blasts, as if I'm standing in front of a confetti cannon. It sticks to my lashes. I blink it away and walk faster.

The sidewalks—the ones that have been shoveled—are more slippery than I expected. With each step, I struggle not to fall flat on my back. My nose runs. I've stopped wiping it because I don't want to take my frozen hands out of my pockets.

That stillness I found magical at home now seems eerie. Like I'm the last person alive after a snow apocalypse. Carlo's, the pizza place where Izzy and I used to split a small pie with Yoo-hoos every Friday afternoon on our walk home from middle school, posted a sign in the window: Closed due to storm. Stay safe.

I imagine Izzy's voice in my head: "When even a crusty old Italian guy's scared, you know you're screwed!"

Izzy. I've completely ruined things with her. She hates me and I don't blame her. After James and I kissed at that New Year's Eve party almost a year ago, I'd slept over at her house. We ran back to Izzy's through the snow with seconds to spare before her special extended New Year's Eve 1 a.m. curfew expired and snuck into her house through the side door. Not that it mattered. Becca was staying over at a friend's, and the rest of the family was asleep. Kicking off our boots, we flopped down on the beat-up futons in Izzy's basement.

"I knew it! I knew he'd love you," she said. "I should be a matchmaker. I'm going to start a business. Maybe this is what I'll do now since I can't find love for myself."

Her words rushed together, slightly slurred, tinged with truth. She was in the mood to talk but I wanted to be quiet. I tried to remember the feel of James' lips on mine, his hands in my hair, holding my face, his skin cold, his mouth warm as we kissed goodbye under the white, white moon. I needed to replay it four thousand times in my mind before drifting off to what I imagined would be the best sleep of my life.

"You did good, Iz." I yawned, hoping she'd take the hint. "I really, really like him."

"I knew you would," she squealed and ran to the mini-fridge in the garage where her dad kept extra six-packs. She came back, bounced onto the couch, and handed me a bottle of cheap beer.

"I'm sorry Russell is so basic," she sighed, making fun of her dad. "This tastes like cat pee—or what I'd imagine cat pee tastes like— but hallelujah for twist offs!"'

We clinked bottles and took cautious sips. I agreed about the cat pee.

"So, listen, I know this is going somewhere great for you, and you totally deserve it, but just remember, whatever happens, it's hoes before bros! I'm still your top priority."

I'd laughed, buzzed and slightly nauseous from mixing cocktails and the warm champagne Fix poured—or spilled, really, into our red Solo cups—at the stroke of midnight as we watched the ball drop and some singer have a colossal lip-synch disaster on live television.

"Hoes before bros! Always!" I'd said, certain I'd keep that promise.

Izzy loved that phrase, not that either of us had any experience that would qualify us as "hoes." I'd once kissed Matt Atherton on the middle school ski club bus, but it was on a dare, so that didn't count. At eighth-grade graduation parties, some kids played spin the bottle or seven-minutes-in-heaven, which the girls insisted be dropped down to one minute because the boys were greasy and aggressive.

Izzy never played. Sometimes she said she had strep throat. Other times she'd say she was seeing someone from another town. The boys' disappointment was painfully obvious from their moans and groans. Izzy, with the biggest boobs in our grade, was healthy as a horse, and she wasn't seeing anyone. Only I knew her secret.

"Just remember: Hoes before bros," she'd said each time I'd told her I had a crush on someone.

"Of course! Always!" I'd agree.

But that motto had never been put to the test because nothing and no one ever mattered more to me than Izzy. Until James.

Now here I am, ditching her birthday dinner, which I'd never missed in seven years of friendship, to pick up a stranger at an airport in the middle of a blizzard. And this was no ordinary celebration. Tonight is it. The night. She is finally going to tell her parents. I remember the day she told me. We'd been watching iCarly in her basement.

"I like this show," she'd said.

"Yeah, me too." I didn't care what we watched; I was just happy to be at Izzy's house and not my own, where my regularly scheduled program was Dad wandering around the house sighing and making more coffee as he tried to write "something meaningful."

"I think Miranda Cosgrove is crazy gorgeous. Do you?"

"Yeah, totally," I said, downing fistfuls of bright yellow microwave popcorn. Mom only believed in air-popped with the world's smallest pinch of salt. Izzy's mom bought the fluorescent movie theater butter kind.

"Toxic. Put it back," Mom said whenever I tried to hide a box in our cart at the grocery store.

"I like her." Izzy pointed to iCarly.

"Yeah, she's funny," I mumbled, cheeks bursting like a greedy chipmunk.

"No, Tess. I like her. Like, 'like her' like her."

I turned away from the screen and my almost-empty bowl. Izzy's eyes locked onto mine. My friend, the first one with a joke or sarcastic remark, wasn't kidding. She stared at me. Waiting. Expecting what? Me to flinch? Laugh? Look away? Disappear?

It was the summer between seventh and eighth grade. In that moment, I saw something. It was the first time I'd ever spotted a trickle of loneliness lurking behind her usually bright, bold eyes. The ones that stared down Trey Larkin when he told her to hand over her pizza money in fifth grade just before she laughed in his face and said, "Piss off."

Something in her face said, "I've been keeping a secret. Not because I want to, but because I have to. And I can't do it anymore. I have to tell someone."

I didn't need to look around the basement to know why she'd kept this to herself. Above our heads hung a Celtic cross. First holy communion photos of Becca, Izzy, Michael, and freshly-added Sean surrounded a framed picture of the pope. What she was telling me, this part of her, might not be welcome in her Irish Catholic family.

I knew I could watch that trickle of loneliness turn into a flood that rushed toward a sea of loneliness, where she'd be stuck treading by herself indefinitely. Or, I could offer her a life raft. Acceptance. Unconditional support. I didn't even have to think about it.

"That's cool," I'd said.

Because, really, I've always thought everything about Izzy is cool—even after she called me selfish and a shitty friend when I told her I wouldn't be there tonight.

Another thing about Izzy: She's usually right.

There aren't many cars in the train station parking lot. Still, I have to brush snow off three license plates before I find the ancient Volvo. I climb in. The car is as old as I am. Dad bought it right after I was born, and they'd left Manhattan for the suburbs.

"If you don't have a station wagon or a mini-van, they kick you out of this town," Dad always joked.

"Yeah, but they probably don't mean you have to keep the same one for decades," I'd groan.

The leather on the steering wheel is cracked. The ceiling upholstery sags, and there's a frisbee-sized hole in it that exposes the ugly orange foam beneath. When the windows

96

are down, the slightest breeze makes the fabric flap and fan out, filling the whole back of the car.

"How can you drive like this?" I'd asked Dad while he taught me to parallel park.

"Pretend we're in a sailboat on the high seas, or you're parachuting over the Amazon. Use your imagination, Tess," he'd said.

"Or you could get a new car? Imagine that!" I'd laughed while I tried to find a radio station that wasn't pure static.

"This jalopy is good for my starving artist image. Maybe the college will pay me more if they think we're destitute," he'd reasoned.

I think Mom makes him keep this clunker as a punishment for not being more successful. I put the icy cold key in the ignition. Part of me hopes the car won't start. Then I'll have a legitimate reason to tell James, "Sorry, I tried, but I can't get your pal Nick after all."

I turn the key, and of course, it sputters to life. I sigh, sounding like Dad when he's out of ideas. I grab the scraper from the glovebox and clear the front and back windshields, the mirrors, and windows. Snow falls so steadily I can barely keep up. I get back in and wait a solid five minutes before everything defrosts enough for me to see. The car smells faintly of cigarettes from the days when Dad would still sneak them.

I've never really driven in snow before. Do you turn into a skid or away from it? Maybe those rules will come back to me the way the Heimlich did. I put the car in reverse and pretend my hands are shaking from the cold.

At the first stop sign, I can't take it anymore. The guilt is destroying me. I pull out my phone and text Izzy.

"You've got this! Remember: new year, new you!"

I add thumbs-up, heart-eyed cat, and party hat emojis, hoping they'll make her smile, and end my message:

"Everything is going to be great! XOX"

There I go. Lying again. I want to believe everything will be great, that her family will support her, rise to this. She's met someone. Someone amazing, she says. When Izzy talks about her, her eyes go all megawatt. Her name is Carol, and she lives in Connecticut. They met at field hockey camp in July, and they've been Snapchatting or texting ever since. Izzy wants Carol to spend Christmas break at her house, and then the four of us—Izzy and Carol, James and I—will go to Times Square to watch the ball drop on New Year's Eve.

Izzy says she's sick of pretending and denying who she is. Who could blame her?

"I'm done hiding," she told me Thanksgiving night when we sat in her basement, both of us stuffed, neither of us thankful.

I missed James, and I was pissed that Mom and Dad wouldn't let me visit him and bummed that James' dad was such a cheap asshole, he wouldn't fly his son back for the holiday. James Sr., aka "Jimmy," had the money, but preferred to spend it on the young women he met online at OKCupid or Plenty of Fish.

"You knew this was part of the deal when you chose to go half-way across the country," James' dad told him after he volunteered to take the red-eye both ways if his dad would help out with the cost. "Lots of great schools here in New Jersey, but they're not good enough for you, are they, Jimmy?"

James, who hates being called anything but his proper name, was disappointed but not surprised.

"I'll be surprised when he doesn't act like a complete jerk all the time," James had said when he told me he'd be going to a friend's home in Oak Park for the holiday. "I'll be sampling my first Turducken, so at least there's that."

We'd laughed though, really, I bit my lip to choke back tears.

Meanwhile, Izzy was upset because she'd hoped to visit Carol for Thanksgiving weekend, but Carol's family decided to go skiing last-minute. Selfishly, I was happy she was stuck in town with me.

"I'm going to invite Carol to come here for winter break," Izzy said. "I want to be—I deserve to be—excited about this."

"You totally do," I told her, meaning every word.

She'd always been happy for me about James. Hell, she'd orchestrated it. I'd die if I couldn't talk about him out in the open all the time or if we had to fear hate from all directions just for holding hands in public. Especially in the beginning, just saying his name gave me the best tingly feeling. Maybe I'm a sap, but I want that for Izzy.

"I've come up with a plan," Izzy said. "I'm telling them on my eighteenth birthday. December sixteenth. I need you there, sitting next to me, squeezing my hand under the table for courage, okay?"

"Of course!" I promised her. "Have I ever missed your birthday?"

Izzy came to my house every afternoon for the first two weeks of December to go over what she'll say. This is a BFD, and I've blown it.

Everyone knows being a teenager is pretty much the lowest human life form on the planet, second only to the elderly, when it comes to being treated like you—everything about you: your thoughts, your opinions, your feelings, don't matter. Now add being a little different in a town where everyone is pretty much striving to be exactly the same, right down to their matching Vineyard Vines t-shirts and cartoon stick-figure family minivan decals. Okay, so pretty rough, right? Then, throw in being part of an over-the-top Irish Catholic family. Poor Izzy.

"How fantastic would it be if Grams reveals she'd taken a lady lover in Belfast before she came to America," she'd grinned after perfecting the speech she planned to give on her birthday.

I'd looked at my delusional friend and shaken my head. Her grandmother, who's always encouraging us to sit and say the rosary with her, seemed about as likely to have had a lesbian affair as she was to have spearheaded car bombings for the IRA.

"Becca will support you, right?" I asked, knowing that even though the sisters fought sometimes, there was a ton of love between them. "She's got your back for sure."

"Becca's known since we were little, and I'd hide Ken under the radiator and make my Barbies kiss each other. But still, I've never said it out loud." Izzy stopped and stared up at the ceiling in disbelief. "That's crazy, isn't it? All the crushes, all the boyfriends Becca's gone on and on about for years, and we've never talked about this."

"This is your time, Iz. You've got this," I told her.

"When my mom brings out the cake, she'll tell me to make a wish like she always does. This is what I'm going to say, 'I know I'm not supposed to tell you my wish, or it won't come true. But this year I wish that each of you will accept me for who I am, and not as you'd like me to be, or who you think I could be if I just tried harder, but exactly as I am. I'm gay. I didn't choose this, but I am choosing to be honest with you, and I want to choose happiness over shame and fear. Please don't insult me by telling me it's a phase or something I'll outgrow. I'm still the same person I've always been. I love all of you exactly as you are. My wish is that you will do the same for me."

She varied it a little each time, but it always made me tear up.

"They love you, Iz. Give them the benefit of the doubt. They'll understand," I said with fake confidence, like the way I always tell myself I've studied hard enough for a math test, hoping I'm right, but knowing deep down, I'm probably going to fail it.

That I won't be there to hold her hand beneath the table, to see their reaction—and if it's bad, help her deal—makes me hate myself. But I can't turn back. I promised James.

Maneuvering the car along the icy downtown streets, I keep a steady foot on the gas pedal, scared to accelerate, terrified of spinning out. At the very end of Main Street, just before you come to the highway, there's a traffic light that stays red for what feels like days. When Becca drives us to the mall, and we approach it, Izzy sings, "Catch the green, yes, queen! Arrive on red, good as dead!"

Coasting toward it, I will the light to stay green, panicking that even tapping the brakes will cause me to fishtail into a tree.

Sweat beads above my lip as I watch it change to orange, then bleed into red. It feels like a bad sign.

A Job to Do

"You asked for my professional opinion. I'm giving it to you. It's too soon."

I hear Lydia. She's outside my room. Her tone is firm, her voice so quiet I can barely hear.

"She's trying to be strong, but her mind is fragile. I'm telling you, she's not ready. The shock could be debilitating," she insists.

Debilitating? I remember this word from my SAT prep course. It either means "to weaken" or "something that's used to remove unwanted hair." Wait, no, that's depilatory. I wonder who Lydia's talking to. Mom? Dad? A doctor? And what "shock" is she talking about? Maybe it's not about me at all. I hear another voice, a man's, gruff and mumbly. Lydia cuts him off.

"Of course, I understand the urgency, but you risk making an already-tragic situation worse. I know you're eager to get in there and question her, but I'm telling you she needs more time. What you're suggesting will almost certainly guarantee a setback."

Tragic situation? I'm straining so hard to hear if it weren't for the guardrails I'd fall out of this narrow bed.

"I know you have a job to do, but so do I, and now I'm respectfully asking you to let me do it."

The person she's talking to reminds me of the adults from *Peanuts*. All I hear is more *wah wah wah*. I can't understand a word.

"Two days, maybe three. Until then, please just sit here and protect her until we know exactly where he is."

"Where *who* is?" My brain itches with questions as Lydia strides into my room. Her stern expression morphs into a smile when she sees me watching her. I can't tell if it's genuine or the face she wears to work. Is she at all concerned that I might have overheard her? Or, did she want me to? I imagine when you're a psychologist, every word is weighed, every move calculated. Or maybe I just watch too much TV.

"Tess." She rubs the top of my right hand gently before she sits. "How are you feeling today?"

She's wearing a green wool skirt, black boots, a white cable knit sweater with red candy cane pin. I'm so disoriented. I've lost track of the date. It must be almost Christmas Eve. I don't ask because I don't want to know, it's too depressing—and I've got bigger things to worry about.

"Were you talking about me, just now, in the hall?"

Lydia smiles again. Maybe the fact that I'm paying attention strikes her as a good sign.

"Tess, I'm trying to get you all the time you need, but there's an urgency to this, to your case, that you're obviously unaware of. Carolyn—your mother—tells me you asked about Nick Lawrence."

"Yes." A small shiver creeps down my spine, and the hairs on the back of my neck prick to attention the same way Daffy's ears do when she hears me opening a can of food. "The name's stuck in my head, but I can't picture him. Like at all."

"Are you using the journal? Is it helping you recover any memories, any pieces of Saturday?"

"It's helping." I nod, hoping she doesn't ask to read it. I wish I could change the subject, but what is there to talk about other than this?

"Tess, I'd like to spend more time with you, but the holidays, this season—it makes people—well, let's just say this is my busiest time of the year."

"No problem, I get it." I debate telling her that I'm used to it. Neither of my parents has had much time for me. Even now. Even after all this, where are they?

Lydia stands. She rubs her forehead. I brace, wondering if she's about to give me more bad news.

"I'll be back tomorrow with something that may jog your memory—if you feel up to taking a look it." She smiles. I think it's for real, not just a work face. "In the meantime, keep trying to remember. I know it's not easy. But sometimes, Tess, the only way out of a bad situation is to go straight through it."

Saturday, December 16, early evening

It's only 5 p.m., but already it's dark, so dark I wonder if one of the headlights is out. The storm's causing major power outages. Along the highway, whole towns appear to be nothing more than silhouettes, like fake scenery in a high school play. The only light comes from the moon reflecting off the snow on rooftops.

I should be home with Daffy and a cup of cocoa, making a birthday cake for Izzy like I always do. She's right. I am a selfish and shitty friend.

Snow crunches beneath the tires, and the steering wheel shimmies and shakes even though I'm holding it so tightly my fingers cramp.

According to my GPS, I'm almost there. Newark Airport is just three miles away. That alone feels like a miracle. I've never driven to the airport before, and the highway signs are beyond confusing. I'm lucky there are so few other cars on the road.

On the off-ramp, the Volvo slips and slides into the other lane. A horn blares beside me. I jump as an SUV that must've been in my blindspot swerves to avoid a collision. Even in my dim headlights, I see the driver give me the finger. My knees tremble. I want to get the hell out of this car. It feels like midnight. I glance at the clock on the dashboard; it's taken me fifty minutes to go eleven miles.

I try to read the signs through the snow. Long-term parking. How long is long-term? Are these things everyone just knows—like how to iron a shirt or balance a checkbook? Maybe I am "totally unprepared for real life" like Mom's always insisting.

James sent a text saying Nick will be waiting at arrivals Terminal C.

"I told him you'd look for him near the United baggage carousel even though he's got no baggage."

"We've all got baggage," I wanted to joke but couldn't be bothered typing all that; my fingers were stiff from the cold.

I coast at ten miles per hour toward hourly parking, praying I have enough money in my wallet to cover it. I want a credit card, but Mom says she's afraid I'll lose it. She's convinced I've been taking the house key we hide under the planter on the front porch and leaving it in odd places. I keep telling her I didn't.

"I have a key, why would I take the spare?" I've tried to reason with her.

"Then how did this end up on my desk?" She held the key in front of my face and frowned at me last week.

"Maybe you or Dad left it there?" I wanted to say but didn't. You can't win with her sometimes.

"You have to stop being so careless, Tess. Your father and I aren't always going to be here to fix everything for you," she scolded me on her way to return the key to the porch.

I park the car and rest my head on the steering wheel. A mix of exhaustion, gratitude, and disbelief washes over me. I made it. Now, if only I can find Nick and we can get home safely, the rest of the night should be NBD.

Rushing toward the building, I remember that I never googled "Nick Lawrence" to see if I could find a photo. I pull out my phone. The battery's down to three percent. I start typing when another horn wails. I freeze just in time to avoid getting run down by a hotel shuttle bus as it skids away from the curb. I'm distracted because my search turns up a gazillion Nick Lawrences. Some are middle-aged men; some are kids with baseball caps holding Little League trophies or puppies. But there's no sign of a brown-hair, brown-eyed guy holding a bulldog. I stare at the phone again. It's after six o'clock. More than two hours have passed since James asked me to get Nick.

"He'll be waiting." I hear James' voice in my head.

What if he didn't? What if he ran into someone he knew or bummed a ride from a stranger? The airport's only exciting when you're heading off on a trip. When you're standing around waiting to go home, it sucks. I'm no world traveler, but even I know that.

A blast of heat smacks my face as I walk through the automatic doors. I look at the monitors. If someone gave me a dime for every time the word "canceled" appears beside a flight, I could buy a private jet.

Stranded holiday travelers sleep on the floor using their suitcases for pillows. Families eat dinner slumped against garbage cans. Two men scream over who's been waiting longer for an outlet to charge their phones. The stale air smells like French fries and feet. It's chaos, and though I don't want to drive again anytime soon, I'm jumpy to get out of here as fast as possible.

Circling the baggage carousels like a shark, I'm bursting with adrenaline after that hell ride. My shirt, damp with sweat, sticks to my skin. I feel chilled beneath Mom's coat. I'm wondering how I'll ever find Nick Lawrence in this sea of people when a guy walks up to me. At first, I think he's going to ask me for money or a ride, but then I take a closer look. Dark hair, dark eyes, empty-looking duffel bag slung over his shoulder. He's wearing a lightweight hoodie over a t-shirt. The neck is stretched out and wavy. He looks sloppy, not like a guy who attends a top university, but maybe he's shot from finals too. His eyes, vaguely familiar, meet mine. He holds out a thick, clammy hand.

When our palms touch, an electric shock passes between us. He holds my hand a beat too long and smiles, a weird, goofy grin. I have the sudden urge to pull away, turn around, leave him standing there. He doesn't look like the kind of guy James would befriend, but James always reminds me: Don't judge a book by its cover.

I should be relieved that I found him, or he found me, whatever. Instead, I feel creeped out. This guy—possibly Nick—looks as twitchy as I do after that awful ride. I ought to be less judge-y. He's had his stuff stolen, endured a long, probably turbulent flight, and then waited several hours for a ride from someone he's never met. He probably couldn't relax for a second because he had to scan the crowd to try to recognize me based on photos hanging in a dorm room in eight hundred miles away.

He continues staring, taking me in. Part of me wants this to be just a lonely random dude who's going to do some stoner, "Hey, baby, what's up?" thing, and I can say, "Eww," and keep on walking in search of James' friend, who I imagine looks nothing like the hot mess in front of me.

That hope vanishes when he opens his mouth and says, "Nice to finally meet you, Tess. I'm Nick."

Walking Through It

I put down the diary. A wave of nausea overwhelms me. I look for the wastebasket. I think I'm going to be sick. I know Mom would chalk it up to all the medication on an empty stomach. I haven't eaten—actually chewed food—in days. But it's not that. It's Nick. His slimy hands, his awkward stare.

As much as I want to remember every minute of Saturday night and how I got here, I'm scared. Picturing Nick's face makes me break out in a cold sweat like I did driving to the airport. I can't shake the sense that I'm on the verge of remembering something awful, like I'm peeking behind a door that's better off closed. I tuck the diary under my cast. That's enough for today. Then I hear Lydia's voice from earlier: ...*sometimes, Tess, the only way out of a bad situation is to go straight through it*.

But what if I just avoid it? Like the way I decided to drop statistics this semester and take a study hall instead. I'm not going to college to get a degree in mathematics, so who cares? Does it really matter what happened Saturday night? Regardless of what took place, the outcome is the same. I'm stuck here, trapped like a clueless patient in an episode of *House*. My point is: Why

109

go through something brutally unpleasant if you can skip it? I'm not proud of this attitude but, hey, whatever works.

Except, in this case, it won't work because, according to Lydia and Dad, no one else has the answers. Only I do. I close my eyes and wish this was a bad dream like I thought it was when I first opened my eyes Monday afternoon. I want to get up, walk out of here, and return to my regular life. But that feels impossibly far away now.

I think of Izzy, her brave plan to tell her family who she is and how she wants to live. My mind drifts to Emmett, starting new schools, new diets, new therapies, never quite understanding why, all in the hope of becoming more independent, more comfortable in his own skin. I picture Samira, her endless practicing, forcing herself to do something she's sick of because she doesn't want to disappoint her parents.

After James introduced me to Emmett, he asked me to watch a movie with them. It's the story of this amazing woman, Temple Grandin, who has autism. When she's a young girl, and even after she's an accomplished adult, she's misunderstood by pretty much everyone except her mother. But even with an awesome mom, it's incredibly difficult for her to navigate the world around her. In this one scene, the automatic doors at the supermarket freak her out. She can't seem to anticipate when they'll open, but she knows if she wants yogurt, which is kind of all she eats, she's got to overcome it. It becomes a matter of survival.

She says something like, "I see a door. I'm walking through it." At other points in the movie, when something really challenging gets in her way, she repeats that like a mantra and keeps going.

That courage, it's everything. I look down at the diary.

I see a door. I'm walking through it.

Saturday, December 16, early evening

"Any chance you'd want to drive back?" I ask Nick as we cross the empty parking deck. "I got my license eight months ago, but tonight was my first time ever driving in snow."

"This isn't just snow, it's a freakin' blizzard," Nick says, peeking out from the hood of his sweat jacket. "But, hey, you made it here, didn't you? That's the main thing. Toss me the keys."

He's right. I did make it. That's something. I drove to an airport in a massive snowstorm without crying or crashing. I kept my word to James. Still, I'm glad Nick's willing to take the wheel. As I flip the keys over the Volvo's roof, I remember his wallet was stolen.

"Wait, you don't have a license. Can't you get a ticket for driving without one?"

"Well, I can't exactly speed, now, can I?" His laugh comes out like a sneer, but he has a point.

Nick opens the back door and tosses in his bag before crouching down into the driver's seat. He's taller than I imagined, taller than I am by at least six inches, putting him at a good 6'2", 6'3". He slides the driver's seat all the way back to the point that it looks like he's in the middle of the car.

"So, you're pretty trusting, I see," he says, finding the headlights, turning on the wipers.

His arm is around me, well, not me exactly, but the back of the passenger seat. I feel his fingers brush my neck through the opening in the headrest, and a chill ripples through me—not in a good way. He's looking at me while driving in reverse, while actually backing out, and even though the lot is deserted I imagine Mom screaming, "Watch where you're going!"

She was such a spaz when she attempted to teach me to drive that she eventually gave up and let Dad take over. She said her nerves couldn't handle it—and that was even before Mr. Miller's accident.

"What do you mean?" I ask, turning toward the window, hoping that breaking eye contact will remind him he's driving.

It works. He puts the car in drive, and we head toward the gate to pay for parking.

"I mean, you're pretty trusting. You know, you pick up a stranger at the airport, you let him drive your car."

He looks over at me, and I give him $10, which he hands the parking attendant. Instead of saying "Thanks" or waiting for change, he pulls away quickly. The tires spin, and snow slides down from the car's roof, momentarily blocking the windshield. The wipers clear it, and I realize I've been holding my breath.

I exhale and think about asking him if he and James have any classes together when he says, "I mean, what if I were a madman or even just a terrible driver?"

The roads are icing up. The car slides as if it's on skis. I laugh, more out of nervousness than because I think he's funny.

"Well, are you?"

"Am I what?"

"Are you a madman or just a terrible driver?" I ask.

"Both!" He laughs and puts the pedal down to prove his point, causing the back of the wagon to swing left then right.

As I grip the seat, spongey yellow foam pokes through the cracked leather. Gross. I'm pissed and want to tell him, "Give it up, Ricky Bobby. This isn't 'Talladega Nights,'" but no one else is on the road, and I don't want things to get off to a bad start since he's staying over at my house.

"Well, if James says you're a good guy, then that's enough for me," I say, forcing myself to sound cool and laid back, like this—driving through a snowstorm with a stranger—is just a typical Saturday evening for me.

"Wait, who's James?" he asks.

I glance over. He's still got the hood of his sweat jacket up but his odd grin is gone. He's serious.

My knees go weak. My armpits turn into fountains of sweat.

"Kidding! Kidding!" He punches me in the shoulder.

"Ha! Good one." I don't laugh, but I do take a longer look at him. There's something so familiar about his face—his eyes, the set of his jaw.

"Are you sure you haven't been in any of James' Instagram posts?" I ask. "I feel like I recognize you from somewhere."

"Nope, doubt it."

"It's just that I feel like I've seen you before."

"People say I have a familiar face."

He switches on the radio. The classic rock station Dad always listens to comes in fifty percent static, but Nick turns the volume up anyway and attempts to sing along to "The Reaper."

"Come on, lady, don't fear the reaper! Lady, shake my hand, don't fear the reaper!"

I roll my eyes as he screws up the lyrics. Where did James find this guy?

"Bet you can't name the band!" Nick challenges, speeding up and changing lanes for no reason.

"Blue Oyster Cult," I say, picturing the album cover.

Dad's been buying vinyl records since he was twelve. "Paid for my first Led Zeppelin with my paper route money," he repeats each time a visitor admires his collection. For years, Mom has been after him to get rid of them.

"They take up so much space. Why do you need all these—especially now when you can just download music and keep it on something as tiny as your phone?" she asks every few months.

"If I have to explain it, that proves you don't get it," Dad always responds, shaking his head, saying, "Look at this cover, Carolyn! That's art! And the sound! That warmth? There's no comparison."

"Impressive," Nick says, turning it up louder.

Our small talk is over. That's fine. I wish my phone weren't almost dead. When I'm stressed out, I watch how-to videos on YouTube—everything from ways to perfect a fishtail braid to applying makeup to look like a celebrity. It relaxes me the same way cooking and following a recipe does. But if my phone dies and Nick ends us driving us into a ditch, we'll freeze to death. I try not to think about that and focus on the road instead. Every mile means we're that much closer to home and getting out of the car alive.

I hope that James has arrived at my house ahead of us, that he's inside, giving Daffy dinner, maybe even lighting a fire. My heart beats faster thinking about seeing him in person again.

He'll Be Waiting

After what feels like days in the car, we finally pull off the highway and get stuck at the endless red light. I hear Izzy's voice: "Arrive on red, good as dead!" But we're almost home, and the town hasn't been plunged into darkness by a power failure. Nothing bad can happen now.

Nick barrels into the driveway, attempting to break through the wall of snow the plows have made clearing the street. The wagon only gets a few yards in before can't go any further. Nick cuts the engine after we hear the tires spinning. I'll need to dig out the car tomorrow, refill the gas tank, and return it to the train station so Mom and Dad don't know I took it. But James will be here to help me.

Nick grabs his duffle bag from the back seat as I leap over mounds of snow and hurry up the porch steps to the front door hoping James might be inside.

I turn up the empty planter to grab the spare key but it's not there. My heart soars. James must be here. I turn the knob. It doesn't budge.

Nick, still holding the car keys, hovers over my shoulder and then slides the house key into the lock and opens the door. My excitement disappears. Only Daffy comes running to greet us. I look at the Christmas tree in the corner. The only gift I really want this holiday—time alone with James—hasn't been delivered yet.

"I'm gotta take a piss," Nick says, stepping over the cat and walking toward the bathroom.

Crushed James isn't here yet, I remove the keys from the lock, toss them into the bowl shaped like my outstretched five-year-old hand, take off Mom's coat, and hang it back in the closet.

Mom always says I'm unobservant, not paying enough attention to things.

"I hope you're never called as a key witness," she says. "How can you have a mother who's an attorney and a father who's a novelist and still have no eye for detail? Seriously, Tess!"

"Just lucky, I guess," I reply to annoy her. It works.

But I'm suddenly aware of a few details I wish I could ignore. Like, how does Nick know his way around my house? He kicked off his boots and headed toward Mom's office, where the downstairs bathroom is, with the confident swagger of a frequent guest.

It also occurs to me that he didn't ask me for directions—or even my address.

Though we've never met before, Nick knew exactly where I lived.

Bathroom Surprises

I stare at the diary in my lap, thinking about the bathroom. Mom's home office bathroom. Not too many people would want to hang out in a smallish room beside a toilet, but for days last spring I wandered in there and sat on the edge of the tub, feeling all tingly and happy remembering Memorial Day weekend.

Even though the night I desperately want to recall shows up in fragments, the memory of that spring weekend returns to me now fully formed. I close my eyes and see it all, starting with that Friday night back in May.

Mom, Dad, and I sit around the kitchen table, splitting a pizza I made using a cauliflower crust. (FYI: It's as gross as it sounds—not even smoked mozzarella and prosciutto could save it.) Mom, who's usually the polar opposite of spontaneous, says, "Let's have a barbecue tomorrow!"

"Really?" Dad asks, as surprised as I am. "The three of us?"

"Well, it could be just us, or I thought Tess could invite James, and maybe I'll invite Natalie."

Natalie is Mom's friend from Legal Aid, where she'd volunteered years ago before she made partner and her caseload blew up. Natalie's been through a rough divorce—her second—and despite vowing never to marry again, Mom's determined to help her find her next husband.

"Let me guess, it didn't work out with the young model-slash-personal trainer?" Dad asks, burying a pizza crust inside a napkin.

"No, it didn't, which is why I thought I'd invite Ned Miller."

"Wait, like a set up?" Dad raises his eyebrows.

"Sure, why not? Natalie's met one jerk after another through those dating sites, and I think Ned could use a nice day out of his house."

"Why? What's happened to him now?"

Mom's tendency to be drawn toward people in need has grated on Dad over the years.

"The things you initially love about someone are the same things that will eventually drive you crazy," he's said, half-joking whenever she invites the young, homesick law students from her firm over for Thanksgiving or Christmas dinner.

Ever since she bumped into Mr. Miller in New York that day and found out about his wife's cancer, she's been worried about him. I think Dad's getting sick of hearing about "poor Ned."

"He lost his wife, Jack. Isn't that enough?"

"Fine, invite him," Dad says, sifting through junk mail. "But what are you going to do if he and Natalie fall madly in love? Who will you fix then?"

"You!" Mom tosses a crumpled napkin at him playfully. "Maybe I'll just have to fix you."

Late Saturday afternoon, I look out the kitchen window over the sink and watch the four of them sitting beside the pool, dipping chips in guacamole, drinking Frosé from stemless glasses. I'd shown Mom the recipe on Pinterest when she said she wanted to make a "colorful cocktail," and they seem to be going down easy. Too easy.

Mom sent me into the house to blend up another pitcher. James excused himself seconds before to use the bathroom. He's still in there. The Frosé can wait. I run down the hall, through Mom's office, and stand just outside the bathroom door, hopping from foot to foot like I'm the one who has to pee. I don't. I have to tell James something before I lose my nerve. There's no privacy here. The back of the house is almost all windows or glass doors. Our basement is a disgusting breeding ground for spiders. Cobwebs decorate the steep flight of concrete stairs, making it look we're celebrating Halloween year-round. Mom and I do everything we can to avoid going down there. A few years ago, when she added her office, she had a laundry room built off the kitchen. Now we pretend the basement doesn't exist. Only Daffy is brave enough to venture down there, probably to search for mice among Dad's tools and empty paint cans.

James and I can't go up to my bedroom—especially not in bathing suits. The last thing I want is for Mom to give me her birth control and STD lecture again.

I wait outside the bathroom. My pulse throbs in my ears but not loud enough to drown out the squeaking sound the faucet makes as it's turned off. James opens the door.

"Hey." He smiles.

I put my right hand on his chest and push him back inside, locking the door behind me with my left. Before he can say anything, I kiss him, urgently, the way I've wanted to since he rang the doorbell with tulips for Mom and a lush and leafy basil plant for me, knowing I've become mildly obsessed with perfecting my pesto recipe.

I stop, look into his blue, blue eyes. "I love you." I blurt it fast before I can stop myself.

Izzy warned me not to say it first when I told her I couldn't hold it in much longer. But then she said, "Screw it. Say it if you want to. Life's short, and what the hell do I know about love or romance?"

I stare into his eyes, focusing on that small black freckle. Time stands still. Will he say it back, or will I forever be the weird girl who professed her love to her first official boyfriend while standing beside a toilet?

"And I love you, Tess," he whispers, matching the intensity of my gaze, turning my legs to spaghetti. He takes my face in his strong hands and kisses me again, long and slow.

I pull back, smile 'til my face hurts, then laugh. "I'm sorry, I know this isn't a very romantic setting." I point to the rubbery black toilet plunger in the corner.

"Well, I doubt Chris Harrison would choose it for *Bachelor in Paradise*." James smiles. I'd recently begged

121

him to watch reality TV with me. "But I think as long as there's a clawfoot tub in the room, it's cool."

We kiss again. The rest of the world melts away.

For the rest of the day, I'm floating. I love James. Yes, I said it first, but who cares? He loves me back. Nothing can ruin it. Not the overpowering scent of the citronella candles. Not the way Natalie keeps calling James, "hon," as in, "Pass me that coleslaw, hon!" and "Tell me, hon, what are your summer plans?" Not even the disagreement with Mom that happens after dinner.

I bring out the dessert, a triple-layer strawberry shortcake with blueberries ringing the bottom tier.

"Oh, Carolyn! It's beautiful," Mr. Miller says and claps his hands like a toddler at a birthday party.

After they finished all the Frosé, Dad poured a couple of glasses of Scotch for himself and Mr. Miller. Mom and Natalie moved on to white wine.

"I can't take the credit. Tess made it. But I did buy the ingredients if that counts for anything." Mom laughs, refilling her glass.

"You like to bake, Tess?" Mr. Miller asks.

"I love to." I place the cake in the center of the table and begin to cut slices and pass them around. I try to make them stand up on the plate rather than lay them flat on their sides, but it's tricky.

"Do you think you'll go to culinary school? I'm always so impressed when a young person knows exactly what she wants to pursue. My daughter was like that. Just knew she had to go to art school."

"What does she do now?" I ask, more out of politeness than because I really care.

"Graphic design for a tech company in San Francisco. Her rent is outrageous, and I miss her like crazy, but she's happy. That's the main thing, I guess. Now, if only my son could get his act together. He loves computers, but he lacks direction."

"Well, that's huge, Ned," Natalie says, rubbing his arm in a way that feels too familiar even if he doesn't seem to mind—or even notice, thanks to the Scotch. "Computers are the future," she continues with a hiccup. "They're everywhere."

"Yes, but unfortunately, he's gotten more into the subterfuge side—hacking, spyware. I try to tell him to use his talents for good but...well...he's having a hard time..."

"That's understandable," Dad says, pulling his chair closer to the table.

I know what he's doing, and it makes me cringe. I've seen this act before. He's hoping Ned will share some heartbreaking personal details that may spark an idea for his next story.

"Good writers borrow, great writers steal," Dad always says, paraphrasing T.S. Eliot, who some say lifted that line from Picasso or vice versa, which I guess proves the point. Mom must sense it too because she jumps in.

"Well, for Tess, this is just a hobby. Right, Tess? You don't want to spend your life standing around a hot kitchen, filling other people's orders. You'll find

123

something better, something more suitable, more lucrative."

"But I love it, and I do want to pursue it." As I say this, the slice I'm cutting for her separates and falls over on its side. I pass it to her anyway. I had been thinking about applying to culinary school, and now Mom's disapproval makes me more determined than ever to go for it. I know that makes me a teen cliché, choosing a future to spite my parents, but, hey, as Mr. Miller said, you have to find direction somewhere.

"Well, you know the old saying, 'Do something you love and you'll never work a day in your life!' Dad chimes in, masking his disappointment over not getting to hear Mr. Miller pour his heart out.

"Yeah, but look where that's gotten you," Mom says with sudden sharpness.

Natalie gasps and then covers her mouth like she didn't mean for the sound to escape.

"Ouch!" Dad says and clutches his heart dramatically, trying to play it off.

Wine is like truth serum to Mom.

"Does anyone want coffee?" I offer, hoping she'll take the hint.

"I should probably go," Mr. Miller says, "but thank you for a lovely evening. I don't want to overstay my—"

He stands and sways a bit. James jumps up and steadies him before he falls into the pool.

"Ned, you shouldn't drive," Mom says. "Why don't you stay over? We have plenty of room."

James and I look at each other—Mom suggesting an adult sleepover?

"Thank you, but no, I don't want to leave my son alone for much longer—even though he probably hasn't even realized I'm gone," he says, his head hanging like a wilted flower.

"How old is your boy?" Natalie asks.

"Oh, he's no boy. He's nineteen, but still, we've had a rough year. I'll call him to pick me up. It'll do him some good to get out of the house."

"Tell him he's welcome to come and have some cake with us," Mom says.

Mr. Miller smiles politely. "I think he'll probably just want to go back home, but thanks, that's very thoughtful."

James and I lie in the hammock. My head rests on his shoulder. Faint traces of chlorine, sunscreen, and smoke from the grill cling to his skin. They mix with his warm, familiar scent, and I wish I could bottle it. I want to stay here forever. There's a light breeze, and we can see stars through the swaying treetops. What I think are fireworks in the distance turns out to be Mr. Miller's son's car.

"Sounds like someone needs a new muffler," Dad says.

"Ah, my chariot awaits," Mr. Miller stands again, steadier this time.

Mom and Natalie hug him good-bye. Dad shakes his hand and grips his elbow, making sure he doesn't stumble into the pool. From the hammock, I watch as Mr. Miller struggles to work the latch on the garden gate. As soon as he's on the other side, I hear him sigh, shrinking as he wanders deeper into the darkness.

I think about loneliness, death, sadness in general, and snuggle tighter to James.

"I love you," I whisper it again, meaning it even more than the first time I said it.

Everyone else has gone home, and it's just Mom, Dad, and me in the kitchen when Mom says, "Poor Ned. This last year has aged him. When we met twenty years ago, he looked like a young Robert Redford. Now his face has gotten thin, and he looks so tired. I think he's anxious about his son."

"I'm sure the kid will come around in time," Dad says.

"I don't know." Mom scrapes the plates over the garbage and arranges them in the dishwasher. "I think it's more than that. I think the son might be a little 'off.'"

"'Off'? what do you mean 'off'?"

For once, I'm glad James isn't here. He's sensitive to people making a diagnosis about anyone else's mental health. Mom's out of line talking about Mr. Miller's son when she doesn't even know him, but at least whatever anger she felt toward Dad earlier seems to have passed.

"Ned is so funny and charming; I'm sure Sarah must've been too. But from the way Ned describes him, his son's always been sullen. He doesn't have a lot of friends or interests—outside of computers. Poor Ned. He tries so hard. He invited his son to come to the office once, to take him to lunch, maybe spark some interest by showing him around our IT department. The guy scowled the whole time. He seemed intense. There's a lot of anger there."

"The kid had just buried his mother, Carolyn. Give him a pass. Wouldn't it be more concerning if he'd shown up as bubbly as a game show host?"

"I don't appreciate your sarcasm, Jack," Mom snaps.

I wonder if that's a line she got from the marriage counselor they've been seeing.

"All relationships require maintenance, Tess," she'd said when she and Dad sat me down in the living room to tell me they were "having issues" and getting help.

Even now, I'm embarrassed thinking about it, but when they told me, I started to cry.

"Does this mean you're getting divorced? Do we have to move?" My thoughts spun—and, selfishly, they were all about me. James and I had only been hanging out for a couple of months, but he'd already told me about his parents' divorce and how miserable it was. Plus, if we moved, I worried I wouldn't see him or Izzy as much.

"We're committed to working things out," Dad had said.

"That's right." Mom nodded. "We're going to do everything we can to get things back on track."

What were these "things" they both mentioned? Still, it sounded promising in theory—sort of. After they told me, I couldn't stop analyzing every conversation they had. Were things improving? Were they getting worse? I couldn't tell. I'd been in my own world, thinking about James, spending time at Izzy's, attempting to study for the SATs, I hadn't realized there were problems to begin with, so how could I know if they'd fixed them?

"My apologies," Dad says now, clearing his throat. "Let's change the subject. Do you think you were able to make a love connection between Ned and Natalie?"

"That would be nice," Mom says, switching off the lights over the kitchen island and turning on the one over the sink. "Who doesn't want another chance to fall in love? I think they're both ready to start their next act."

I want to tell her if there's one thing I've learned from binge-watching too many Netflix series: Things tend to fall apart after the first season.

Mom and Dad go to bed, and I slip back outside to dip my legs in the pool. I want to FaceTime Izzy. There's no way I can sleep. James and I said it again—I love you— when I walked him to his car. I'm so happy my heart might explode. I feel as if I, the most un-athletic girl on the planet, could run a thousand miles fueled by pure joy.

I see Samira watching TV with her parents. I wave to her. She comes out to talk to me over the fence.

"Hey, party girl," she says.

"Hey, yourself. Want to join me for a swim, or will the chlorine damage your delicate musician's hands?" I tease.

"I can't stay out long, Tess. I'll be eaten alive by mosquitoes. I'm too sweet, you know this," she says with a cheeky grin.

I smile.

"What?" she asks.

"I told James I love him." I have to tell her. I can't keep it in. "And he said it back!"

"Good, you should love him. He's kind, smart…" She's ticking off attributes on her long, slender fingers. "He's got the looks of a sexy, young weatherman, and a nice bottom too. And you are a darling girl who makes a perfect lemon poppy seed pound cake. What's not to love? Although we both know you should try harder in school."

"You see everything, don't you?"

"Yes!" She nods with a faint smile on her lips. "And did you know that I'm also a body language expert?"

"I know you have many talents, but no, I didn't know that was one of them."

"It's true. And it looks like someone at your party has a serious crush."

"Oh, yeah, my mom's trying to set up her friend Natalie with a man she works with. I think it has potential. She seemed into him, right?"

"Yes, and no. She is into him; he is not into her."

"So, then, who's crushing who?"

"Samira! Samira! Get back in this house at once, dear! It is almost midnight," her mother calls.

"Tell me before your coach turns into a pumpkin, Cinderella!" I say as Samira rolls her eyes in the direction of her mother.

"That wobbly man, the one who nearly fell into your pool like a tipsy flamingo? Keep an eye on him."

"Where do you get this stuff?" I ask her.

She stares up at me, her big brown eyes serious beneath her enviable lashes. "Trust me!" She squeezes my hand and sprints back to her house.

"Okay, Samira the Spy, if you say so," I call and watch her disappear.

***

Why am I remembering this? The bathroom. Mom's office bathroom. After James and I shared that amazing moment, I found myself going back in there to try to relive it, that feeling of pure bliss, again and again. Mom has this white tea body lotion that smells like vacation in a bottle, and the scent alone takes me back to what I now think of as the best day of my life.

"I love you." Are there three better words in the English language? No, I don't think so. Not even "maple pecan scones" or "math test canceled" can compete.

On an afternoon in mid-June, I sit on the edge of the tub, closing my eyes, picturing James' hands on my face, the warmth of him pressed against me, when I hear Mom on the other side of the door.

"Tonight? Sure, I'd love to." She's on her cell phone. Mom and Dad have gotten in the habit of calling each other even though they're in the same house to avoid screaming from one level to the other. I'm guessing it's another trick suggested by the marriage counselor.

"That sounds fantastic. Can't wait. See you soon. Bye-bye!" She's using a different voice, not her regular fake phone voice. This one's soft and deep, like Daffy's purr, but human.

That therapy must be working. I wonder where she and Dad are going. Will they be out for a while? Can I invite James over? Can we finally be alone for a full hour—maybe even two? I want to text him, but I left my phone charging in the kitchen. If I come out now, I'll have to explain to Mom that sometimes I hang out in her bathroom like a weirdo sniffing body lotion and thinking about love.

I wait a few more minutes, moisturizing my knees and elbows to pass the time. Izzy's always saying if you don't care for your elbows, they end up looking like cracked nipples. With summer about to begin, she's made me paranoid.

I hear the car start in the driveway and bolt out of the bathroom to text James. When I reach the kitchen, Dad's there, sitting at the island skimming the newspaper.

"Looks like it's just you and me tonight, kid. Feel like whipping up a feast for a grateful old man, or should we just order pizza?"

"Wait, you're not going out with Mom?"

"Nope. She's got some work thing. She told me we shouldn't wait up."

I want to tell him about the way her voice sounded on the phone, but what would I say? And maybe she is at a work thing? I decide to express myself the best way I know how—with comfort food.

"How does chicken Alfredo sound?" I ask.

"Like heaven," he replies without looking up from the newspaper.

Mom's phone call. The pocket watch. The note. Nick walking straight to the bathroom. They feel like puzzle pieces I need to connect. I want to talk this through. Where is James? He hasn't been here today. And Izzy. Even with our fight, I can't believe she hasn't visited me. I'm lonely and confused. I rest my head against the pillow. The staples in my scalp itch like crazy. Mom says that's a good sign, the healing has begun. But can I trust anything she says? Can I trust anyone?

Wanda, the woman from Food Services, wheels in a silver cart, the triple-decker version of the ones flight attendants use.

"We've got something real special for you tonight," she says exactly like she did last night, even though it was a slice of unappetizing brownish meat and lumpy potatoes garnished with a limp sprig of parsley. But it's fine. The medication kills my appetite.

"Thanks," I say as Wanda places tonight's meal on the table on wheels beside me. When I hear my voice, I realize I haven't spoken to anyone in hours. Tears spring to my eyes against my will.

"Ah, honey, don't cry. It's not that bad. It just needs a little salt. Here, I'll slip you some, but shh! Don't tell anybody!" Wanda reaches into the pocket of her gray uniform and pulls out her cell phone as she digs around for a tiny packet of salt.

"Thank you!" I perk up, wipe my eyes, and reach for the salt. "Wanda, can I ask you a favor? Can I borrow your phone real quick?"

She looks over each shoulder, probably worried that the patient in the next room will ring for the nurse if dinner isn't delivered soon.

"I don't know, baby. We're not supposed to use our phones while we're working. Where's your phone? I'll hand it to you." She glances at the chair, table, and windowsill. She rearranges and fluffs my thin hospital blankets, checking for it.

"My cell is at home, and this room doesn't have a landline because the jack is broken," I lie. "It's just that my mom was supposed to be here an hour ago. With the snow and the icy roads, I'm worried that something has happened to her."

It requires virtually no effort to bring more tears to my eyes. I feel like a manipulative jerk, but I sense Wanda's about to give in.

"It'll just take a sec, I promise," I sniffle.

"Okay, okay, sure, honey. Why not?" She hands me the phone after punching in a passcode with her long nails, which alternate between red and green for the holiday. "Here you go." She looks over each shoulder again as if she'd just handed me a dime bag, not a Samsung Galaxy.

I'll deal with the guilt over lying to this nice lady later. Right now, I'm giddy. I dial James' number, reminding myself not to say his name in case Wanda's listening. The line rings. My heart races. It rings again. Maybe he's eating dinner or Christmas shopping or ice skating with Emmett. The ringing continues. It's going to voicemail, but at least I'll hear his voice, even if it's just the recorded "Hey, it's James. I'll call you back as soon as I can!"

I'll leave a message, ask him to visit me asap. I don't care how needy I sound. It rings a final time. An automated voice catches me off guard. "The voicemail box is full and cannot accept any new messages. Goodbye."

My heart rate slows to a sad crawl. I hand Wanda back her phone. "Thanks, she's not there," I say, not exactly a lie.

"I'm sure she's on her way," she nods reassuringly. "Now go ahead, pick up that fork and dig in! Wednesday night's my personal favorite—lasagna."

Saturday, December 16, evening

I light the flame under the largest burner and put the stockpot back on the stovetop, determined to make James' lasagna, when Nick walks into the kitchen.

Water beads dot his forehead. Either he washed his face and forgot to use a towel, or he's sweating, which seems impossible because the house is freezing. I remember James saying that Nick came back to the dorm pretty drunk last night, maybe he's hungover.

"Whipping up something special for Jimmy, are you?"

"You don't call him that to his face, do you?"

James has zero tolerance for this nickname because it reminds him of his dad—a perpetual disappointment.

"We're pals. I call him whatever I want."

James has a soft spot for people who are a little different. Izzy and I figure it's because of Emmett. It's as if James consistently tries to pay it forward. Like if he's always kind to everyone, he's generating good karma that'll flow back toward his brother. I don't have the heart to tell him the universe doesn't work like that. But Nick? He's beyond "quirky," as James called him, and he's more than just a little different. Even being in the same room with him is awkward because he stands so uncomfortably close that my back presses against the sink.

"Hey, would you mind plugging in the Christmas tree and starting a fire?" I ask.

He stares.

"In the fireplace?" I point toward the living room.

He grunts and walks off. I get the feeling that he's one of those guys who prefers to give the orders rather than take them.

I pull the package of ground beef from the fridge and start browning it in a pan. Seasoning it with dried herbs and garlic powder, I listen to it sear, hoping to get the lasagna into the oven before James gets here.

"Sweet collection," Nick says, pointing to hundreds of record albums Dad has alphabetized in the bookcase he built under the window. Instead of starting a fire like I asked, he puts on The Clash's "London Calling." I recognize the early drum beats of "Spanish Bombs."

Even Izzy had been impressed the first time she sat down on the floor to check out all that vinyl.

"Wow," she'd said. "Pretty cool." She studied one after another, her fingers tracing Janis' giant sunglasses on "Joplin In Concert."

"How freaking adorable is a young Janis Joplin? Seriously."

"My crush has always been Derek and the Dominos-era Eric Clapton," I revealed.

"I could see that," she said. Then she laughed, turning "Aja" over in her hands. "OMG, did I tell you that up until like a year ago, I thought Steely Dan was just one dude named Dan? Then I find out it's a bunch of dudes named after a sex toy."

We were sprawled out on the floor, listening to "Peg," looking at the faded cardboard record jackets—John Lennon, Mick Jagger, Joni Mitchell, with her perfect full red lips on the cover of "Clouds." Their faces were so familiar to me. Like uncles and aunts who lived in a cabinet, I could visit them whenever I wanted, whenever I needed to hear their voices, their words seeping into my subconscious even when I had no idea what their hypnotizing lyrics meant.

"I don't know, I'm kind of over it," I said. "I used to think my dad's taste was so unique, but, really, it's like a classic hits library. Big deal. It's like he was afraid to branch out and be original, you know what I mean?"

If Dad had ever heard me say that, it would gut him, but that's how I felt.

"Yeah, but still, at least your dad has an interest, a hobby," Izzy said. "All my dad does is eat and fart."

I'd laughed so hard iced tea streamed out my nose. Izzy could always make me snort with laughter just by saying the most simple and honest thing.

Izzy. I look at the clock on the microwave: 7:25. Has she blown out the candles, made her wish? Will our friendship survive the fact that I bailed on her when she needed me most? We both have other friends—hers are from field hockey and lacrosse. I met mine at the cooking club I started freshman year. It was Mom's idea.

"You need to put something on your college applications, Tess! Something that proves to people that you can lead," she'd insisted.

Once a month, a bunch of us go to a new restaurant or try a different cuisine. Then, throughout the year, we hold bake sales for worthy causes. Having a charitable component was the only way the club got approved. After I'd told James about it, he asked if I'd write reviews of the new places we tried for the school paper. I did, of course. So then I made a few more friends from writing for

The Chronicle. But none of those relationships could ever come close to what Izzy and I share.

I think back to when we first met. Fourth grade. She was the new kid, fresh from Brooklyn. We were in math class, and the teacher, Mrs. Blake, asked her to solve a word problem. Some guy at a fair was going to buy four lemon ices and one zeppole, and, given the cost of each, Izzy was supposed to figure out how much money he'd have left.

"Isabelle, can you solve this one for us, please," Mrs. Blake had asked.

Izzy shook her head. "I can't," she said calmly.

Some kids laughed, because, really, it was early in the year and the problem wasn't that hard.

"Can you try?" Mrs. Blake asked. "Where should you begin, Isabelle?"

"I can't because I'll never understand why this kid would buy a lemon ice when he could just spend all his money and get six more zeppoles."

Everyone laughed—this time with Izzy, instead of at her—even Mrs. Blake, who realized Izzy's issue wasn't with the calculation.

At lunch, I stopped by Izzy's table. She sat alone, pretending to be captivated by the tower she'd built out of Nilla Wafers.

"Hey, how did you know how to say that word?" I asked.

"What word?" She stayed focused on her cookie creation.

"Zee, zep, the thing from the math problem."

"Seriously? How could you not know how to say zeppole?" she said, kind of tough, like she was coiled and ready to fight. Whenever she gets like that now, she'll say, "Sorry, my Brooklyn is showing."

"I thought it was zee-pole," I confessed.

"Wait, have you never had one?" She frowned as if I'd just admitted I never changed my underpants.

"Nope."

"Come to my house after school tomorrow. My mom will make them, and then you'll understand why nobody'd pick some pee-colored ice over hot balls of fried dough."

Now, Izzy's mom makes me a heavenly half-dozen every year for my birthday, presented in a brown lunch bag tied with a bow. When I shake it, the confectioners' sugar that lines the bag's bottom coats them perfectly. Sweet white clouds as soft as baby powder puff out and swirl around, dusting my hands.

I think I'll die if that tradition doesn't continue.

My phone lights up, catching my eye as it buzzes against the countertop where it's charging. A text. Please, please, please let it be from James saying he's almost here. Or Izzy telling me that I was right, and everything went well with her family. I reach for the phone and see Nick stacking logs in the fireplace in between bursts of playing air guitar as "Lost in the Supermarket" throbs from the speakers Dad mounted in each corner of the living room.

It's Samira. I look out the window over the sink. She waves and points to her phone, meaning I should read her text asap.

"What's up, busy girl? Who's the raven-haired hottie? You're not cheating on James, are you? (Holiday side piece, LOL!?!) Can't see his face too clearly, but the musician in me is picking up dark, brooding Kurt Cobain vibes. Spill it! You know I live vicariously through you. Yours truly, Samira the Spy."

"He's def. grunge-y…"

139

He'll Be Waiting

I start typing but then delete it. Why am I so harsh and judgmental? I'm turning into Mom. I don't know how to respond, but she's staring at me out the window, so I can't ignore her.

"Ha! No, he's James' friend Nick from school. Needs a place to stay 'cause of the storm. James should be here soon!

I add hearts and praying hands emojis.

"I'd come over. We could double date. But I must practice for state symphony auditions."

Frowning and nerd faces follow.

"TBH, he's kinda odd."

It's mean, but at the same time, it's a relief to confide in another person.

"Not everyone can be as perfect as your knight-in-shining-armor, James!"

She's probably being sarcastic, but she's right.

"So true! Good luck with practice!"

I'm about to look for the clarinet emoji when I feel hot air on my neck. Nick stands right behind me, leaning over my shoulder. I jump. I never heard him come into the kitchen because of the blasting music. I turn around, forcing myself to be extra nice in case he read my text.

"Hey, great job getting the fire going. It's warmer already." It's true, I'm sweating but mainly because he scared the hell out of me.

I try to picture him as a "hottie," like Samira wrote. Nope, not seeing it. But there is something familiar about his face, his mannerisms. I can't place it.

"You got any wine? Let's open a bottle. You seem a little tense, and, shit, I've had a rough few months. Years, actually."

"I can only imagine," I say, reaching for a bottle of red from the crisscross wine rack on the side of the island.

140

I've only touched Mom and Dad's stash a few times in the past, and when I did, I was always sure they'd catch me, so I couldn't enjoy it anyway. Now, I don't even give it a second thought. Nick's right, it has been a rough few months and the last few hours haven't exactly been a picnic.

"The pressure to get into a school—especially one as good as yours—it's insane. I just finished my applications this week. I wanted to be done with all that before James got home. So I definitely feel like celebrating."

I expect him to open up, commiserate about personal essays, SAT and ACT scores, begging for letters of recommendation. When he says nothing, I hand him the bottle and pull a corkscrew from the drawer. The water comes to a rolling boil. I count twelve lasagna noodles and place them in the pot.

"You got any crackers?" The cork's pop punctuates Nick's question.

Before I can answer, there's a knock at the door. A tornado of excitement swirls inside me. It has to be James.

James

James sits a few feet away. Finally. He's here, and I should be bouncing up and down in my hospital bed to have him close after all this time. But Phyllis stopped by with another plastic cupful of pills around eight o'clock. There's nothing quite like narcotics for dessert. If only they'd help me forget that flavorless lasagna Wanda delivered.

After she brought my dinner, I stared at the door, hoping James would show up any second. I don't know if I slept for two minutes or two hours, but now I'm trying to swim up to the surface. Reality feels distance-y, out of reach.

Of course, I'm happy to see James, but something's different.

"Hey," I manage to say, "when did you get here? I told you not to let me sleep."

James lifts his face, smiles, and closes the book that's in his hand. He's one of those people who's always devouring a story, and it's paid off. During the past year, during college and job, interviewers asked, "So, what are you reading at the moment?" Of course, he could pull a paperback copy of *The Amazing Adventures of Kavalier & Clay* or *The Goldfinch* out of his messenger bag.

"You are the ultimate dork," Izzy had said when he'd told us, wanting to give us a heads-up so we'd be ready if we found ourselves in the same situation.

"Me? I'd have had to say, 'Well, I'm halfway through Ina Garten's *Barefoot in Paris*. Do cookbooks count?'" I'd laughed.

"Stick to your culinary school dreams, and you'll be just fine, my friend," Izzy had said.

Through the sheer curtains, the night sky is black, starless. I can't see the moon, only the fluorescent light behind my bed shines down on the scuffed-up linoleum floor. James remains largely a silhouette. A handsome shadow. I look at the cover of the book in his hand — pink and blue flowers.

My journal.

That's what he's holding. To pass the time, I picked it up while I waited for him, but things started to get hazy, and I had to shut my eyes. Maybe it fell on the floor, and he picked it up.

I gesture toward it lamely, embarrassed but too groggy to care that he's seen it.

"Lydia, my psychologist," I take a beat to roll my eyes, "thought it might help. I don't know. I'm scared, James. Nothing feels normal anymore."

He gets up, walks over, sits on the right side of the bed, and presses his lips to my forehead. Too bad I'm wrapped so tightly in a fog of painkillers and exhaustion that I can't feel it. He leans back and takes my hand.

I want to cling to him and hope it will make everything else melt away like it did when we held each other in Mom's office bathroom. I want to give him all my attention. How can I not focus on the person I've longed to see more than anyone else? I want to hear what he's been up to, find out how Emmett's doing, make plans for when I get out of here. But my brain spins, memories mix with dread. The metallic taste of fear lingers in my mouth.

Saying Lydia's name out loud caused my mind to flood with bits of the conversation she had with that mumbly person in the hall this morning. Was that just this morning? It feels like years ago. Time stands still in a hospital—especially when you spend almost the entire day by yourself.

Though it makes me seem like a spoiled baby, I'm angry and upset that James has hardly visited me. I tell myself that his mom and Emmett are probably taking up most of his free time, but still, my feelings are hurt.

When I first met Mrs. Potter, she was pretty stressed out and not very friendly. I think she worried that if James had a girlfriend, he'd have less time to help with Emmett. I wanted her to like me, but I had to get Emmett to like me first for that to happen. Initially, I was scared. Autism. What does it even mean? James explained that it affects people differently, but there are certain things that are fairly common, like struggling with communication or having trouble enjoying social settings or interactions. Sometimes Emmett will stare at his hands or look at his Matchbox cars for hours, and he'd rather do that than anything else. For people with autism, there are times when the outside world is just too much. Lights are too bright, voices are too loud, smells are too strong, and all that can cause them to retreat inside themselves or have a meltdown. I get it. I guess I wasn't really scared of Emmett; I was afraid of doing something accidentally that might upset him. Because if he didn't like me, would James still like me?

Once I got to know Emmett, I realized he's unlike anyone I'd ever met. Even though his vocabulary's pretty limited, he tries his best to express how he's feeling. Before long, I could understand his secret language. His high-pitched squeals mean he's having fun. His hands clamped over his ears, or his fists clenched into tight little balls signal he's anxious or overwhelmed.

When we make cookies together, he hums and bounces up and down with excitement, and it makes me happy to know that he's having fun.

As Emmett and I developed a friendship, Mrs. Potter and I did, too. Once, when she was working late during tax season—she's an accountant—James, Emmett, and I went to the store and bought everything to make dinner. It wasn't anything too exciting, just a roasted chicken, some honey-glazed carrots, and mashed potatoes because those are Emmett's favorite.

"It smells like Thanksgiving outside. One of our neighbors must be cooking up a feast!" Mrs. Potter had said when she walked through the door to their condo not realizing the scent was coming from inside her home.

James and Emmett had set the table, and when she saw me pull the bird, stuffed with lemon, rosemary, and garlic, out of the oven, she marveled, "Oh my gosh, Tess!" like I'd presented her with a Birkin bag full of diamonds.

Then, as we ate, she said something that I still think about a lot.

"For a long while, it felt like our world was shrinking. I'm glad it's growing again."

Emmett squealed and took another forkful of mashed potatoes as James' leg brushed against mine beneath the table. I knew what she meant. There were times when I'd swear I could feel my heart expanding. I guess sometimes you don't realize how lonely you are until you aren't anymore.

After James left for college, I visited Emmett a few times a week. We'd make granola bars together in the food processor. "No preservatives, just pure ingredients," Emmett would say, repeating a TV commercial, while tossing in almonds, dates, apples, and a sprinkling of cinnamon. Sometimes, I'd stay after Emmett's sitter left and I'd start dinner to give Mrs. Potter a break. She'd invite me to stay. We'd bond over talking about the latest Netflix series we'd watched and how much we missed James.

Sometimes I felt more a part of their family than my own.

So why do I feel so alone now? I would've thought Mrs. Potter would visit me. Even a homemade "Get Well Soon" card would be a nice gesture. I guess the fact that they haven't made any effort bothers me—a lot. I think about mentioning it to James, but who wants to hear someone complain about their family? Nobody. Still, I can't shake the feeling that they're avoiding me.

Did I do something horribly dumb, dangerous, or embarrassing, and that's why I'm here? The last thing I remember is Nick opening a bottle of wine. Did James ask me to drive and pick him up somewhere? If we were in an accident, then, of course, his mom would be furious with me. It would also explain why Mom and Dad seem so stressed. Is Mom so busy because she's preparing my legal defense?

But I still don't even know if I actually saw James on Saturday. It's crazy that I'm able to piece a lot together, but he's still missing from my memory of that night. When I asked Mom about him when I first woke up here, she looked upset, like she didn't even want to hear his name.

Does James have more to do with what happened than anyone is telling me? He's the one who asked me to go and get Nick. Where is Nick now? That guy was definitely odd, but was he dangerous? What was it Lydia said this morning? Something like "sit here and protect her until we know exactly where he is."

If James were a threat to me, he'd never be allowed inside my room. Unless no one knows but me—and I can't remember.

I'm spiraling. My thoughts don't make sense. I take my hand out of his and rub my eyes as if that will help me see things more clearly. It doesn't.

"James, is there someone outside the door? Like a cop or a security guard? Did you see anyone just now? I think someone's out there." I sound crazy, paranoid, but I don't care.

"I don't know. I slipped in through the window." He smiles. When I don't laugh, he continues, "I didn't notice anyone, Tess. But I was focused on seeing you."

He kisses me long and slow. Butterflies fill my empty stomach. Still, I wonder if he's lying to prevent me from freaking out.

"I love you," he whispers, staring into my eyes. I lose myself there. He kisses me again. I want to savor the familiar feel of his mouth on mine, but all I taste is shame for doubting him—even for a second. I know he'd never hurt me, even if he's hardly been here.

He holds up the journal. "I hope you don't mind that I looked at this."

If anyone else had, I'd be mortified, but James understands me, he really sees me. He has from the moment we shook hands in the library more than a year ago.

"Who needs another 'young woman wakes up in a hospital with no memory' story, right? Maybe if I ever remember how I ended up here, I can write the whole story, and you can edit it. We could turn it into a bestseller. Can you imagine? My dad would die from jealousy!" I try to joke, but James isn't laughing.

"I know you hate writing. Reliving that night can't be easy either."

"It's crazy, James. It's like all my memories are there, I just have to concentrate, and most of them come back. At least I think they do. But it makes me so tired, and I'm scared of what might pop up next. I mean, obviously, it's something bad, based on all this." I point to my casts, the bruises on my face.

I want to tell him about the pocket watch and the note I found, the way my parents are acting around each other now, but that has nothing to do with us and why I'm here.

"You're close, Tess. I can feel it. Close to putting it all together. And then, in time, you'll heal, and you can go home."

"And we can spend more time together." I reach out to hold his hand again. "After this, there's no way I'm not coming to visit you at school. Screw my parents."

James shakes his head. "I won't be there, Tess."

"You're not going back? Wait. Why? Because of this? James, you—"

"I can't. Not after everything that's happened. But, Tess, whatever memories may resurface next, I want you to know, meeting you—this—it's the best thing that ever happened to me. You didn't remember me last year, but I had a crush on you since you sat in front of me in photography class your freshman year. I was crazy about you from the moment you turned around and passed me the syllabus and said, 'This better be an easy A,' and I said—"

"And you said, '*Lens* hope so.'" I laugh, hoping it hides my rage at my ability to recall something that happened three years ago with no effort when parts of just four days ago are still missing.

"It sounded so much better in my head." James smiles.

I reach up to trace the dimple in his chin.

"I'm the one who begged Izzy to introduce us," he continues. "I asked her not to tell you. I was sort of embarrassed that I didn't have the courage to just ask if you wanted to hang out sometime. So I pleaded with her to help me. And she kept my secret. At least I think she did."

"She did." I nod. Good old Iz. Thinking about how she's always looked out for me makes me feel worse that I wasn't there for her. "Wait, have you seen Izzy since you've been home?"

"Only for a second."

"Did she say anything about me? About me and her? Will she ever forgive me?"

James frowns. "You were there, Tess. You talked to her."

I shake my head. How can I not remember seeing my boyfriend and my best friend? Tears of frustration spring to my eyes. When did I see her? Where? If she hasn't been here to visit me, does that mean things are actually worse between us now? I need to know what happened.

James looks down at his wrist, a reflex. His watch, the one I gave him for graduation, isn't there.

"I have to go," he says.

Tears slip down my cheeks now.

"Each time you leave, I feel like you're never coming back."

"I know. I think that's how Emmett feels too."

I nod and try to be an understanding girlfriend and not a self-centered crybaby, which seems like my new default setting.

"Okay," I nod. "Tell him I said hi."

My stomach makes an embarrassingly loud rumble, but if James hears, he doesn't mention it. He kisses me goodbye and hands me back my journal. Even though it's a crazy thing to ask, food is on my mind, and I can't help it.

"Did we eat the lasagna I made Saturday night?"

"No, Tess." He shakes his head. "No, we didn't."

Train in Vain

Dad sits in the chair beside my bed with his right ankle resting on his left knee. He's frowning at the manuscript in his lap.

He sticks his reading glasses on the top of his head when he realizes I'm awake and staring at him.

"There's my girl," he says. "How are you feeling?" He doesn't wait for my answer. "Listen, I'm sorry I didn't make it here last night."

At least he didn't finish that sentence with "for my shift."

"Roads were closed. Power lines were down. I was halfway here when I had to turn back."

I know he's lying. James made it here. They were coming from the same area. I don't bother saying this because he'll just offer some other excuse I won't believe anyway.

"But the good news is all my classes were canceled so I can spend most of the day here with you," he says.

"With me or with your manuscript?" I want to ask him.

I've been complaining to Izzy that my father prefers his fictional families to his real one for years.

"Can you blame him? You have total control over the people you dream up," Izzy would point out. "You can put words in their mouths, make them do whatever you want. You're the ultimate puppet master, and the best part is, you don't even have to pull any strings."

When she put it like that, it made sense. Still, it sucks to consistently come in second to people who don't actually exist.

"Your mother and I have an appointment with Lydia this afternoon, and then the four of us are going to sit down and talk. Lydia thinks it's time to share some information that might help."

I nod but don't say much else. He returns to his manuscript. I've noticed with adults, if you want their attention, ask them a question about themselves.

"How's your new book coming along?"

For the past couple of months, this topic has brought a light back into Dad's eyes. Maybe I'll actually read this one when he's finished.

He frowns, his shoulders sag, and he shakes his head. "I'm afraid I'm going to have to shelve it. I keep rereading it, realizing now that I didn't really know the characters the way I thought I did. I didn't understand their motivations. I had it figured out all wrong."

He's losing me, like, how hard is it to make fake people do what you want?

"I think I may have to scrap it. Wait for the next idea to show up, start over."

Does he mean start over with this book or in general? He'd been so sure of this one, so positive. It's sad to hear him sound so defeated. I'm about to ask him if he can fix it when I hear gentle tapping. Even though the door's wide open, Phyllis, the nurse, always the professional, knocks anyway.

"Hey, Phyllis," I wave, hoping it's not time for another sponge bath, which has to be, literally, the most embarrassing thing I've ever experienced. I'd almost rather send a dozen nude selfies to the football team than be washed and dried again by a stranger. But what are my other options?

"Good morning, Tess, Mr. Porter."

She's all business. I expect her to launch into her usual list of acronyms that'll make up my schedule for the day: PT (physical therapy), OT (occupational therapy), the MRI (magnetic resonance imaging) the doctor might want to be sure my leg is healing right.

I'm exhausted just thinking about it, and I haven't even attempted to get out of bed.

But instead of talking to me, Phyllis turns toward Dad.

"Mr. Porter, if I could speak with you in the hallway for a moment, there seems to be an issue with your insurance. Mrs. Porter, or Ms. Winslow, is named as the policyholder, but since you and Tess are on there too, I'm hoping you can clear up something for us in her absence."

Ms. Winslow, aka Mom, kept her maiden name professionally. She'd been Mrs. Porter when I was in preschool, when Dad was a rising literary star. She resumed being Ms. Winslow when she went back to work after I started kindergarten. I'd overhear her on the phone telling friends and relatives that she'd decided to return to the firm because she wanted to be a role model for me. That was a good one. She never mentioned what I'm sure everyone on the other end of the phone was guessing: Dad was struggling. There was no second bestseller in the works.

Maybe she believed her own words because she threw herself back into her career wholeheartedly. Still, it's hard to admire your role model when that person is more like a ghost. Most mornings, Mom was gone before I ate breakfast. Usually, she didn't return home until after I'd begged Dad to read my favorite bedtime story—*Chrysanthemum*—at least three times.

Whenever Dad suggested she scale back a bit, Mom quoted studies that said children whose mothers worked outside the home turned out smarter and happier. I wanted to say, "Tell that to the kids stuck in aftercare looking at the same used coloring books and buckets of sticky Legos until five-thirty every afternoon."

They finally stopped sending me in fourth grade when Dad started teaching morning classes at the college, and I began spending time at Izzy's. That's where I got a real taste of what a family could be. Hot cocoa, snowball fights, dinners with salads and side dishes. Izzy's mother would yell funny things: "No, I don't know how old that donut is, I didn't have a birthday party for it!" Or, "Just wear your sister's snow pants! They're snow pants! Let me know when someone from *Vogue* comes to photograph your backyard

155

sledding expeditions, and I'll be sure to run out and get you a new pair." With her Brooklyn accent, Mrs. Collins was like a character from a familiar sit-com. But no matter how harsh she sounded, everyone knew there were a million layers of love beneath her tough tone.

During school breaks, Izzy's mom would pile us all into her van, and we'd go to the beach to fly kites. On other days, we'd go to the Bronx Zoo. Sometimes Becca would bring a friend, and Mrs. Collins would have seven of us to watch, but she never acted like it was a big deal.

"When you have this many kids, you have to keep moving, or they'll tie you to the furnace," she'd joke, looking directly at Izzy's little brothers.

Meanwhile, Mom resented even taking me for a haircut. It ate into her billable hours.

So for all Mom's talk about wanting to be a role model, it was Izzy's mom I hoped to be just like. Mrs. Collins nailed the marshmallow-to-cereal ratio in her Rice Krispie treats every time. She knew how to get gum out of your hair without using scissors. She had a Pinterest board before anyone else I knew had even heard of the site, and she found cool crafty projects for us to work on in the afternoons.

When I showed Mom a photo of the butterfly costumes Mrs. Collins made for Izzy and me in sixth grade, she said, "It must've taken her hours. Couldn't you just buy all that? Surely, there are better uses for her time."

"But, Mom, she *made* them! And we helped!" I tried again, but my excitement wasn't enough to convince her it was worth the effort.

"Well, if Izzy's mom finds joy in working with a glue gun, good for her, I guess," she said and went back to reading her briefs.

I wanted her to be open-minded and support my interests, even if they were different from her own. But I knew how she felt. So for a long time, I didn't mention all the cool crafts I did at Izzy's. I pretended to be interested when Mom talked about the cases that brought her closer to being made partner, which she did when I was in eighth grade. And, boy, you'd have thought she'd been appointed to the Supreme Court. Still, it was nothing compared to how impressed I was when Mrs. Collins attached our sparkly butterfly wings to our bodysuits and said, "If I didn't know better, I'd expect you two to fly."

"What's the issue, Phyllis?" Dad asks, turning in his chair to face the always-serious nurse.

"We're trying to get pre-approval in case the doctor goes ahead and orders the MRI. But we've each tried a couple times, and we're getting the same notification that says your insurance has been canceled."

Dad frowns. Insurance is typically Mom's department.

"Okay, let me see what I can do. I've got my insurance card here somewhere," he says, pulling his wallet out of his back pocket.

He'll Be Waiting

He puts his glasses in his pocket and sets the manuscript down in the folding chair. He's "old school" and claims he's only able to edit when he's holding a paper copy.

Dad reaches out, touches my good leg. "Be right back, Tess," he says and follows Phyllis into the hallway.

I look down at his manuscript and make out the first few paragraphs of a chapter titled "Train in Vain," a reference to The Clash's final song on the "London Calling" album.

I begin reading:

Ted Morrison had plenty on his mind as he folded himself inside his Prius that early September morning. Beyond his windshield, he saw the sun peeking through what once had been a dense forest of trees across from his home. Most of them were leveled now ahead of another colorless cul-de-sac that would soon be littered with those cheap cardboard houses that sprang up overnight like a series of ugly jack-in-the-boxes.

How he missed the simple joy a fresh sunrise represented. It used to seem almost magical, like a perfect orange drifting steadily back up toward the invisible tree from which it had fallen. Another new day filled with promise. Potential. Those words, like rich, ripe fruit, belonged in other people's vocabularies now. He was painfully aware that every endless day had little in store for him. He was a widower, a middle-aged man raising a troubled son.

"How did it come to this?" he wondered as he fastened his seat belt.

If he'd known, in that moment, that it would be the final time he'd ever slide the silver buckle into the cartridge, would he have at least savored its gentle click?

The voice I heard yesterday morning roars back: *"Your father is a loser. A pathetic has-been. He doesn't have an original thought left in his head."*

I wince, not only at the words but the tone. The voice. I recognize it now. The hairs on the back of my neck stand up, and everything goes cold and hot all at once.

The room is silent except for the drumming of my heartbeat as it throbs in my ears. And, of course, I can still hear that voice. His voice.

I must be confusing things, mixing up memories. Because if not, what I told James is true: Something horrible comes next.

Saturday, December 16, evening

The knocking continues. I race out of the kitchen, sliding along the hardwood floor in my socks, and yank the door open ready to leap into James' arms like something out of a romcom.

"You're here!" I shout a second before my heart sinks. I picture it hitting the floorboards and dropping all the way to the basement. It's not James. It's the twins, Parker and Perry, who live three houses down. Dad always says, "Parker and Perry. Perry and Parker. Sounds like an upscale lounge. Or maybe it's a corner coffee shop or an independent bookstore where a young writer discovers a first edition of 'David Copperfield' and travels back in time."

"There's your next book!" Mom would exclaim back when it had been okay to imply that a "next book" was a given. "I'm sure the twins' mother would love that."

The boys stand on the porch wearing Angry Birds hats, one black, one red. Identical metal snow shovels poke out of their gloved hands. They look like a surrealist twist on that "American Gothic" painting.

"What's up, guys?" I ask, trying hard not to weep with disappointment that James still isn't here.

"We'll clear your walkway, steps, and driveway..." Parker or Perry —I can never tell them apart — says.

"...for $70," the other finishes his brother's sentence.

"Um, I don't think I have that much cash on me," I tell them, not lying.

"We take checks," they say in unison.

"Um," I turn around and expect Nick to be a millimeter behind me like he's been since we walked through the front door. I'd hoped we could do a little good cop/bad cop thing where I say "I'd love to hire you..." and Nick would jump in with something like, "I dunno. That's a little steep, fellas. Thanks, but I've got this covered."

But he's nowhere in sight.

"Um," I stammer, "I think I'll probably do it myself, you know, good exercise."

I watch their hopeful faces fall.

"But, hey, why don't you ask Mrs. McAllister? She could probably use the help."

"We tried," one of them says. "She's too cheap. She offered us $20 to do everything. That's practically illegal."

I laugh. Mrs. McAllister, who looks about three days older than God, always tried to convince me to sell my Girl Scout cookies to her for half-price, and I'd have to explain that it didn't work like that.

"Sorry, guys, maybe next time," I call as they jump off the porch into piles of snow.

I close the door and turn toward the kitchen. Nick's nowhere in sight. His disappearing act reminds me of some of the more annoying kids I babysit, the ones who wander off and hide in a closet or under their beds just to scare the crap out of me.

But Nick's got to be exhausted. Maybe he's setting up the pull-out couch in Mom's office. Or, better yet, what if he's already asleep? That'd be a relief. Just when I let myself believe this awkward stretch could be coming to an end, he walks into the living room, holding something behind his back.

"What do you say you and I play a game?" he asks with a smirk.

Before I can answer, he shoves Scrabble at me.

"Sure, why not?" I say, hoping it'll pass the time. "But let's play at the kitchen table so I can keep working on the lasagna."

I head back toward the stove, drain the fat from the meat, and turn off the flame under the noodles.

"Whatever," he says, opening the box, lifting the board, and placing a tile holder at opposite ends of the table, "as long as you promise that while you're standing over there, you won't try to look at my letters."

"I promise," I say, dumping the noodles into a strainer.

"Yeah, you don't strike me as a cheater," he says.

Even though I'm opening cans of crushed tomatoes to make the sauce, I swear I hear him mumble something under his breath, something that sounds like "unless you take after your mom."

"What did you say?"

"Nothing." He looks at me and smiles. He's roaming again, opening and closing cabinets. "Ah-ha, here we go."

He pulls down the oversized margarita glasses someone gave Mom as a birthday gift inside a sombrero along with an expensive bottle of tequila, which I'm guessing is long gone.

"Um, those aren't meant for wine." I sprinkle oregano and parsley over the crushed tomatoes and stir.

"Jeez, Tess, sorry I'm not as cultured as you are. Sorry I'm not some fancy pants sommelier." He pronounces it "some-mull-leer" instead of the correct pronunciation, which is more like "somm-ul-yay." The only reason I know is from watching every season of 'Top Chef.'

Sensing I've offended him, I try to make it right. "No, these are totally fine, just a little big, don't you think?"

"Well, that's good because I'm pretty thirsty," he says, filling each glass to the rim. As he pours, the wine makes that glug, glug, glug sound I've come to hate because it reminds me of how Mom spends so many evenings and late afternoons, pouring a glass, then another, staring out the picture window, not answering when I ask what she'd like me to make for dinner.

I try to get her talking by asking about work, but she says, "Same old, same old."

I've wanted to tell Dad it's bad, that it's bigger than something that can be fixed with flowers or 'Hamilton' tickets, but he's preoccupied with teaching and writing his new book. So I just watch Mom slip into a wine trance and pretend everything's normal.

I sit across from Nick and take a long sip, willing it to work its magic on me, loosen me up, make me stop worrying about why James isn't here and help me forget about how I've completely let Izzy down on the most important night of her life.

"Not bad, right?" Nick says and raises his glass. "A toast: to a home-cooked meal, a warm house, and getting to know each other."

"Cheers." We clink glasses and cabernet spills all over the board.

"Kinda looks like blood," Nick laughs.

When it's his turn, I preheat the oven and work at the island, layering sauce, noodles, meat, cheeses, and spices.

"I'm not cheating," I reassure him. Not that stealing a look at his letters would help me. Scrabble has never been my game. I'm only playing to avoid making awkward small talk. Once the lasagna is prepped, I cover it with foil and stick it in the oven. James and I hate when the noodles get all hard and crunchy, so I set the timer for thirty minutes and pray he arrives before it rings.

My phone buzzes on the countertop. Samira again.

"Wine and scrabble? Look who's so sophisticated!"

"OMG, do U have binoculars?"

"You live in a fishbowl. Want privacy? Buy curtains!"

"If U can see everything so clearly, help me make a seven-letter word, and win this thing."

"My advice: Never waste an 's'."

"??"

"Always make 2 words with it. Say the word 'jam' is on the board horizontally, make it 'jams,' and then make the word 'swan' vertically if you can."

"??"

"Focus, Tess, you're smarter than you think!"

I return to the table and look at the board. The wine, which I've been sipping while putting the lasagna together, makes me feel as if I'm floating above my chair, like I'm liquid, like I could slide under the French doors, and make snow angels without ever feeling cold. Everything seems better. Nick is sixty percent more likable since he poured me that second full glass. Unlike some of my classmates who love bragging about their drunken antics on Snapchat, I don't drink very often. When I do, I'm definitely not the blackout or throw-up-in-the-bushes-every-Saturday-night type. I might have a couple of drinks at a party or in Izzy's basement—a shot of vodka here, her dad's watered-down domestic light beer there. But this wine? It gets better with each swallow. I'm starting to see why Mom's such a fan.

"Your move," Nick reminds me.

I think about Samira's 's' strategy. I have one 's'. I pick it up and check out the words I've made so far: "cow," "love," "boot." Nothing much to work with there. I glance at the scoresheet expecting to see that I'm losing by a ton when something else catches my eye. My name looks normal, but Nick's is odd, like he wrote another name first and then wrote over it. Maybe he's got a goofy nickname at school or really sloppy handwriting. What do I know? I'm drunk. I start laughing.

"Your words are so much bigger than mine." I point to the board. "I mean look at them: danger, lying, broken, sinister.' Pretty impressive, though Samira would say you shouldn't waste your 's's like that."

"This is just a little friendly competition, right?"

"I don't know, is it?" I try to sound dramatic. "It's almost like your words have a dark theme."

"Yeah," he laughs and drains the rest of his glass in one gulp. "It's almost like I planned it that way. Maybe I'm the one who's cheating."

I ignore him. The wine gives me the courage to ask about something that's been bothering me for months.

"So, speaking of cheating..."

"Listen, Tess, if you're going to ask me about Jimmy hooking up at school, I want you to know, I'd never throw our boy under the bus like that."

"I know, of course not. I'm not asking you to."

I regret even bringing this up because I'll never figure out if Nick's telling the truth no matter what he says. Still, I started it, I have to continue.

"It's just that you always hear about how it's impossible to make a long-distance relationship last. But, I don't know, I can't imagine being with anyone but James. Like I'm not even tempted. And I guess, I know it's stupid and makes me seem totally insecure, but I want to believe he feels the same way."

Nick looks at me. Blank stare. I can't tell if he heard what I said or if he's busy thinking about his next creepy Scrabble word. He gets up and pulls another wine bottle from the rack. Working the corkscrew, he clutches the neck as if he's trying to strangle it, before he finally says, "Listen, Tess, it's obvious that Jimmy cares about you— probably a lot. But nobody's a saint. Not even your mom," he pauses and pulls the cork from the bottle. Pop! He looks right through me. "Or your dad."

"Wait, do you mean my mom or dad? Or are you talking about parents in general?"

"What do you think?" His eyebrows arch toward the top of his forehead, and he refills his glass. Glug, glug, glug.

I frown. I'm getting a headache. I pull my hair out of the rubber band and rub my temples. How did we get off James and onto my parents?

"You're cute when you're confused." He sits across from me again. "Look, Tess. Jimmy's one of the good ones."

I smile. He smirks.

"That's what you want to hear, isn't it?"

I'm not taking his bait.

"You're drunk," I say, trying to laugh off the whole stupid conversation. I shouldn't have brought it up. I've never had any reason to doubt James, why should I now? "I told you these glasses were too big."

I think about texting Samira, asking her to come over so I'm not alone with Nick any longer when he says, "No. James is the real deal. I mean, he's always talking about you. And the way he cares for his brother? There's nothing he wouldn't do for you or Emmett. You're not gonna find too many like him. And look at tonight—how he went out of his way to rescue a friend stranded at the airport? Well, I guess technically you're the one who did that. But that just proves you two are a great couple."

"Thanks," I say, liking Nick more even though I can't tell if he's just saying what he knows I want to hear. "I feel really lucky just to have met him."

I mean it. James is like someone from a different time. He holds doors for people. He waves at toddlers in strollers. If we go to a store and a cashier says, "How are you?" he doesn't ignore them and stare at his phone. James answers, asks it back, looks them in the eye, and waits for a response. Those things shouldn't seem like a big deal, and yet they are. They're rare.

I'm about to ask Nick how he and James met when there's a knock at the door.

"James!" I scream.

I jump over Daffy and run to the door.

I can't believe it.

James is here.

Standing in front of me.

"Oh my God, I've missed you so much." I wrap myself around him like I'm part boa constrictor.

"Tess!" he whispers, soft and gentle as a prayer, his face buried in my hair.

We stand like that for I don't know how long, the snow swirling around us, the world perfectly still. "I thought I'd never make it."

We kiss. His skin is cold, his scent wonderfully, dizzyingly familiar.

"I can't believe you're here. You're finally here!" I understand now what people mean when they talk about crying tears of joy.

"I can't believe I'm here either. I'm so sorry it took forever. An old Jeep, an eight-hundred-mile road trip, and a blizzard are an awful combination."

"I'm so, so happy to see you." I'm up on tiptoes, squealing like a kid who just got a puppy on Christmas morning. "Come in. Come in!"

Reluctantly, I let go so he can step inside and puts his bags down. I take his jacket and hang it in the closet beside Mom's coat. The note and pocket watch I found a few hours earlier flash through my mind. The whole thing upsets me, so I force it right out of my head. I look at James' shabby old barn jacket. It isn't nearly warm enough for a New Jersey or a Chicago winter. I can't wait to give him the new navy pea coat I bought him for Christmas. It's upstairs in a box under my bed. I wanted to have it wrapped and ready but ran out of time because of having to go pick up Nick. Where is he now? I expected him to rush out and start fist-bumping James. Maybe he's being considerate and giving us some privacy.

"It smells amazing in here," James says. "I'm starving. We were going to stop, but we were afraid the storm would get worse, so we kept driving. I had no idea it was snowing like this here, Tess. You should've told me. I never would've asked you to go get Nick."

"I made lasagna."

I can't stop smiling. The drive to and from the airport feels like a lifetime ago.

He kisses me again and my knees go weak. Before James, I'd thought that was just an expression. But, no, a good kiss has the power to do that. It's real. And it's just about the best thing I've ever experienced.

I want to take him upstairs, continue this, make up for months of lost time, but then I remember Nick is just a

168

few feet away, probably watching. I pull back to let James take off his boots. I sway a bit and grab the back of the couch to regain my balance.

"Looks like somebody's had some wine," James says. He glances at the pair of bottles on the kitchen table, one empty, one half-full, then at the Christmas tree in the corner, the picture-perfect fire. I suppose it might look like a romantic scene and not what it is: two strangers trying to make the best of it until their mutual friend arrives. I can't tell what James is thinking, but he's got to know that there's no way anything would ever happen between Nick and me. Still, if I turn the tables, would I love seeing him alone with a girl, a roaring fire, and lots of wine? Definitely not.

"So, Nick's in the kitchen," I say. "We were playing Scrabble to kill time until you got here."

"Tess, I'm so sorry. I thought I'd be here hours ago. I can't believe you drove in this. Thanks again for doing that."

"It's totally fine." I'm embarrassed by how my words slur together. "Everything's fine now that you're here."

It is fine, just not how I'd imagined it when I thought about this night, which I have one thousand times since James left. I'm still wearing jeans with holes in the knees and the same striped shirt I sweat through while searching the airport for Nick. I'd hoped that once I stuck our dinner in the oven, I could shower, straighten my hair, put on makeup, and change into the sweater dress I bought at Anthropologie. It was super expensive, but Evie's mom gave me a gift card last week, so hey, merry Christmas to me! The dress is pretty much perfection because it's really soft and a cool mossy green that makes my eyes look bright and not like boring, drab olives. But telling Nick I'd be upstairs showering seemed too weird, so now I'm stuck looking like I made zero effort and couldn't care less, when James is actually the person I care about most.

I'm about to say something, like, "Sorry, I look like I just cleaned out the garage," when Nick walks out of the kitchen. James looks at me, then back at Nick.

"Hey, buddy! You finally made it!" Nick reaches out and claps James on the shoulder.

"Yeah, it was a rough one," James says and extends his right hand. "I'm James Potter. Nice to meet you."

I don't know if it's all the wine I've had on an empty stomach, the heat from the fire, or a combination, but I suddenly feel super-hot and have the oddest sensation, like I'm in a dream and the room is tilting.

"Um, James? You feeling okay?" I ask, worried that maybe lack of sleep from finals and driving through a snowstorm have left him exhausted and disoriented. But to the point that he wouldn't recognize his friend? That freaks me out a bit.

"Thanks again, man, for letting me crash here. Tess is as awesome as you're always saying," Nick says, grinning.

James shakes his head. Then smiles at me.

When we first started hanging out, I used to play these dumb pranks on him. Like we'd go to Starbucks, and I'd come back from the restroom and tell him I'd accidentally dropped my phone in the toilet. Then, I'd tilt my head, fluff my hair, and ask if he'd do me a favor and go get it.

"Are you serious?" he'd ask and jump up like he would actually retrieve it for me.

Another time I'd told him the pizza delivery guy was waiting on the front porch.

"He said he either wants a bigger tip or he's going to come in and eat half the Margherita pizza with us."

James had pulled a few more singles from his pocket, headed toward the door, and said, "I'll tip him extra, but we are never ordering from this place again."

When I'd confessed that I was kidding, he'd said, "I love you, Tess. But sometimes, I think your sense of humor needs work."

It was random dumb stuff, and the jokes never lasted long because I couldn't keep a straight face. I eventually gave up because James caught on right away.

I realize that's what he must be doing to me now – retaliating for all my goofball gags. He's pretending not to know Nick, so I'll think I picked up some stranger at the airport and brought him into my home. I admire his attempt, especially after a crazy-long road trip, but I'm not that gullible.

"Okay, Tess, you got me. Who is this?" James frowns.

I'm not falling for it. "Ha! Now, who's the jokester, James? Well played!" I say, waiting for him to crack up and tell me he's kidding.

"I'm serious, Tess. I've never seen this guy before. Who is he?"

"James, stop. It was a good try, but it's over. I'm on to you." I punch him gently in the shoulder.

"Tess! Come on. I do not know who this is." He looks at me, then Nick, and then me again. He's definitely not smiling like this is something we'll all laugh about later.

"Dude, stop!" Nick says. "You're scaring her." He turns and walks into the kitchen, laughing.

"Tess," James lowers his voice, like he's trying not to lose it, brushing his hair back from his forehead. "I'm not kidding. If this isn't one of your jokes, then we have a serious problem."

He stares at me. I recognize his expression. Expectant. It's the same one he wears when he's waiting for me to burst out laughing and say, "Gotcha!" That's what makes me think maybe he's not turning the tables and trying to trick me after all.

"I'm not joking," I say, my insides starting to shake. Everything's happening too fast, and thanks to the wine, I'm processing in slow motion. "But, James, he knows things about you. About you and me, about you and Emmett."

"Tess, I swear to you, I've never seen this guy before in my life."

"Neither have I."

We stare at each other. I go from hot to freezing cold in a split second. Who did I bring home? Who did I let into my house? My mind spins, trying to recreate the moment I met him. Did I just assume this guy was Nick? No, that's not what happened.

"He came up to me at the airport, James. He introduced himself. He told me his name was 'Nick.' He knew exactly who I was."

"Yeah, but who is he?" James asks. His eyes travel from me to the guy neither of us knows standing just a few feet away.

My stomach pitches the way it does when you go flying down the steepest drop on a roller coaster.

James strides into the kitchen. I follow behind him, legs weak.

The man I picked up hunts through the fridge.

"Hey, buddy," James says. "Why don't you tell us who you are and what the hell you're doing here?"

"Aw, c'mon, Jimmy," the stranger says casually, closing the fridge door. "Your girlfriend and I were having such a good time, now you come in here and ruin it. I was hoping we could all get to know each other. Let's not spoil it so soon."

Maybe it's pure adrenaline, the fact that this guy called James the name he hates, or the whole "good time" business, but suddenly James spins the guy I thought was Nick around and throws him up against the fridge.

I scream as the magnets Mom, Dad, and I have brought back from family vacations rain down, clattering against the floor. Daffy darts for the basement stairs and disappears. James and the guy are the same height, their noses almost touching, when James shouts, "Who are you?"

Fake Nick just keeps staring, his lips form a pout, like he's about to answer, but won't. James attempts to shake him. He's got fistfuls of the imposter's sweat jacket in his hands, but he's as immovable as a mountain, and his eyes reveal nothing.

"Who are you?" James demands again, in a threatening tone I don't recognize.

Now James seems like a stranger. I've never seen this side of him. My heart pounds. I can't catch my breath. Is this what a panic attack feels like? I look for my cell phone so I can call nine-one-one, but it's not on the countertop where I left it.

"James?" My voice wavers. I reach for his arm just as the microwave beeps. The lasagna's done. I've lost my appetite.

"Time's up," says the guy, pushing James off him. He turns up one corner of his mouth in a satisfied smirk, and he winks just before he adds, "Things are about to get interesting."

The Real Nick Lawrence

Just outside the door, I hear Dad's voice, the click of Lydia's heels. I tuck the journal under the cast on my left leg. A layer of cold sweat beads above my lip, behind my knees, in the cracks of my elbows, as my heart trampolines inside my chest. I want to tell them everything I've remembered, but how? How do I explain that I'm responsible for all of this? This nightmare that I brought down on myself. And them.

Even though I have broken bones and a head injury, there's no way they'll ever be cool with the fact that I took their car, drove to the airport in a snowstorm, and picked up a stranger because my boyfriend—who I invited to sleep over while they were out of town—asked me to. I may have been a terrible friend to Izzy, but I'm an even worse daughter. Where do I start this conversation, and how much do they already know?

I want to be alone, not only to avoid facing them but because I need to call up the memory of what happens next, no matter how terrifying it might be. Seeing James again, even if it's just in a memory, and thinking about how he kissed me, gives me that happy, fluttery feeling in my stomach, which is kind of insane because I should be focusing on who the hell Nick really is. But I also know I'm here. I'm not in great shape, but I'm alive, and James has visited me every night, so maybe things don't turn out so bad after all? Focusing on these thoughts saves me from having a complete breakdown.

Dad lumbers through the door first. He looks like he's aged ten years in the few hours since he left to solve the great insurance mystery with Phyllis. I hadn't noticed the dark rings under his eyes before. His hair sticks up in all directions, which means he's been dragging his hands through it, his signature move when he's stressed out.

"Oh, Tess," Mom whispers as she moves in close and pecks me on the forehead. The imprint of her cold, wet nose makes me cringe. I have a hard time not wiping away her kiss with the back of my hand. Does she think I lost my sense of smell along with my memory? I can't use the left side of my body, but my nose still works. She reeks of wine. If I ask her about it, she'll deny it. That's been her strategy.

One morning right before Thanksgiving, she was in full cling-on mode and hugged me hard as I was leaving for school.

"It's a little early, isn't it?" I'd said, adjusting my backpack.

"Early for what?" she'd asked, her eyes glassy and bloodshot as a textbook drunk's—literally—they've shown us photos in freshman health class.

"You've been drinking. Already." I'd looked directly at her, which was easy because we're the same height, and hard because I no longer liked what I saw.

"Honey, no. It's Listerine," she'd lied.

As if proving my point, she'd swayed, lurching like a seasick passenger on a cruise ship, and steadied herself by grabbing on to the small table by the front door.

"Whatever," I'd mumbled and walked out, not bothering to close the door behind me.

When I'd reached the sidewalk, I glanced back at the house and saw her hunting under the planter for the spare key.

"It's gone again, Tess!" she'd called. "You have to remember to put it back!"

"Jesus Christ, get a grip," I'd muttered, fighting the urge to flip her off.

Mom barely looks at me now as she backs away, dabbing at her face with a crumpled tissue. She's been crying. Again.

Lydia's the only one who appears even remotely normal. Wearing black pants, a turquoise blouse, and a tweed jacket that ties it all together, she looks like she just stepped out of one of those Talbots or J. Jill catalogs Mom gets. Does anyone even order by phone or mail anymore? Why keep slaughtering all these trees and forcing mail carriers to deliver this crap, is what I'd wonder as I tossed them straight into our recycling bin.

Still, seeing her, with her statement necklace and matching earrings, reminds me how much I miss real clothing. I'm sick of these faded and flimsy mint-colored hospital gowns. Lydia's style is definitely granny chic, but she, too, looks a bit messed up today even with her coordinated ensemble.

Since there are only two chairs, she gestures for Mom and Dad to sit.

"I'd rather stand," Dad says. He squeezes my hand before backing up toward the door, staying as far from Mom as possible, a challenge in such a tight space.

When Lydia's eyes meet mine, I can see she's trying to compose herself. Is it wrong that it makes me feel slightly better to think that spending time with Mom and Dad has taken its toll on her the way it often does on me?

"Oh my God, Tess. I don't know how you tolerate them!" I picture her ranting. "Their egos! Their neediness! They pack the emotional drama of an entire season of *Grey's Anatomy* into a single conversation!"

"I know, right? They're beyond annoying!" is my imaginary response.

Like she's reading my mind, she smiles. This time I can tell she's covering up other emotions—annoyance, impatience, exhaustion. Are they directed at me, my parents, or her other patients? Does she know about the series of bad decisions I've made?

Whenever we leave Izzy's to go to a party or even just out for a drive, a cheap way to escape our suburban boredom, Mrs. Collins kisses us each on the top of the head and says, "I love you, girls. Make good choices."

Never before have I strayed so far from that.

"Tess," Lydia says, settling into the recliner, placing a folder on her lap, "as I mentioned yesterday, time is of the essence. You haven't met Detective Warren yet, but he's eager to talk with you, and I've stalled him as long as I possibly could. Unfortunately, my professional recommendations only carry so much weight once the police are involved."

When Lydia first mentioned the police, I'd hoped maybe she was doing it for effect—a trick to scare my memory into returning faster. Now, thinking about Nick—or whoever pretended to be Nick—it doesn't seem far-fetched. At all. Waves of nausea ripple through my stomach. You'd think having Mom and Dad nearby would help. It doesn't.

"I know you asked your mother about Nick Lawrence," Lydia continues. "We understand from your phone records that you were googling someone with that name. We also know that you went to Newark Airport on Saturday night, is that right?"

"Yes," I nod. There's no point in lying.

"Do you remember being at the airport, Tess?"

I nod again.

"And you were there because your boyfriend, James—"

Mom bows her head and lets out a sob at the mention of his name.

"— asked you to go and pick up Nick Lawrence? Is that right?" Lydia's hands rest firmly on the folder.

"That's right," I say, wishing she'd hurry up and get to the new or helpful part.

"And this person, this man you met there, he told you that he was Nick Lawrence?"

Hearing Lydia list my actions makes them seem so much worse. And if she knows the whole story, why is she making me go through it all again?

178

"Yes," I whisper and look down at the cast on my arm.

Now I'm the one who's avoiding eye contact. No wonder Mom and Dad have barely visited me. Before, I was just a mediocre student with few talents beyond a comprehensive knowledge of kitchen gadgets. Now, I'm the absolute idiot who brought home a stranger, played Scrabble with him, and cooked a meal while he watched. My face purples at my stupidity.

"I want you to take a look at something, Tess," Lydia says, opening her folder slowly and deliberately.

Great. This is probably one of those stupid inkblot tests where I say I see a guillotine when it's actually a lemonade stand, or I think it's a vagina, and it's really a butterfly, and then they send me off to the funny farm for good.

She pulls out a photo, an 8"x10" of a brown-haired, brown-eyed guy. He looks about my age, maybe a year older. He's wearing a white, button-down oxford shirt. Freckles dot the bridge of his nose like sprinkles on a cupcake. They soften his strong jaw and make you not hate him for his perfect, white teeth. The photo cuts off mid-chest, but you can tell he's got broad shoulders. He could be anyone's hot older brother.

"Have you ever seen this young man, Tess? Don't answer right away. Take your time."

He looks familiar, like, in an Abercrombie & Fitch model way. I know immediately he's not anyone I've met—or seen before IRL. His face is the kind you'd remember. But Lydia wants me to try, so I squint and act like I'm concentrating.

"Anything, Tess? Any recognition?" she asks.

"No," I shake my head. I look at my parents, hoping maybe they'll jump in with answers, but they're on opposite sides of the room, both staring down at the floor.

Lydia nods.

"Who is he?" I ask.

"This is Nick Lawrence, Tess. This is the man who was waiting for you at the airport."

"But I never —" my voice trails off.

"We know, Tess. This isn't the man who left with you." Lydia pauses, letting that last sentence land. It's disturbing, but it also means that my memories are real.

"This young man came forward after seeing the story on the news. Police are still investigating, but they have reason to believe the person you picked up at the airport was impersonating Nick Lawrence. They think he was there waiting for you. Waiting for you specifically."

"This has been on the news?" My head spins. I know the media will pounce on any stupid story these days, but why would this be newsworthy? Once again, hot coals of rage burn in my belly. It was bad enough when just Lydia, my parents, and James knew more about what happened to me than I did. Now I find out the whole world does too.

I think about the other thing Lydia said: *He was waiting for you. Waiting for you specifically.*

"Me? Why me?" I ask, panic rising in my chest as an image of James throwing wannabe-Nick up against the fridge flashes through my mind. I shut my eyes as if that will make it disappear.

"What, Tess? What do you see?" Lydia asks.

The urgency in her tone scares me even more than the scene playing out in my head.

"The guy who said he was Nick was in the house with us. With James and me. He was strange. Like sometimes, he seemed okay. Other times he was creepy. But he knew things, things about us. That's why I thought James was joking when he said he didn't know him." I rub my head. It feels impossibly heavy. I lean back into the mountain of pillows and close my eyes again.

"Why don't you tell us who you are and what the hell you're doing here?" James growls in my memory, and I flinch.

"It's okay, Tess, we're here with you now," Lydia says gently. "I know it has to be frightening for you, but do you know who he is? Did he tell you his name or why he was there? What did he say to you?"

I shake my head. "I don't remember that part yet." In my mind's eye, I see Nick kicking off his boots and walking toward Mom's office. "But it was like he knew our house. The layout. Where the bathroom was—at least it seemed like he did."

Mom inhales sharply. I don't know if it's related to anything I've said or if she's trying to choke back a hiccup. Dad shoots her a harsh look. Suddenly I'm crying. It comes out of nowhere. I'm filled with bone-deep embarrassment.

"Why? Why would anyone pretend to be James' friend? No one knew I was going to the airport except James and that guy, the real Nick." I point toward the photo in Lydia's lap. "So how could someone be waiting for me? Someone other than Nick, I mean. Even I didn't know I was going to end up there. I swear."

Tears slide down my cheeks. I wipe my nose with the back of my right arm as Lydia hands me a tissue, then the whole box. I look at Mom and Dad. Do they believe me? Why should they?

Lydia glances at Mom, then Dad. Neither speaks.

"Detective Warren has some theories that he'll share with you tomorrow, Tess," she says, sliding the photo of the real Nick Lawrence back inside the folder. "But before then, I think it's important that you and your parents talk."

The way she says it, this isn't a suggestion, it's an order.

She stands and brushes imaginary lint off her pants and reaches out to squeeze my hand, but it's full of used tissues, so she settles for my wrist.

"If you can remember anything else before then, write it down, okay? Any—all information will be useful." She gives me a half-smile as she's almost out the door. "You've been very brave, Tess. I'm just sorry you've had to be."

Mom chokes on another sob as Lydia disappears. It's just the three of us now. The awkward triangle again. Dad moves in closer and stands beside the bed. Mom is still in the recliner by the window. I wish I could burrow under my covers like a groundhog and wait this out for a few months.

"Jack, would you like me to start?" Mom asks.

I realize it's the first time she's spoken to him directly since I've been here.

"Is now the best time, Carolyn?" There's a nasty edge to his voice, which gets louder as he continues. "Do you really think you're in any condition?"

So Dad knows she's drunk, too. Once upon a time, he'd been the one who'd overdo it. One glass of Scotch led to two, and soon he'd be ranting about "what was wrong with the publishing industry today." Mom and I knew he snuck cigarettes in the garage when the words weren't coming, or his agent wasn't responding to his emails. Back then, Mom would have a glass of wine once in a while, maybe champagne on New Year's Eve. But over the summer, she began drinking almost daily, like it was a favorite hobby she'd only just remembered. But the real drinking—or what I've come to think of as the serious drinking—began shortly after Mr. Miller's accident.

Mom had gone to his funeral mass. It had been her idea that the firm should host a luncheon afterward since his kids didn't have much money. I remember I was in the kitchen starting dinner when she stumbled out of an Uber and went straight to bed. At the time, I thought the whole scenario—that her friend had died in such a violent way right up the street from our house—had caused her to go into some kind of shock, one that she was hoping to numb with alcohol. I assumed that once she "processed" it, as Lydia would say, she'd return to normal. Wrong.

What freaks me out is that I'm pretty sure I heard Mr. Miller's accident. I'd been half awake, half asleep that early September morning. I was experiencing a rare burst of new-school-year enthusiasm brought on by the shine of fresh notebooks and the thrill that comes with wanting to wear your just-purchased fall sweaters and boots, even though it's still eighty-five degrees. Everything hummed with that clean-slate vibe. Of course, it wasn't the same with James away at college, but I was determined to make the best of it.

I was rolling around in bed, debating whether I should get up early to straighten my hair when I heard the train whistle. Not like the usual, "just passing through" *peep! peep!* This was thunderous. Life and death. Maybe it's my mind playing tricks on me because, of course, now I know what happened, but I swear I remember the sound of the crash. Metal slamming up against metal. The railroad crossing might be blocks away, but I'm convinced if we lived closer it would've shaken the house.

For years, residents petitioned to have an elevated train bridge built and the crossing removed. They'd warned it was only a matter of time before a car got stuck on the tracks—most likely at rush hour. The town council always shot down the idea, claiming it would cost millions and take years to build a bridge. Plus, they pointed out, everyone was aware of the danger by now. Signs cautioned drivers not to stop on the tracks. The reason I know all this is because it was always on the cover of the local paper that gets tossed in our driveway every Thursday. I used to scan it for babysitting gigs back when I was ambitious. Now it's just one more thing I recycle.

But the crazy part is, it wasn't rush hour. It was the crack of dawn when Mr. Miller was hit and killed. In my imagination, it's always just him in his tiny car versus the enormous locomotive. For weeks after it happened, I pictured his Prius spinning around like one of Emmett's Matchbox cars, snapping off those candy cane-striped crossbars, sparks spraying from the train's wheels like fireworks.

That's what I thought of after. But in that moment when I heard the horn, the screeching, then the deafening thud, I simply rolled over, and chose sleep over straight hair.

What woke me later was the screaming. It was a sound I'd never heard Mom make before. It was worse than the shriek she let out when Daffy hauled a dead mouse into the house and laid it at her feet. It was sadder than the groan she'd expel when she'd get a call that a jury was back too quickly, meaning the verdict probably wouldn't go in her client's favor.

Dad and I almost collided as we ran downstairs and found her doubled over at the front door, her robe pulled tight around her, police officers getting back into their car. They'd already been to Mr. Miller' house and told his son.

It still strikes me as odd that Mom was their next stop. But my knowledge of police protocol is based on "Brooklyn Nine Nine" episodes, so I'm hardly an expert.

I look at Mom now and realize she's staring back at me, almost through me. She leans in closer but doesn't stand.

"Tess," she says softly, "there are some things I think we should talk about before you meet with the police."

"Carolyn, stop it. Now is not the time." Dad's voice is firm, insistent. It's weird to hear him like this. Usually his anger is self-directed, but Mom seems to be his target. Or, is it me? Or this whole situation?

"I'd like to prepare her, Jack."

"Prepare me? For what?" My eyes dart to each of them.

"Prepare you before you talk to Detective Warren tomorrow," Mom says, coming around to sit on the right side of my bed, which makes Dad sidestep toward the window. They're like chess pieces strategically moving around a tight board, never touching.

"Am I in a lot of trouble? I know I've made unbelievably bad choices and some huge mistakes, and I can't even begin to tell you how sorry I am." I'm babbling and crying all at once, morphing into a pathetic, snotty mess. "Are you going to prepare me like you prepare a witness? Is that why you've been working so much?

"Your mother hasn't been going to work, Tess." Dad jams his fists in the pockets of his jeans like they're safer there. "She quit her job in—when was it exactly, Carolyn? Mid-to-late September?"

"Jack, please, I want to talk to Tess privately about that." Mom looks at Dad, but he's staring at me. I sense he's sizing me up, wondering how much more I can handle.

"Why the need for privacy, Carolyn? So you can fill her head with more lies?"

"Jack, I—"

"That's why we have no health insurance, Tess. The three-month extension your mother paid for expired yesterday. She quit her job and didn't bother to tell us. There's a lot she hasn't bothered to share actually."

Mom hangs her head, shoulders shaking as she sobs soundlessly.

Dad's shoulders shake, too, but because he's laughing. Like a mad man.

"And here I thought I was the creative one, you know? The master storyteller. But, no, this whole time, it's your mom, Tess. She's been selling us one piece of fiction after another for months now. Isn't that right, Carolyn? And we're too, what's the word—naive? gullible? kind?—to ever question her, especially not at the peak of her depression. Not after losing her old pal Ned, right?"

"Jack, stop it," Mom says, almost pleading. "We agreed that we weren't going to talk about that now. This isn't the part she needs to know before tomorrow."

"Well, gee, sorry that this is what I feel like talking about, Carolyn, not that you give a shit about my feelings."

That's it. The floodgates open. I'm ugly crying, worse than when they told me that they'd started seeing that marriage counselor. I'm blubbering because so much more than just my arm, leg, and memory are broken. My family is broken. Beyond repair, it looks like. Neither Mom nor Dad attempts to comfort me or pretend that things aren't as awful as they seem.

"Jack, that's not fair. You know I care." Mom's trying to get Dad to look at her, but he stares out the window. As if acknowledging defeat, she adds, "But you're right, this isn't the conversation we should be having now."

"You should go, Carolyn," Dad says, and when he finally turns toward her, his stare is so cold, I get chills just looking at him.

Mom's face falls. After months of Dad doing everything he can to make her happy, this shift is seismic.

"And call a cab—or an Uber. You've caused enough damage already."

Dad sinks heavily into the recliner and drags his hands through his already messed-up hair.

There are a thousand questions I want to ask him: What were you and Mom going to tell me? What is it I'm supposed to know? And probably a thousand more that I don't want the answers to, like: Where does Mom go when she says she's at work? Why is she lying to us?

"Dad—" My voice cracks, eyes sting from crying.

"Get some rest, sweetheart," he says, tilting his head back against the chair and closing his eyes. "It can wait until tomorrow."

Saturday, December 16, Night

The microwave timer continues beeping as the guy I thought was Nick starts a creepy, non-rhythmic slow clap that ends in a fist pump. "Yes! This boring-ass night is finally about to get interesting."

James and I look at each other. I've sobered up fast after realizing that I've been hanging out with an imposter—who may or may not be a complete psycho—for the past several hours.

"Listen," James says in the calm voice he uses when Emmett's on the verge of a meltdown. Seeing that screaming in this guy's face didn't work, he's changing his strategy. I'm praying he knows what he's doing. "The joke's over, okay? You got us. Whatever it is you want, just take it, and go. Please."

"Wow, gee, thanks, Jimmy, that's big of you, but I've got a headline for you: You're not the one in charge here," Fake Nick says. "And, unfortunately, what I've come for isn't something I can box up and take with me."

James straightens to his full height, around 6'3", and crosses his arms. While he was away at school, I hadn't forgotten how handsome he is, but seeing him in person again, I can't believe he's actually my boyfriend. Maybe I'm still feeling the effects of the wine, but all I can think about is being alone with him again. I'm imagining taking him upstairs, when a voice inside my head shouts, "Get it together, Tess, there's a stranger in your house, and you have no idea if he's crazy, dangerous, or both! Now is not the time to be planning a steamy make-out session."

I force myself to focus. All we really know is that this guy definitely isn't James' friend. I look back at the countertop where I'd left my phone, sure it's where I left it. But, no, it's gone.

I glance over my shoulder at the cluttered desk, past the bills and magazines, where the landline usually sits in its charger. That phone's also missing. Could this guy have taken them while James and I were on the porch or in the living room? I get a weird prickly sensation on the back of my neck.

What if we need a weapon? It seems insane to be thinking like this. A few hours ago, I was preparing for the most amazing night of my life. Now, I'm in a 'Twilight Zone' episode. My eyes dart beyond the island to the corner near the sink. The block of knives stands empty. All nine slots are wide open. Even the scissors, typically tucked in the back, are nowhere in sight. I need to tell James, let him know we're in real trouble here. But how? What if I freak out and make things worse? My thoughts bounce back and forth. Panic! Don't panic. You're going to be fine. You're going to die!

"So, why don't you tell us what you've come for then?" James' voice strains to remain even.

I can tell he's trying to use the techniques he learned when he became a peer mentor to teens with disabilities or emotional issues, kids whose behavior can turn aggressive or even violent at a moment's notice. He's attempting to diffuse the situation by staying calm, steady like he was taught. But will that be enough?

"Well, it's a bit of a long story," Fake Nick sighs, "but, shit, we've got the time. Why don't we all sit down?"

He gestures toward the table where the Scrabble board and wine mock me.

"Thanks, but we'll stand," James says. I stay right by his side, my knees buckling with fear.

"Suit yourself, Jimmy," Fake Nick laughs, "I can tell it just as easily from here."

He comes around from behind the island until we're just a few feet apart. James moves closer, ready to step between me and this stranger. I want to grab James' hand, push past this creep, and run through the French doors to freedom. But I'm frozen to the floor, too scared to make a move.

"Now, Tess, take a good look at my face. I saw you staring at me in the car. I know it's been a while, but I look familiar, don't I? You said so yourself."

I hope it's a rhetorical question. It isn't. He glances out into the living room, toward the fireplace, waiting for me to respond. With his eyes cast off to the side, I feel like I have seen him somewhere before.

"Maybe a little, I think. I'm not so sure anymore," I say, nervous that James will think I actually know this person after all.

"Let me give you a hint," Fake Nick says, his dark eyes lock onto me. "'Christmas is here with New Year's Eve close behind! We hope this season puts you in a festive frame of mind! From our home to yours, blessings and good cheer, here's wishing you all the best in the coming year!'"

Dizziness sweeps through me. I clutch the island as if that'll make it go away. I picture the small stack of cards tucked in the back of my closet, the family of four, now shrunk to two. The beautiful St. Bernard, Louie, probably gone also. The boy's eyes always staring off into the distance, never at the camera. He must've worked hard to overcome that. But the eerie otherness about him, it's still there.

"Luke?" My tongue feels so thick I can barely say the four-letter word.

"Ding! Ding! Ding!" He alternates between tapping his nose and pointing at me. "Bingo! Good for you, Tess!"

"So, you do know this guy?" James asks, confused as I stare back at both of them speechless. My heartbeat drumrolls in my ears.

"Our families used to exchange Christmas cards." Luke's voice fills the tense silence. "Nice of you to save them, Tess."

He's been in my closet? Each second is more disorienting than the last. It feels like a nightmare, especially when I open my mouth to speak and can't get a single word out.

"But no, Jimmy, Tess and I have never actually met. Though there have been times when we've been in this house together."

Luke pauses, letting the impact of that sink in. I'm biting my nails, gnawing away at the cuticles, a habit it took me forever to break. I stick my hands inside the pockets of my jeans, hoping Luke hasn't noticed how terrified I am. As if he can read my thoughts, he turns away from James and toward me.

"But, of course, Tess, you weren't aware I was here." His grin gives me chills. "Sometimes, we were so close, I could've reached out and touched you."

He extends his hand toward my face slowly and then draws it back again as if giving me a glimpse of what I'd missed during those visits. I flinch.

"You've got a really nice singing voice, by the way. Hope you don't mind, I usually let myself in using the key you keep under the planter. Probably not the smartest hiding spot. Just sayin'."

"Wait, what? You've been letting yourself in? To this house?" James sounds like he's the drunk one, struggling to catch up. His calm tone's gone, replaced by anger and disbelief. "Jesus Christ, Tess. Who is this?"

"Wait, Tess, before you answer, let me give Jimmy here a little clue."

I'm too numb to speak. Thoughts ricochet inside my brain. I'm scrambling to connect the dots, figure out what he's doing here, why he'd pretend to be someone else, and what the hell he wants.

Luke pulls a cell phone from the inside pocket of his hoodie. The voice inside my head, the one that told me to focus, screams for me to get out of the house, to grab James' hand, and run far and fast. But it's like a horror movie where the kids stay inside the haunted house looking for the killer instead of fleeing to safety. I can't make my body do what my mind tells it. Instead, I watch dumbly waiting for pieces of a bizarre puzzle to slide into place.

"How's this for a refresher...wait for it..." Luke scrolls through text messages until he finds what he's looking for. "'You mean that sad old guy who got wasted in your backyard on Memorial Day and nearly fell in your pool? That's too bad.'"

I study James' face. I can't tell if he's put it together yet, but I know what Luke's reading and brace for the next part.

"Now, Tess, here's your response: 'Yeah, same dude. He just got creamed by the 5:44 a.m. express train. My mom's freaking out, losing it big time.'" Luke waits, letting my cold, heartless words hang there. Then he points to James, "Jimmy, here's you again, 'That's awful. Gotta run. Multimedia storytelling waits for no man.'" Luke slides the phone back inside his jacket. "Real compassionate there, Jimbo. Thanks so much for your heartfelt condolences."

James and I continue to stare, shocked to hear our texts, written months ago, spewed back at us off.

The microwave keeps beeping. I can't tell if it's the wine, the fire, the lasagna burning, or white-hot fear, but the kitchen feels like an inferno. I want to yank open the French doors, let in some fresh air, and scream for help. But James and I stand still, hypnotized by the insanity of it all. It's like Luke's placed us under his spell, and we're powerless.

"That sad old guy—" Luke exaggerates his air quotes "—was my dad!" He slams his hand down hard on the island, sending a jar of cooking utensils spilling over the edge. Slotted spoons and spatulas hit the ground and sound like a smattering of applause. "That was my dad, you assholes!"

"How...how did you get those messages?" I know that's not the most important part, but it's definitely the creepiest.

"Well, Tess, I may not be so good with people. Like, maybe I don't understand their motives, what drives them, you know. For example, why would a middle-aged woman like your mom mess with the emotions of a lonely widower like my dad? Lead him on and then break his heart just for the fun of it? No, I'll never understand people. Maybe I don't even want to. But computers? Software programs that allow me to see every text, view every site you visit, track all your calls, and, what is it the cool kids say? 'Slide into your DMs'? Now that's the kind of shit I understand."

James shakes his head. I'm watching the whole picture shifting into focus inside his brain. I can tell he's getting ready to charge Luke. I hold his arm. Some part of me wants to believe that this guy is just confused, depressed, lonely, grieving, pick whichever shitty adjective applies after losing your parents in separate but horrifying ways. I block out the fact that the phones are missing, the knives gone.

"Luke, I know my mom cared about your father—a lot—but I don't think it was like that." I inch backwards as Luke leans in closer.

"You don't think it was like what, Tess? Let me guess, you don't think your mother's responsible for my father killing himself in one of the most violent ways imaginable? For his brains exploding all over the windshield? You can tell yourself that, but from where I'm standing, she might as well have been driving the fucking train."

"Luke...." I want to sound as calm as James did, but I can't. My voice squeaks out in a nervous, shaky plea. "I'm so sorry about you losing your mom and your dad, too, but I'm sure that was nothing more than a horrible accident. Your dad was just in the wrong place at the wrong time. I don't see how that has anything to do with us, with my family."

"Then let me break it down for you," Luke says, his voice growing louder, his words tumbling out faster. "About twenty years ago, my dad was in love with your mom. But he was a shy guy from the Midwest who was scared of rejection, afraid of screwing things up. Then, just when he'd worked up the nerve to tell her, some hotshot writer swept in and—bam! It's over for my dad just like that."

Sweat beads on Luke's forehead as he kicks out his leg and sends one of the stools beneath the island flying toward the French doors. It crashes to the ground but doesn't shatter the glass.

"Luke, believe me, we're truly sorry for everything you and your family have been through," James interrupts, attempting to short-circuit whatever Luke's about to say or do next. "Why don't you let me drive you home? It's been a long day, and maybe tonight's not the best time. Why don't you come back tomorrow when Tess' parents are around?"

"Oh, Jimmy. Are you even listening? I'm just getting started." Luke's crazy laughter makes the air feel electrified, dangerous. When he starts talking again, he's deadly serious. "Fast forward, to like three years ago, my mom got sick, and my dad just lost it. He panicked, couldn't function. Rather than rise to the challenge, my old man shrunk. Lost his job. Lost the house when the medical bills piled up. Lost everything really, until good old Carolyn Winslow saved the day.

"It wasn't a coincidence that they bumped into each other on the street in the middle of Manhattan. Nope. Turns out, my dad was a bit of a stalker. He knew where she worked. But he couldn't just show up there like the failure that he'd become. So he did a little detective work, found something she'd posted on Facebook, a salad from her favorite place to get lunch. She'd tagged the restaurant. Jackpot, right? He roamed the block for weeks waiting for her, setting up this 'chance' meeting. 'Oh, Ned! What a surprise! How wonderful to see you!'"

He does a spot-on imitation of Mom, reminding me again that he's been in this house. My house. Without us knowing it. The hair on my arms stands straight up as James and I stare back at him in stunned silence. It's a terrible analogy given everything that's happened, but Luke's like a runaway train, and we're tied to the tracks, neither of us able to move.

When someone shares a tale about one of your parents, normally, you listen because it's going to be funny or embarrassing. But this is a story I'd never want to hear.

"She offered him a job, a fresh start," Luke continues, spit foaming in the corner of his mouth. "She treated him like the guy he used to be before things went to shit. Naturally, he put her on a pedestal. He'd been thinking about her, pining for her for the last twenty years. He told me the whole thing in the car after I picked him up from your stupid barbecue."

He takes a second to wipe the sweat from his forehead with his hand. I pray he's done talking. He isn't. He starts again. Louder.

"So, when he should've been paying attention to my mom—my mother, who was dying a little more every day—he was too busy worshipping this woman who, ultimately, didn't give a fuck about him."

"Listen," James might sound rational to Luke, but I hear a slight tremor in his voice, and I realize he's as freaked out as I am, "my dad has been a huge disappointment too. I don't know what your plan is here, but whatever you're thinking, it's not worth doing something stupid."

"Oh, I know all about your father, Jimmy." James flinches each time he hears the nickname as Luke paces back and forth. "And yes, he's an absolute shitbag. I mean, the way he treats you and your kid brother? But he's still alive, Jimmy, so don't ever compare your situation to mine."

James shifts his weight from his right foot to his left. His eyes slowly scan the room. He's looking for a weapon now, I sense it. There should be a letter opener in the desk behind us, but there's no way to slowly turn around, open a drawer, and fish it out. Plus, a letter opener? There has to be something better, sharper, scarier. I can't imagine actually harming Luke. Even though he's scaring the shit out of me, I just want him gone. As I take a mental inventory of every possible kitchen gadget that could be considered threatening, I realize he's talking to me.

"If we're turning this into a competition, your dad's no prize either, Tess. Actually, your father is a loser. A pathetic has-been. He doesn't have an original thought left in his head. You know that new novel he's been so excited about? He's basically stolen my dad's life."

Luke moves into the living room. He's suddenly light on his feet, like telling this story, having our full attention, has given him newfound confidence. He grabs the fireplace poker, and he stabs at the logs. They crackle to life, sending flames shooting up in jagged bursts of red and orange.

"Don't believe me?" He must've noticed me frowning. "Here's a quick summary: A man gets killed by a train after losing his wife and struggling to raise a troubled son. Except, here's the thing, your dad's missing a major plot point, and it's actually the most interesting part: His real-life wife is having an affair with his main character."

I want to doubt what he's saying, but I flash back to all the times Mom came home from work and Dad would immediately ask her about her day. I was just happy to hear her voice, but for him it was different. Hungry for details, he'd want to know about the cases, the clients—what they looked like, their faces, their clothes, their attitudes.

"Jack, stop, I'm exhausted, and you know a lot of this is confidential," she'd say. "I'm not getting disbarred so you can try to spin this into a short story you hope to publish in Tin House."

It was obvious that whatever magical ability he'd once possessed to make up entire worlds on his own had evaporated.

"Luke, I know you're upset, but my mom said it was an accident. A terrible, terrible accident. Your dad had been putting in long hours, working really hard—"

"Shut up! Just shut up!" Luke hurls the poker at the fireplace screen, and I jump even before it clatters against the slate.

He pulls out his phone again and waves it at us. "This note, it runs through my mind over and over in a sick, twisted loop. It starts up on its own no matter where I am. Day and night, I hear my father's voice—his last words — tormenting me."

He clears his throat and begins.

Dear Carolyn, I lost you once. I can't imagine living through that again. Not now. Not on top of everything else.

I know it wasn't your intention to get my hopes up about us. And yet, you did. You made me want to live again, and I believe I did the same for you. So to hear you say that this— us —can never be, well, it's more than I can bear.

I know you're not happy, and I haven't been either. Not for a long time. But I also know that, together, we could be. I've watched you come alive again, Carolyn. I've seen a light return to your eyes, a joy come back to your smile, and I'd like to think it's because of what we share.

I see you in a way Jack doesn't, in a way maybe he never has. I could make you happy. I know it and I believe you do too.

To feel alive again only to have it all cut short, it's too much for me. I respect your decision to stay where you are. So I hope, in time, you'll respect the choice I've made today.

Love always, Ned

Luke shoves the phone back in his pocket. "Not a very original ending, I'll be the first to admit it, but you know who doesn't mind lack of imagination, Tess? Your dad. I forwarded this to him while you and Jimmy were playing kissy face on the front porch. I thought, 'Shit, maybe he'd want to include this in the novel too.'"

Luke wipes his watery eyes with the cuff of his sweat jacket.

"Luke." James' voice swells with empathy as he steps toward him.

Luke's shoulders sag, like he's done, said everything he came to say, emptied his rage.

Finally, I think, this is coming to an end. I see an opening, and James must too because he's inching closer. I can't tell what James has planned, like, will he put his arm around Luke, guide him to the couch, and get him a glass of water, the way he does when Emmett's upset? Or will he ask Luke to leave again as politely as possible?

Either way, I stop holding my breath. Luke's not dangerous, I tell myself, he's just totally messed up from everything that's happened over the last year. Who could blame him?

But what about the missing phones and knives? What about the times he's let himself into the house? That voice in my head, peppering me with warnings, returns.

200

I try to reason it out when James says, "You've been through a lot, Luke, and you didn't deserve any of it. Let's just sit down, cool off, and—"

Before he can finish, Luke lunges toward the floor, grabs the fireplace poker, and takes a quick jab at James' throat, causing him to jump back. My hands fly to my mouth. I taste blood as I tear off a hangnail with my teeth.

"Stay the fuck away from me," Luke growls. "And don't you dare talk to me like I'm your retarded little brother."

James charges him, reaching for the poker. But Luke, dodges and swings the metal rod in the other direction, knocking picture frames and a vase off the mantle. The poker hits the Christmas tree, catching in its branches. The whole thing crashes to the floor, ornaments smash, the star shatters.

"Get the hell out of this house!" James roars.

I scream as Luke reaches into his pocket and pulls out a gun.

He points it directly at my face as he says, "I'm not going anywhere, Jimmy, and neither are you."

James

I pull the hospital blanket up to my chin, shivering like someone opened a window. The memory of seeing Luke—Luke aiming a gun right at me—leaves me trembling.

I should take a deep breath and calm down, try some of those stupid mindfulness and meditation exercises they make us practice in health class. I'm willing to do almost anything to not think about what I've remembered, but it plays on a terrifying loop in my brain: Luke thrusting the black iron poker at James, James jumping backwards, glass shattering as Luke swings it out of reach, picture frames along the mantle toppling like dominos, glass shattering, Mom and Dad's wedding photo falling into the fireplace. The sound of my screams as Luke pulls out the gun rings in my ears. My sheets are damp from sweat, my hair wet and matted to the back of my neck. I fumble for the button to call the nurse and ask for water and an extra blanket when I look and see James standing beside me. He appeared out of nowhere.

"James, oh my God! You startled me!" Normally, I'd at least try to fluff my hair or lick my crusty, chapped lips, but at this point I'm a lost cause.

"I'm sorry," he says, "I was trying to be quiet. Visiting hours are over."

"C'mere. I'm so happy to see you." I reach out my right hand and pull him toward me. He sits down gently and I wish there were enough room on this narrow bed for him to lie next to me. He smiles. I reach up and trace the dimple in his chin. He still looks so tired, like he hasn't recovered from finals, his road trip through a snowstorm, and then, the kicker, that Luke-inspired hell of a homecoming.

There's so much I want to say, and so much I don't want to think about. I wish I could stare into his eyes, and he'd know everything without me having to say a single word. Why hasn't Google invented an instant download of info through a simple look yet?

"You're shaking," he says, holding my hand in both of his.

"It's all coming back, James, and it's crazy. I mean, if my memories are real or true or whatever, it's like a horror movie, except that it must have a happy ending, right? Because here we are."

He opens his mouth to say something but stops himself. We look into each other's eyes, and it's enough. No, it's perfect. I find that dark freckle, focus, and feel like I can finally breathe. I want to ask what he was about to say, but I have other questions on my mind.

"Why didn't you tell me everything right from the beginning? Why didn't you say anything about Luke or about my mom and Mr. Miller? I'm not mad; I'm confused."

"You'd already been through so much, Tess. How could I add to that? I heard the doctor telling your parents that it would be better if you remembered things at your own pace. And considering how disturbing and unbelievable all of this is, you'd have thought I was the one with the head injury if I'd tried to explain it."

"When did things get so bad? How did I not notice?" I'm thinking out loud as much as I'm asking him. "I was so busy thinking about you, hanging out with Izzy, working on those stupid college applications, checking out what everyone else was doing on Instagram. Meanwhile, my family was imploding. How did I not see it?"

"Sometimes, we ignore the thing that's staring right at us because it's too painful. And sometimes there's nothing you can do to fix it anyway."

James glances off to the side. At first, I think he's looking out the window at the falling snow, but he's staring at my broken arm and leg.

"I'm sorry I didn't tell you everything, Tess, but I was embarrassed. Completely. Instead of doing something sooner, I stood there listening to that lunatic rant about his dad and your mom, like he was delivering a soliloquy from a twisted version of 'Hamlet.' I thought I could stop him by reasoning with him, by showing him some empathy, but it didn't work. I failed you. I failed us both.

When you remember what comes next—the rest of it—I want you to know that I'm so sorry I didn't fight harder to protect you."

"Stop. We're both okay now, that's what matters. And even though the whole thing is terrifying, I'm not scared, James. Yes, it was an awful, freak thing, but I'm here, and you're here, and everything will be better—maybe not right away, but in time. Well, not my parents' marriage, obviously, and I still need to beg Izzy to forgive me. But, really, the main thing is that you and I made it out, right? We survived."

James gives me a smile that makes me think of an SAT word. Wistful: having or showing vague or regretful longing. He must be feeling responsible for sending me to get Nick. It hadn't occurred to me before to ask anything about the guy I was supposed to pick up. I remember the photo Lydia showed me, the handsome, open face. Did I see him at the airport? Rush past him while I circled the baggage claim? Did he see me? Was I so close to avoiding this whole disaster but never knew it? Where did he end up?

"What happened to your friend? The real Nick Lawrence? Have you talked to him?"

"I haven't," James says, again looking full of regret, "but he's left a bunch of messages at my house."

There's a sadness that clings to him like a second skin tonight. It shreds my heart, and I desperately want to find the words that might fix it.

"James, it's okay, I don't blame you for any of this. You have to know that. Even if you hadn't asked me to go pick up Nick, Luke would've found another way to mess with my family. He let himself into my house regularly. That's insane. I'm going to talk to some detective tomorrow, and I'm sure they'll ask me about pressing charges or testifying against him. A year from now, this will be a bad memory, and way in the future, it'll be nothing more than a crazy story we tell at parties."

He lowers his head. My words don't seem to convince him.

"Please, James, this had nothing to do with you. I love you, please don't look so sad."

"I love you too, Tess." His eyes hypnotize me. "When the memories of everything that happens next come back to you, remember that, okay?"

"Of course," I agree and wrap my arms around him like I never want to let him go.

Saturday, December 16, Night

Luke points the gun right between my eyes. Even though he's no more than five feet away and I can see it clearly, I still don't believe this is happening. I've only seen guns on TV or in movies. My first thought is to ask how he got it. Then I remember that this is America, where you can get a semi-automatic rifle easier than you can buy a strong cold medicine.

Still, none of this feels real. But tell that to my heart. It's banging against my rib cage as if it's trying to claw its way out of my chest like a lobster in a pot of slowly boiling water.

Mom having an affair? Dad feeling so hopeless that he'd basically write Mr. Miller's biography and try to pass it off as fiction? It all seems too strange to be true. Has Dad read Mr. Miller's suicide note yet, or will he have his phone off in the theater? Now I wish those 'Hamilton' tickets were fake and that they'd come back home—not that I want to see them, but they're the ones who should have to deal with this. This nightmare. They're always nagging me about how my actions have consequences, and yet James and I are paying the price for their mistakes.

Luke stands there, aiming the gun at my head, but at least he's not moving any closer. His smirk returns like he's proud neither of us saw this twist coming. James is still as a statue, half in the kitchen, half in the living room. His hands are up as if this is a bank robbery, an old-fashioned stick-up. I'm by the stairs where I ran for cover when Luke started swinging the fireplace poker.

"Real brave, Tess," I mock myself.

The fireplace tool was nothing compared to the pistol in his hand.

Time feels as if it's standing still, but it isn't. The clock that sat on the mantle for as long as I can remember lies face down and broken on the floor, making a loud, non-rhythmic tick, tick sound. The microwave timer continues beeping, reminding me that each passing second, we're doing nothing to save ourselves.

It's crazy how you feel like you wait your whole life for something interesting or maybe even a little dangerous to happen, and then when it does, you think, "I'd like boring back now, please!" That's how I felt when I was giving Evie Walters the Heimlich—that rush of "Holy shit, this can't be real!" mixed with "I have to do something!" Those same emotions sweep through me now.

James and I look at each other, and for the first time in almost a year of us knowing each other, I have no clue what he's thinking. Part of me expects him to make a crazy move like an action hero in a summer blockbuster. But his face has gone Elmer's glue-white, and he looks more freaked out than that time his mom caught us fooling around in his bed. He's too stunned to move, and I'm hit with a terrifying thought: I, with my crappy grades and lackluster SAT scores, have to be the brains here.

Still, together, we should be able to outsmart Luke. But then I think back to August. Bored and sick of the endless humidity and drizzle, Izzy, James, and I took Emmett and Izzy's younger brothers to an escape room. Time ran out

208

before we got even halfway through the riddles. We just laughed it off and went for FroYo.

No one's laughing now.

How can we escape this? I could bolt out the front while James runs through the French doors to the backyard. That's if Luke doesn't shoot us as we try to get away. But even then, where would we go, how far could we get? I'm trying to think, but it's not easy with my heart pounding, the microwave beeping, and the clock on the floor ticking. Sleet and ice pelt the windows. Could I grab the keys and get the car out of the driveway? The roads are probably ten times worse than they were a few hours ago.

I'm panicking as my mind cartwheels through scenarios that could get us out of this. What if I told Luke where Mom and Dad are staying tonight and let him have the car? It's crazy that I'd even consider something like that, but after all their lectures about being a "good, responsible person," who should "always work hard and tell the truth," it turns out Mom's a cheater and Dad's stolen Mr. Miller's life story. So, yeah, let Luke channel his rage at them. They're the ones he should hate, and I kind of do, too, now that I think about it.

What have James and I done, other than send some insensitive texts? But if Luke wanted to go after Mom and Dad, he's had plenty of chances since he's been sneaking in here regularly thanks to the spare key.

A chill races up my spine. This needs to end. Now.

I look down at the couch that separates me from Luke. What if James distracted him and I jumped over the sofa? If I tackled Luke and he smacked his head on the stone fireplace, that might buy us enough time to grab the gun and call the police. But there's no way James can read my mind, and I'm a terrible athlete. With my luck, I'd probably

209

land in the fireplace. How has it come this? To a place where I'm thinking about assaulting Mr. Miller's son in my living room or suggesting he go attack my parents?

"So, why us? Why now?" Hearing James' voice pulls me back. "Your problems are with Tess' parents, not her. Confront them. Let Tess go. I'll stay until they come back home. Let her leave."

"You don't tell me how this goes, Jimmy," Luke says, turning the gun toward James' chest. "Tess isn't leaving. She's the reason I'm here. You're just collateral damage. Or an added bonus. Take your pick. But it's true, Carolyn is my ultimate victim. A couple of months ago, she stopped by my house, said she wanted to check on me. Like, seriously, how do you think I'm doing, bitch? She tried to return a pocket watch my dad gave her. It was my grandfather's. I guess she thought she could prove she wasn't completely heartless. Whoops, too late!" Luke laughs and turns the gun back toward me.

"I told her, 'Keep it. You already took everything that matters.' I told her, 'My father killed himself because of you. Because of you, Carolyn.' I let that sink in, and then I took a good look at her, a really good look, and tried to figure out what the hell he saw in her anyway." He shakes his head and laughs again. "I couldn't see it. I told her I had the suicide note and that I was going to send it to your father. And you know what she said? 'Go ahead. My marriage has been over for months now, maybe even years.' Turns out, she was only sticking around because of you, Tess. You're all she has left, especially now that she quit her job and drinks all day. So that got me thinking. Wouldn't it only be fair for her to lose everything and everyone just like I did?"

He's going to kill me. Luke is going to kill me. Us.

The voice that warned me about the missing phones and knives is back, echoing inside my head. My chest heaves up and down. I'm hyperventilating.

"You see, the thing is, my dad wasn't always some 'sad old guy.' He was grieving, he was vulnerable, and she knew it. Your mother saw a bad situation and made it so much worse. She took advantage of him to make herself feel better about her own sad life. As I'm sure you know, Tess, you're a bit of a disappointment to her. And your dad, well, I think we've covered that," Luke says, a hideous grin forming on his wine-stained lips. His bottom teeth are yellow and crowded, like kernels on an ear of corn. He's about to say something when the doorbell rings.

We freeze. James and I look at each other. Luke pivots so the gun points at James' head, then he spins back toward me.

"Expecting someone? It's not good to keep secrets, Tess. Though I suppose you get that shady side from your mom."

We're saved, I think, and then, just as fast, start to worry that whoever's here is about to get dragged into this.

The doorbell rings again, followed by relentless knocking.

"I have no idea who it is. Honest. I swear." My voice trembles as my entire body quakes.

"Jimmy, you didn't get fancy and order a pizza hoping the Domino's delivery guy is going to save you, did you?" Luke lets out a big, terrible laugh, like he's a crazy cartoon villain.

"No," James says.

I look at him, hoping he's got a plan. I'm not used to seeing him at a loss for words or ideas.

The knocking turns to banging.

211

"Tess! I know you're there! Open the door, I need to talk to you!"

It's Izzy. I don't care what Luke might do to me; I have to answer it. I move toward the door.

"Tess! No!" James screams.

Suddenly Luke is right behind me. His hand is up under my shirt, the cold metal of the gun digs into the bare skin of my back.

"Get her to go away," he snarls in my ear. His hot, stale breath, tinged with the smell of wine, reminds me of Mom and makes me want to dry heave.

I open the door. A rush of icy wind blasts my face. I blink and squint until I can focus. Izzy. I almost cry out when I see her. She's wearing only her field hockey sweatshirt and fuzzy slippers. Her black curls, coated in snow, hang limp and heavy. Her face is streaked with tears.

"Iz, I'm so sorry, this is not a good time," I say. "I'll FaceTime you later."

"It didn't go well, Tess," Izzy blurts between sobs like she didn't even hear me. "I told them everything—just like we'd practiced. My voice was shaking, and I was so scared, but I just focused on the thought that I would finally be free. They just stared at me. I thought it was going to be fine. I really did. But then my mom started crying. My dad told Michael, Sean, and Connor to go to their rooms. Grams began chanting the rosary—like she could literally pray the gay away."

Izzy stops to catch her breath but only starts crying harder. Tears drip from her chin. I want to tell her that my parents are horrible people too, but I'm scared of Luke, what he might do, so I just keep looking at her and say nothing.

"They acted like I was a freak, Tess. They looked at me like they didn't even know me, like I was a stranger. Please, let me in. I can't go back there."

"Izzy, I'm so sorry." My heart breaks for her because of what her family has done, what I haven't.

For a second, I forgot about Luke and the nightmare unfolding behind me, but now I feel the gun press into my vertebrae. Luke pushes the door a little further closed while I try to block it with my foot.

"Can you come back tomorrow? I'll make us some scones and cocoa, and we can sit and talk. You can tell me everything," I ask, dying at how selfish and heartless I sound.

"Tomorrow? Tomorrow? What the hell, Tess? You're seriously blowing me off again? Really? I am here, literally crying on your doorstep, telling you that I just showed my family exactly who I am, and they rejected me, and you're saying come back tomorrow, and we'll have a tea party? All so you can be alone with your boyfriend? Well, fuck you, Tess. Fuck you!"

"Izzy, wait!" I scream as she backs away, looking at me as if I'm a stranger.

Again, I should be helping my best friend, and yet I'm counting on Izzy to save me.

Can she smell the lasagna burning? Does she hear the microwave beeping? Did she notice the Christmas tree splayed across the floor? Does she see the terror in my eyes? I don't think so because she gives me one last soul-crushing stare before she turns and stomps down the porch and out into the freezing, black night.

"Izzy, I—" Luke shoves me out of the way and slams the door shut. He pushes me toward the center of the living room. The metal tip of the gun presses deeper into my spine, and I cry out.

James spins around. His cheeks are flushed. Was he searching the kitchen for the phone or maybe a weapon while we were at the front door?

"It sucks to lose someone close to you, someone you love, doesn't it, Tess?" Luke growls in my ear, so close his spit hits my cheek. I wince. "I said, 'Doesn't it, Tess?!'" His voice reaches a full-blown roar, and I realize this is not a rhetorical question. He yanks my hair, jolting my head backward.

"Yes, yes!" I yelp, nodding as best I can. "It sucks."

"Well, buckle up, because this is only the beginning."

"Let go of her," James shouts, rushing toward us, Christmas ornaments crunching under his feet.

"Or what, Jimmy? You'll do what?" Luke's points the gun at my temple.

James stops.

"It's okay, James. I'm okay," I say even though I'm pretty sure Luke has ripped out a chunk of my hair.

"You're anything but okay, Tess," Luke laughs. "And your poor old pal Izzy isn't doing so great either. So much for 'hoes before bros,' huh? You're not much of a friend, are you? But again, how can you help it? Look at the people who raised you."

My neck aches from Luke twisting my hair, holding my head at an awkward angle. I shudder as I feel the gun, the outline of the perfect circle the bullet will pass through when he pulls the trigger, pressed to my skin. His words—"hoes before bros"—remind me that he's been reading my texts. Tears slide down my face. There's no way we're getting out of this. Luke's probably been planning this since September. Since he read his father's suicide note.

214

"The thing is, your buddy Izzy should've known better. Nobody likes you if you're different. They can't handle it. Some people will pretend that they're okay with it. Or they want you to think that they're okay with it, but they don't actually want to deal with you, so they build you a safe space. But it's all bullshit."

I'm crying so hard now that it must stir something in Luke because he lets go of my hair. Strands, a wad—I try not to look as I wipe my eyes — fall to the ground. It takes all my willpower not to touch my head. I leave my hands where Luke can see them. He keeps the gun pointed out at me.

"When I was eleven, my dad and I built a treehouse in the backyard. My father was a good man," Luke shouts before shaking his head and lowering his voice. "We built things together. We built things with our hands. He knew I was different, that I had no friends. He told me that when everything got to be too much, to go up in the treehouse, look at the sky, the stars. 'Sometimes it might feel like it's just you and the moon, but it's a great big world, son,' he'd say. 'Somewhere out there are people who'll understand you, who'll like you for exactly who you are. You just need to find each other.'

"Well, I'm still looking, and I can tell you, they're not out there. When I was seventeen, right before we moved back here, this family from around the corner, the Richardsons, they came over. I watched my dad and that dad take the treehouse apart. They reassembled it in the Richardsons' yard. That asshole dad asked if I wanted to help. He didn't know that that treehouse was the only place that ever felt like home to me. It was my safe space. But what I didn't know—what no one tells you—is that there are no safe spaces, only places that suck a little less than others."

Luke lowers his arm, puts the gun down by his side. I'm still crying, but I hope he's starting to realize we aren't his enemies. James senses it too.

"Luke, I can't imagine what your life has been like, but every day I've watched my brother struggle to feel accepted, to have a single friend who isn't a family member."

Luke looks at James. It feels like there's an opening, like we have a chance to stop this, maybe even fix it.

"Your dad sounds like he was a great man," James continues cautiously. "I think he'd want you to keep looking. He'd probably want you to travel the world, have new experiences, find those people, your people. He wouldn't want you to do something here tonight that would end all of that for you."

The room is still except for the ticking of the broken clock and microwave's steady beeping.

"Why don't you give me the gun, so no one gets hurt?" James says. "Then we'll go into the kitchen and have dinner. Like friends."

I'm scared he's going too far, overdoing it, laying it on so thick Luke will see right through it. The air crackles with tension while we wait to see what happens next.

"Can someone stop that goddamn beeping?" Luke yells, suddenly agitated. "I can't think! I can't think straight!"

He wipes the sweat off his forehead with the back of his hand that holds the gun. It points directly at my face. I'm so afraid he's going to pull the trigger; I start crying again.

"I-I can do it," I stammer through tears. I take a step. My legs feel like linguini. I can barely move.

"I've got it," James says, turning to go into the kitchen.

"No!" Luke shouts. "Stay where I can see you!"

216

James walks over slowly so that he's standing in front of Luke and beside me. He raises his eyebrows at me hopefully, like maybe we'll walk out of here alive. I want to believe he's right, but I don't feel it. That voice in my head tells me this isn't over. Luke's story, his words, "there are no safe spaces," give me chills though the fire blazes on the other side of the room. I'd reach over to hold James' hand, but I'm frozen with fear.

Luke gestures with the gun for us to move forward. I stagger, wobbly as a newborn foal, struggling to put one foot in front of the other. As we walk into the kitchen, I see Daffy, back from the basement, pacing in front of the stove where grayish-black clouds of smoke escape. The lasagna must've bubbled over. Sauce and cheese burn on the bottom of the oven. Is it enough to set off the smoke alarm? If that happens, will a neighbor hear it and come help us?

"Make it stop! Make the beeping stop!" Luke yells again.

I walk toward the microwave, and that's when I see it. How did I miss it before? The barbecue fork I gave Dad for Father's Day rests on the back of the stove's top. Its pointy tines shine like daggers even through the smoky haze. I know James calmed Luke down moments ago, but he's volatile. I don't trust him. At all. If James distracts him, I can catch Luke off guard and stab him in the neck with the barbecue fork. We'll have just seconds to grab the gun and get out of the house, but I think it could be enough.

My trembling arm feels like it weighs a thousand pounds as I extend it toward the timer, terror forcing me to move in slow motion.

"I'm going to turn off the stove to stop the smoke," I tell him.

Do I dare reach for the fork? One wrong move and it's over.

"Make it stop! Turn it off!" Luke chants. He covers his eyes with the back of his hand. The hand that holds the gun. Can he still see me? I can't tell.

I have a chance; I have to take it. I grab the fork and lunge toward his neck just as he takes his hand away from his face. Our eyes lock as I'm inches from his throat.

"You fucking bitch," he sneers. He grabs my arm and twists it. The fork crashes to the floor. Luke shoves me hard across the kitchen. The door to the basement is wide open. For a second, I think I'm going to go flying down the stairs. James' eyes meet mine. He thrusts out his arm to stop me before I go over the threshold. It works. I clutch the doorframe, panting, more scared than ever.

In the distance, I hear a siren. I look at James. He nods. I don't know how he's done it, but my heart soars. Help is on the way. We're going to be make it out alive.

"What the fuck? You called the cops, Jimmy? This is not how it was supposed to go!" Luke howls, his eyes wild with pain and fear. "I didn't want to do this. I mean, I wanted to, I just didn't know if I'd go through with it. But now you've left me no choice. You've left me no fucking choice."

Through the French doors, I see flashing cherry lights. A police car. Is it a reflection coming from in front of my house? Or is it straight ahead and one street away? I'm squinting, trying to figure it out when I see something else. Samira?

"This is not how this was supposed to go!" Luke screams as he spins in a circle, and light floods the kitchen floods. "You've given me no choice. You did this, Tess! Your family did this!"

Luke, bathed in white light, raises the gun and points it at my head. "I decide, Jimmy. Not you. Not Tess. I decide! This is how it ends!"

James' arm suddenly crosses my chest. He jumps in front of me, knocking me backward. I'm falling down the basement stairs when I hear it. The shot that makes my ears ring. The last sound I actually hear. It's all fuzzy static after that. I'm tumbling. There's nothing to grab. I can't figure out which end is up, like getting clobbered by a wave at the edge of the ocean.

I hit the ground head first, so hard my teeth rattle. The metallic taste of blood fills my mouth. Everything goes dark.

"James! James!" I'm screaming, but no sound is coming out, or if it is, I can't hear it.

Where is Luke? I don't know. I can't see anything. The air's so cold and damp. I try to crawl under the stairs in case Luke comes for me, but my leg doesn't work. It's going the wrong way. There's a buzzy, fading-out feeling in my head when I try to sit up. My arm, it's dangling at an odd angle. I don't feel any pain. Shock. So much damage. Why? For what? I'm slipping. Can't think clearly. A single phrase loops through my mind as I drift away: There are no safe spaces.

No Words

Sunlight spills through thin shades. For once, it's not snowing. Mom sits at the foot of the bed, my journal in her lap. She's the last person I want to see. Well, almost the last.

"Tess—" she says. "Sweetheart, how are—"

"Why are you here?" I cut her off. There's so much more I want to say: "Wouldn't you rather be home drinking?" and "You stopped caring about Dad and me a while ago, so don't bother showing up now." Or, more to the point: "Your relationship with Mr. Miller ended up with him dead and me pretty damn close to getting shot."

But why waste my breath? She doesn't deserve my time or what's left of my energy. I hate her and can't imagine that feeling ever going away.

"Tess, I wanted to talk to you before Detective Warren comes in. I don't know how much you remember from Saturday." She holds my journal, absent-mindedly tracing the pink and blue flowers on its cover. Her words aren't slurred together, and she's sitting up straight, like she's bracing for something. She's probably on her best behavior, knowing the detective will be here soon.

"There are certain things your father and I want to tell you, things we don't want you to hear from anyone else."

If she's trying to explain why they wouldn't give me back my phone, she's doing a crappy job. I can't believe I'm trapped in this bed, forced to listen to her. I want to tell her that if she's come here to make some big confession about her affair, that's old news.

"I don't know what you and your father talked about last night because...well, you know, he asked me to leave," she continues.

"What are you doing with my diary?" I switch the conversation, short-circuiting her impending pity party. "You have no right to—" I'm tempted to grab it, but what's the point now? She's already looked through it.

"Tess, your diary..." She lowers her voice to a whisper and thumbs through it, ruffling the pages.

She cranes her neck, seeking me out, trying to establish eye contact. I refuse to look at her. "Tess, it's blank. This journal is completely blank."

She's baffled or maybe disappointed that her attempt to spy on me or see what I know has failed.

"Of course, it's blank!" I almost laugh. "I'm left-handed!" I hold up my cast. My fingers poke out, boney and ghostly. "I figured you'd know that considering you're my mother. But you're too wrapped up in your own world to think about me." My voice shakes with rage.

"Tess—"

"Don't," I yell and stare straight at her. It feels so good to finally say what I've been thinking. "For years, you've

221

acted like I'm the screw-up, like I'm the disappointment. But that's backward. It's your life that's an absolute mess!"

I may not have been able to write them in the diary, but my memories are clear, and now that the torture Luke inflicted on James and me has come flooding back, my relationship with Mom is over. It's time she knows it, too.

"We're all human, Tess. We all make mistakes." Tears stream down her cheeks, but I have to give her credit, she doesn't look away. Instead, she looks humbled. Still, I wonder: Is she going to talk about her mistakes or mine—bringing a stranger into our home, caring more about doing a favor for my boyfriend than about anything or anyone else?

"There are things that you could never understand about my life, Tess. I'm not making excuses for what I've done, but it's been so hard, having to be your father's constant cheerleader. For so long, it's been about him and his writing. Would he ever get back to where he once was? It drained me because there was nothing I could do to help except work, pay the bills, and try to keep everything together. Do you think I wanted to spend that much time working? All those hours away from you, missing your childhood, the school concerts, and playdates? I didn't, but someone had to. I wanted to believe it was all for the best, that I was a role model for you, as if climbing this stupid ladder to nowhere meant something. But you didn't care. You idolized Izzy's mom, and that hurt too, childish as it may sound. So when Ned came back into my life, he reminded me of who I used to be, before everything got so…so heavy."

I want to scream, "Shut up! It's too little too late!" But I can see how painful this is for her, so I let her keep going.

"What Ned had gone through, losing his wife, I felt like I could help him, like I actually mattered to someone again."

She pulls a tissue from the pocket of her sweater and shakes her head. I'm furious that just when I hate her the most, she decides to be honest and real with me. But maybe it's an act. I've spent years watching her prepare her closing arguments, perfecting the way she stresses certain words, monitoring her expression in the mirror, deciding which side her head should tilt toward for maximum sympathy. Maybe this is all a game to her.

"I was flattered by his attention. I got swept up in it. I wasn't thinking clearly, and by the time I did, it was too late. You have to understand, Tess, I never intended for anyone to get hurt. When I ended things with Ned, I'd thought I'd stopped it in time."

She's crying harder. Her shoulders gently bob up and down as she stares out the window into the blinding sun.

"No words can ever express how sorry I am, Tess. A young man is dead because of me, and that's something—that guilt is something—that I'm going to have to live with for the rest of my life."

At first, I think she means Ned, but he wasn't young.

"Wait, Luke? Luke's dead?"

Her head snaps in my direction, her face twists, contorts, a hideous mask of confusion, pity.

"Tess, no. Luke is missing. No one knows where he is. That's what Detective Warren wants to talk to you about."

Weakness washes over me, sweeping up behind my knees, settling in the crooks of my elbows. My heart rate goes from sluggish to cardiac arrest.

No one knows where he is. Her words echo in my head. How is that possible? I suddenly remember the deafening sound of the gunshot.

"Who's dead? Did Luke shoot a police officer?"

"Oh, Tess." Mom's hands inch toward mine and hold the fingers poking out of my cast. "James was shot. James is dead, Tess. I thought you knew."

The room spins. Dizziness swallows me.

No. It's not possible.

"No," I say. I pull my hand out of hers. "No, James was here. He was here last night. I saw him."

"Oh honey, you're on some very strong medication. I think maybe there's a chance you imagined—"

"Shut up! Shut up! You are a liar and a drunk, and I'll never believe you!"

I scream, trying to focus, to think of every time James was here. I know he was here. I fight against my mind to block the weird bits that float to the surface, like the navy-blue pea coat I'd bought him for Christmas. How did he get it? Where were the coffee and flowers he brought me? How did he always seem to appear out of nowhere and leave just as quickly? Why did Mrs. Potter and Emmett never visit or even send a note? If anything happened to James because of me—because of my family—they'd never speak to me again.

No, it can't be true.

"Tess, I'm sorry, I thought your father had told you last night after I left. We didn't want you to hear it from the detective. Lydia thought it would be better—"

"Why should I believe you? Why should I believe anything you say? You've been lying to Dad and me for months," I scream through tears, squirming up the bed as much as I can to get away from her.

A nurse passes by the door and stops. I don't care who hears us.

"Why are you doing this? Why are you saying this to me?" I shout.

"Tess, if you'll just listen, I'll try to —" She leans closer, attempting to take me in her arms. And do what? Hug me?

I shove her back with my good arm. I have to get out of this bed. I put my right foot on the ground and try to swing my left leg in its cast over the side. I need to leave this room. There's no air. I can't breathe. I look up, the nurse is gone. I have to find her. I need a phone. I need to call James, I need to hear his voice, I need to tell him my mother's gone insane, I need him to say he'll be right over.

"Tess, Tess, you can't—"

Mom is in front of me now, trying to hold me back, to lower me onto the bed. I wind up my cast like it's a bat and swing at her head, sending her backward. Pain shoots from my fingertips to my shoulder.

"Don't touch me!" I scream.

This isn't happening. It's not possible. James was here. I saw him. I held him. It was real. He is the only good thing I have left. He cannot be gone, too.

"Nurse! Nurse!" Mom yells through sobs, fumbling for the call button.

I stand on one leg, pain taking my breath away. James. It cannot be true. I hop toward the door. I'm going to be sick. I lean on the folding chair. It gives way beneath me. I'm falling to the ground—the last things I see: nurses, a needle, then nothing.

Holes

The man in the recliner stares at me. Am I imagining him? Sunlight streams directly into his face, but he doesn't squint. He holds his phone in one hand and a legal pad in the other. His white hair is cut short. With his piercing dark eyes and stubby neck, he reminds me of a bald eagle. His head rests at an odd angle, like he's studying something. That something is me.

Detective Warren.

I can't do this now. My arm, my leg, my head, everything hurts. Two nurses caught me just before I hit the floor when I tried to escape from Mom and this room. They sedated me and put me back in bed. That could've been minutes or hours ago. I have no idea. The worst part of all floats to the surface: Mom's voice saying, "James was shot. James is dead, Tess." I think I might throw up.

I wish a canyon would open beneath my hospital bed and swallow me. My world is empty without James. For the past year, he's been on my mind from the second I woke up until I drifted off to sleep each night. It's impossible to imagine a day without him. It was hard enough to go from late August to mid-December not seeing him in person, feeling his hand in mine, his arms around me.

Tears fall like raindrops, dotting my hospital gown. Lydia hands me a tissue. I take it but don't acknowledge her.

Dad's here too. I see their mouths moving, but I don't listen. My mind buzzes with steady static. There's an ache, a void, widening in my chest, like someone cracked my ribs open and my removed my heart, then smashed it into small pieces. The only bit of relief is Mom's not here. I close my eyes. I don't ever want to open them again.

But I have to because the man in the recliner wants to get things moving.

"Tess, I'm Detective Warren." He doesn't stand, shake my hand, smile, or make any attempt at pleasantries. Not even, "How are you?" No, he gets right down to business.

"I'll try to bring you up to date on where we are with our investigation, which isn't very far, unfortunately. After shooting and killing James Potter in your kitchen, Luke Miller fled the scene moments before officers arrived. We're hoping you can recall some details from your time with Mr. Miller that will help us determine his whereabouts."

I don't respond. "Your time with Mr. Miller." He's got to be kidding. I can't believe this asshole thinks that I'm going to answer his questions as if we're casually chatting about a day Luke and I spent together at a theme park.

Because of my "time with Mr. Miller," the maniac who murdered my boyfriend, my life will be forever divided into the blissful "before" and the awful "after." I hover in the numbed-out space somewhere in between, floating on a dark cloud of shock and disbelief.

"Oh, and sorry for your loss," he mumbles.

My loss. He lobs it out there. An afterthought. As if all I lost was a tennis match.

"Tess," Lydia begins.

Calm and reasonable are her default settings but I'm no mood to either.

"I asked Detective Warren to be patient and give you the time you need," she continues. "But, of course, as each day passes and Luke remains at-large, we grow more concerned that other innocent people could be in danger. We need your help."

I want to say something like, "Sorry, Lydia, I don't really feel like it's my responsibility to catch a murderer right now." I narrow my eyes and stare at Detective Warren. Coffee stains dot his yellowish-white shirt. His suit is a cobbled-together mismatch of pants and a jacket in two different shades of navy. No shit, he needs help.

"Bill, why don't you tell Tess what you know so far and maybe she can fill in some details," Lydia, always the peacekeeper, suggests.

Detective Warren grumbles, his words a jumble of sound. He's the one she must've been talking to in the hall a few days ago when I overheard her saying that the "shock" could cause a setback. They've known James was dead all along but never let on. They allowed me to believe that my life would go right back to normal as soon as my head and bones healed. Before, I just hated Mom and Luke, now I hate everyone.

"Luke Miller's car was found at the airport, in long-term parking." The detective reads from notes jotted on his legal pad. "He used your parents' station wagon to get as far as Pittsburgh. Then he abandoned it in a Whole Foods parking lot. We believe he's using cash he stole from the safe in your mother's office because there's been no credit card activity. He left his and your cell phones in your mailbox on his way out of town. Security footage from the airport is grainy, to say the least. Plus, he's got his hood up, so it's tough to make out his face. He deleted all his social media accounts before driving to the airport. It's our understanding that the events of the last two years took quite a toll, and his appearance is vastly different from his high school yearbook photos. His sister, Danielle, has been cooperating with the investigation. She let us search the home, but Luke destroyed all the family's photos, including albums and digital copies. Fortunately, your friend Samira provided a fairly thorough description, so we were able to create a sketch and send it far and wide."

"Samira!" I whisper. She *was* there.

"Your mother confirmed it's a pretty accurate representation."

At the mention of my mother, slowly simmering rage bubbles up inside me. My jaw tightens.

"We'd like to show it to you now," Detective Warren says, "see if you can contribute any additional details."

He pulls the folded-over sketch out of the legal pad. The likeness is uncanny. The greasy dark hair, the dead eyes gazing off to the side. Bile fills my throat, and I vomit over the side of the bed. Detective Warren and Lydia exchange looks as she rings for the nurse. No one speaks, and for the millionth time, I wish I could disappear.

Dad hands me a cup of water and a ball of tissues. I rinse my mouth and spit into the big white wad. Shreds of tissue stick to my tongue. I don't bother to remove them.

"It was Samira who called 9-1-1," Dad says.

I think about all the times I called her Samira the Spy, always there, watching from behind her music stand. Now I realize she was more like a guardian angel.

"But how, how did she know?" I ask, wiping my eyes with fresh tissues.

"She said Mr. Potter—James—signaled to her through your back doors," Detective Warren says.

I picture James now, spinning around, his face flushed after Luke slammed the door on Izzy. I thought he'd been searching the kitchen for a weapon, but that must've been when he alerted Samira. Then it hits me again: She was there. There with Luke. If she could describe him so clearly they must've been face to face. I'm scared to ask, but I have to know.

"How is Samira? Is she okay?"

"She was shot," Detective Warren says.

"What?" My voice cracks.

"A bullet hit her shoulder," Lydia says as Dad buries his face in his hands. "But she's going to be just fine."

My mind races. It can't catch up fast enough. Things keep getting worse with each passing second. I picture Samira, frail as a sparrow, her enormous, dark eyes growing wider as she looked in through the glass door, shining the flashlight of her cell phone in on us. Was she here too? In this hospital? What else have they kept from me?

I feel a surge of relief that Luke wouldn't let Izzy in the house. Then a strange thought hits me. Izzy's brothers are obsessed with this show "Alaska State Troopers." Mrs. Collins says it's not appropriate, but if it keeps them quiet and stops them from leading a life of crime, she's fine with it. You can learn a lot from it actually—like how the cops are supposed to roll up slowly and quietly so they don't startle an intruder and cause him to do something rash.

"Why did the police turn on the lights and sirens?" My voice takes on an angry edge. "That's when Luke completely lost it—when he knew he was really in trouble."

Detective Warren shifts in the chair, and frowns, considering my question.

"When your neighbor called 9-1-1, she said she had reason to believe someone inside your home was in danger, but she didn't know exactly what was happening. Officers arrived at her residence to question her and gain an understanding of the situation before entering your home. But she wasn't there. She'd already gone to your house. Her parents had no idea why she'd called for help. The sirens you heard were units responding to an accident nearby. But in this case, Tess, we don't believe anything would've made a difference. Around 8 p.m. that evening, Luke had sent a text message to your mother telling her it was his intention to harm you and anyone else he found in your home."

Dad starts to cry, no doubt reliving the panic and confusion he must've felt when Luke forwarded Mr. Miller's suicide note to him, and Mom got that text.

"Bill, I think that's enough for now," Lydia says as Dad's sobs, initially muffled by his hands, grow louder.

Detective Warren sighs, annoyed that he's been made to wait days already and now, a bit longer.

"As hard as this is, Tess, it's imperative that you try to recall as much as you can. If you remember anything that could help us find Luke Miller, give me a call right away." He stands and hands me his card.

"Keep it," I tell him. "I don't have a phone."

He ignores that. "I'll be back tomorrow," he says before he turns and walks away, motioning with his bird-like head for Lydia to follow him into the hallway.

I appreciate that he doesn't offer any fake promises like, "We'll find him!" or "Everything's going to be all right!"

Because it isn't.

It never will be again.

Moving On

Dad and I just sit there, the awkward silence so real it might as well be a third person. I wait for him to say something stupid like, "Give it some time, Tess. You'll feel better." But he's trapped inside his own head just as I am in mine.

I stare out the window, the bright sun mocking me, and think about how easy it is to believe that life would be better if only fill-in-the-blank happened. Like, I used to think I'd be so cool if only I had *these* shoes or *that* purse. When I first woke up here days ago, I thought everything would be fine if only I had answers to my questions: How did I end up in the hospital? Why are Mom and Dad acting so strange? Where's James? Why hasn't Izzy visited?

Now that I've got them, I wish I could go back in time. Un-know everything. I finally get the whole "ignorance is bliss" saying. I remember all the things I took for granted: that I'd have more time with James, that Izzy would always be my best friend, that Mom and Dad were good people who were trying their best. What a joke.

I should hate Luke for everything that's happened, and I do, but I also think I understand him a bit better now, as crazy as that sounds.

"It sucks to lose someone close to you," he'd hissed at me in my living room. I agreed just to go along with him—mainly so he wouldn't shoot me. I hadn't even considered how living with as much sorrow as he had could drive anyone crazy.

Still, how could he murder James, shoot Samira, and then just drive away? I think about Detective Warren asking for my help. But I don't know where Luke is. How would I? It's not up to me to solve this. I'm empty. I've lost everything. There's nothing Detective Warren can say or do that will make me want to think about this — Luke—anymore. Yes, he's completely unhinged, and innocent people might be in danger, but we're all in danger. How many mass shootings do we hear about, and nothing changes? How many lunch meat and lettuce recalls kill people every few months? And don't forget about drunk drivers and terrorists. We're all walking that thin line, one split second, one decision to go left instead of right, to say yes instead of no, away from disaster every day. The world is pretty much fucked the way I see it. So don't act like it's up to me to save anyone, Detective. I'm out.

That's what I told Lydia when she came by earlier this afternoon to check on me. Dad had gone to get more coffee, which was a welcome relief. He'd been crying on and off and, at different points, I think he expected *me* to console *him*. I can't even pretend to care about his problems.

I almost smiled when Lydia walked in, which made me instantly hate myself because James is gone, and all I should feel is grief. But she was wearing this sweater with rows of tacky green and gold garland separated by red-nosed reindeer. Of course, she had her usual tasteful pearl earrings, but this silly side of her caught me off-guard. I nearly laughed until I remembered. Christmas. The image of Luke swinging the fireplace poker and sending our tree crashing to the ground flashed through my mind. I felt the blood drain from face and thought I might be sick again. I guess that's my regular look now because Lydia didn't ask if I was okay or needed anything.

Instead, she said, "I'm on my way to an ugly sweater luncheon."

"Yeah, I got that," I told her.

"Tess, I know that the last thing you want to do is think about Saturday, especially now in light of everything you know, but Detective Warren, the police, could really use your help. If you can think of anything, maybe you could—"

"Write it down in my journal?" I said sarcastically.

"I'm sorry, Tess, I had no idea you were left-handed. I should've noticed that in your chart. I would've given you a voice recorder. I can get one for you now if you'd like, if you think it will help."

I wanted to tell her something like, "Don't beat yourself up, Lyd, even my own parents didn't think of it." But because she didn't throw the blame back on me by saying, "You should've told me you're left-handed!" I felt kinder toward her.

"It's okay, I'm not much of a storyteller anyway. I think watching my dad struggle with words for pretty much my whole life may have something to do with that."

Lydia nodded. "Understood."

"When I held the journal in my hand and thought about what you said about how I should imagine that I'm telling the story to a stranger because I'd pay closer attention to the details, I do think that helped."

"I'm glad to hear that, Tess," she nodded again.

"Of course, now I'd give anything to forget it all."

"Assisting the police in finding Luke could offer a small bit of comfort, perhaps even closure."

"Comfort? Closure?" I snorted. "I am a very long way from either of those." That's when I told her that the universe was basically screwed, and that I had no interest in helping Detective Warren. "You of all people should understand that I need time."

That shamed her, like I hoped it would. She took a beat, and lowered her head before speaking again.

"I do understand, Tess, and I want to give you all the time you need to process these devastating events. I'm in no way making light of any part of what you've survived. I wouldn't ask this of you if it weren't for the fact that apprehending Luke may prevent someone else from getting hurt."

"Thanks, but I really can't worry about anyone else right now," I said, tears springing to my eyes. "I mean, look at me. My life as I knew it is over. I don't want to stay here but I can't bear the thought of going home either. I wish I could just evaporate."

She nodded but didn't say a word. For all her fancy degrees and worldly wisdom, she had no more advice to give.

"I'll be back later this afternoon," she said.

"Enjoy your party," I called after her with a snotty edge to my voice. Then I turned toward the window, closed my eyes, and hoped she'd give up on me and go away for good.

Now she's back. I don't know how much time has passed, but her ugly sweater has been replaced by a black cardigan with bell sleeves. She carries a plate with gingerbread people and sugar cookies decorated to look like wreaths. I hadn't even thought about all the baking I was missing. Every year, I try a new, more complicated cookie recipe and force Izzy to sit in the kitchen while I screw it up, re-do it, and then, five batches later, perfect it. Now, when I picture my kitchen, all I see is Luke, filled with rage and confusion, screaming and spinning in a circle. I shut my eyes tight and try to block it out.

"I thought you might like something sweet," Lydia says, placing this peace-offering on my tray.

It's a nice gesture, but I have no appetite.

"So, Tess, good news. You're moving."

Did the lasagna or fireplace burn down our house? I wonder. Nothing would surprise me at this point. When I don't respond, she continues.

"I know Michelle told you you'd be going to rehab from here, but because of this weather, beds aren't turning over as quickly as they usually do. However, there's a need for this room, and I thought you could probably use a change of scenery."

I don't answer. I'm sure I'll have no say in this anyway.

"Your new roommate is someone very special. I think you two will form a fast friendship."

Roommate? I'm tempted to balk, but then I think a stranger's presence may be enough to force Dad to either pull himself together or go home.

"A nurse's assistant will be in soon to help collect your things and transfer you."

She's so enthusiastic that I don't tell her I literally have nothing to move. Yesterday, Mom brought me my pink bathrobe because she decided the room is drafty, but that's it.

"You'll be going to the palliative care unit," she continues.

"The what?"

"The palliative care unit. It's for patients facing serious or terminal illnesses. The goal is to improve the quality of life for both them and their families."

"But I don't have one of those—a serious or terminal illness, do I?" It's messed up that I even have to ask that, but so much has been kept from me, there's a possibility I could be dying, and no one would tell me.

"No, Tess. But I really think this could be a good spot for you." Lydia smiles gently. "I'll be back to see you tomorrow when you're settled in."

She walks out before I have a chance to tell her that I am dying. On the inside.

Annie Banks

Minutes, maybe hours later, a hospital attendant comes to wheel me off to my new room. He has the round face and curly hair of a Muppet.

"I'm Ernesto. I'll be your chauffeur today." He smiles then frowns like he knows me from somewhere but can't quite place it.

I smile back even though I feel like crying. I don't want to make any small talk with him, and I absolutely do not want to meet any new roommate. I want to wallow in my grief. That is all.

Another assistant comes in, and together they lift me onto a different bed. This one is even narrower, which I didn't think was possible.

"I got it from here," Ernesto says. The assistant nods at him and leaves but not before taking a sideways glance at my face. I must look like something out of a horror film.

Out in the hallway, the lights burn brighter, the beeps and buzzing seem louder. It's all too much. I wonder if this is anything like the sensory overload Emmett experiences. Emmett. My heart splits in two all over again thinking about him. No one understood him the way James did. None of this will ever make sense to him. To any of us. I start to cry, and people—doctors, nurses, patients' loved ones, and even the patients themselves—stare at me as I roll toward the elevator, flat on my back. Helpless.

Even yesterday, I'd probably have been eager to sit up and check out my surroundings, grateful to finally be out of that tiny room. Today, I couldn't care less about any of it. All I can do is think about James. There's a gnawing in my stomach—like hunger but a thousand times worse. It eats away, the hole inside me growing deeper, wider, until I feel almost hollow.

"Excuse me! Pardon me! Beep beep!" Ernesto says as he angles me into the elevator, forcing a young woman into the arms of the man beside her. They hug and giggle.

I close my eyes. Tears slide down into my ears and pool there. I'm grateful that they muffle the sounds around me.

Ernesto barely pushes me inside my new room when the girl on the bed near the door tosses her phone aside and begins talking.

"You're here! It's you! You look so different from the photos on TV. Not worse, of course, I didn't mean that, just, you know, different."

She's about fourteen, maybe fifteen years old, and seems so excited. Oh great, a crazy girl. What meds is she on?

Ernesto whisks me past her toward the window. Another attendant magically appears, and together they lift me onto my new bed.

"You have no idea how psyched I am to have a roommate!" the girl squeals. She removes her shoulder-length brown hair, exposing her bald head, and puts on a spiky pink punk-style 'do. At least that's what I think I see, maybe I'm the one who's taking too many meds.

"It's so boring here on a Saturday," she continues, poking at random tufts of hair, and smiling at her reflection before turning to me. "I finished the book I was reading this morning—the new John Green—do you like him? You can have it. Anyway, this is perfect timing! I'm Annie, by the way. Annie Banks, like the girl in the movie 'Father of the Bride.' Ever see it?"

"Nope, I don't think so."

"I have acute lymphoblastic leukemia. ALL, for short. Don't worry, I'm not contagious."

I look at her, really look at her, and the first thing I notice is her lack of eyebrows. It makes her face seem open, a blank slate, free of judgment, up for anything.

The second thing I notice is her wig collection. Resting on faceless mannequin heads on her meal tray are two shades of red—one's ginger with curls like orphan Annie, the other is fiery with pigtails that probably make her look like Wendy from the fast food place. She's also got one with a long, blond braid like Elsa's from "Frozen." I recognize it because every time I babysit Evie, she insists we watch it and sing along.

Perched on a nest of blankets, Annie turns to face me, still talking, "When you spend days, weeks, even months of your life in treatment or being forced to rest, you see just about every movie ever made. Well, not the R-rated ones, but, anyway, check it out. It's cute."

"Noted," I say and turn toward the window. I may be on a lower floor in a different unit, but the view is just the same. It's getting dark now. In the distance, the sky is that deceptively optimistic shade of pink, like tomorrow will be a better day. Doubtful.

I hope that if I keep staring in this direction, Annie won't see the tears welling up in my eyes and, maybe, after staring at the back of my head, she'll take the hint and stop her endless chatting. She seems pleasant enough, but after almost a week of being on my own, silence and I have become pretty well acquainted.

"And you need no introduction—you're Tess!" she continues. My attempt at discouraging further talking has apparently failed. "Tess Porter! I can't believe it's you. I'd shake your hand, but, you know, germs." She rolls her eyes.

Maybe Lydia told her my name or my whole horrific history, but that seems like a violation of patient confidentiality.

Because I can't bear any more suspense—ever—I come right out and ask, "How do you know my name?"

"Wait, are you serious? Tess, you've been all over the news and in every paper since Sunday. Did you not know? Don't you watch TV? There's a world-wide manhunt for the guy who—"

She stops herself. She doesn't know how to phrase it. I don't blame her. —killed your boyfriend, ruined your life, avenged the death of his dad, which was brought on by your heartless mom. There are so many ways that sentence could end.

"There was a vigil in your town. People were praying for you, that you'd wake up. I can't believe you didn't know."

"I fell down my basement stairs, fourteen steps total, so I've had this head injury, and I wasn't supposed to look at screens, at least that's what they told me. But now I think my parents were just stalling for time, trying to figure out what to do next, how to deal with each other. And me."

Her eyes brighten now that we're sort of having a conversation. She's sitting on her knees, bursting with puppyish enthusiasm but trying to contain it, recognizing that the thing that's catapulted me into the spotlight is actually an unimaginable tragedy.

"Can you tell me what happened, inside your house, I mean? When you're ready, obviously."

Where and how would I begin? My silence must make her think that she's offended me because she shakes her head. "I'm sorry, you probably don't want to talk about it. My mom is always telling me to stop being so nosy. But my dad says I'm insatiably curious, and that's a good thing because that's how you learn."

"I'll tell you about it, sure," I say, surprising myself. Deep down, I guess I'm wondering if hearing it aloud will help me make sense of it all. "How much time have you got?"

"If I'm lucky? My doctors think a week maybe two tops."

Now it's my turn to be sorry.

"I'm an idiot. I didn't mean it like that, I meant—"

"I know what you meant!" Annie laughs. "I couldn't resist."

I take a deep breath and begin to tell her everything. All the details. The events I would've written if my hand wasn't trapped in this cast. I tell her about James' call, the pocket watch and the note, how I foolishly thought the drive to and from the airport would be the scariest parts of the night.

When I tell her about Luke pretending to be Nick, she gasps so dramatically I start to wonder if she's too young to hear the rest. Then I remember that she must know how the story ends from seeing it on the news and reading about it in the paper. And that totally freaks me out—everyone knowing how messed up my family is, probably judging me and my parents in comments sections and on Facebook pages across the world. But none of that matters really, not compared to everything else. Not even close.

I tell her about James, standing there on my front porch, how we held each other, snow swirling all around us. I have to stop because I start crying when I think about how amazing it was to finally see him again. I still can't believe James is gone, that I'll never have another chance to look into his eyes, lose myself in that dark freckle, and dream about our future together. My heart aches, and I can't imagine this feeling ever going away.

I tell her the rest as quickly as I can—about how Luke had been letting himself into our house and tracking all our texts, calls, and social media accounts. Every few sentences, she says, "Oh. My. God…" and then covers her mouth like she's afraid if she interrupts one more time I'll stop talking.

As I near the end—when Luke pulled out the gun—I think about Izzy again. I don't tell Annie that part. I'm so ashamed that I bailed on my friend when she needed me most. It's still too upsetting for me to comprehend that even after that, she still came to my house when her family rejected her. She was there, crying on my doorstep, and I did nothing to comfort her.

I tell Annie that the last bit is a blur for me, that with my shaky hand, I attempted to stab Luke, but he stopped me seconds before we heard a siren screaming in the distance. It's only now that I realize James pushed me down the stairs to save me. He took the bullet that was meant for me.

I'm sobbing, breathless. In telling Annie everything, the shock of it gives way to understanding as the reality of all I've been through, all I've lost, settles in. It's the breakdown that's been building all day, all week. Tears stream down my face and mix with snot pouring out of my nose, forming a disgusting soup that drips into my mouth. I don't even care.

Annie stares like she doesn't know what to do, then she says. "Screw the germs, I'm coming over. I mean, I'm dying anyway, right?"

She untangles herself from her blankets, hops out of her bed, and climbs into mine. She hugs me, her pink wig tickling my nose, making me almost laugh through my tears.

"I wish we could trade places," I tell her when I can breathe again.

"Theresa Annie Porter! Don't ever let me hear you say that again!" She gets out of my bed and stands there, wagging her finger at me.

"I don't have a middle name," I tell her.

"I know, I didn't see one on your chart. A nurse left it over there by the sink before you were wheeled in. So much for patient privacy, am I right? But, seriously, how unimaginative are your parents? No middle name!"

"Um, hello, your name is Ann. It's not like you're Chrysanthemum or something," I say.

"Oh man, I loved that book. And I know, my name is super dull, that's why I had to add the 'ie' at the end. Anyway, I'm giving you my name as your middle name so you can be more interesting too. Just watch, your whole life will be better now."

She sits back down on my bed and hugs her knees to her chest.

I almost say, "Well, it can't get worse," but then stop myself. She's so full of life, I forget that she's so sick. Even though I don't know Annie, like even a bit, she—this, talking about something as silly as names—feels so warm and familiar. It reminds me of all the dumb conversations Izzy and I used to have: *If you had twins, what would you name them? Okay, what about triplets? What if someone gave you a litter of kittens, what would you call them?"* We'd go on like that for hours, sitting on her bed, splitting a bag of Twizzlers.

"Have you seen a girl named Isabelle Collins on the news?" I ask, even though I'm scared to hear the answer.

"Curly black hair, eyes bright blue like mouthwash?"

"Yes, that's Izzy."

"Yeah, reporters have been waiting outside her house. They keep asking her about you, like how you're doing, what your relationship was with Luke, did she know your parents' marriage was in trouble, and she always says the same thing."

I brace for it.

"'No comment.'" Annie shakes her head. "She always says 'no comment.'"

I don't know if that means Izzy hates me so much she can't be bothered talking about me, or if she's protecting my privacy.

"Sorry, I know that's not really helpful. Who's Izzy, anyway?"

"She's my best friend. Well, maybe my ex-best friend. I let her down when she needed me, and I'm not sure how, or if, I can ever make it up to her."

"That sucks," she says. "I'll be your new best friend if you want."

"Thanks, I'd like that," I say.

"Okay, cool. But now that we're best friends, I'm going to need you to do something for me, Tess."

She cocks her head to the side and grins like she's contemplating her request. It's hard to take her seriously in that wig. I have a feeling she's about to ask me to do

249

something crazy, like prank the nurse by asking for an emotional support parrot. But she's taking so long I'm afraid she may ask me to explain what I think happens when we die. I'm not up for either task.

"Promise me that when you get out of here, even if it's on crutches, or in a wheelchair, or you're hobbling like you were just thrown off a horse, promise me that you'll go live this big, fancy, fabulous life," she finally says.

I smile but shake my head. "Right now, I'm living one second at a time. I can't even think about the next few hours. There's no way I can imagine next week."

"That's fair. I get it. Your boyfriend, James, he was really cute, like lost-Hemsworth-brother cute."

"Thanks." I nod, tears returning to my eyes. "He was the best thing that ever happened to me. I know that's a total cliché, but it's the truth. Have you ever had a boyfriend?"

"Nope." She shakes her head. "I've been sick on and off for the last few years so I haven't really gotten to do a lot of 'healthy person' stuff. But when I was in fifth grade, I did have a mad crush on a boy named Will, who was in my chess club. I think he liked me too because he'd always let me win. At the end-of-the-year party, he gave me a note that said, 'I like hearing you say checkmate. Have a nice summer!' Not exactly '50 Shades of Grey,' but it was pretty exciting at the time."

I smile. "Can I ask you a question?"

"Duh, of course. You just told me everything about your life. Go on," she says.

"Where's your family? Why are you all alone here?" I have no right to ask, and I know it makes me a really bad person, but part of me wants to think that I'm not the only one whose parents are a disaster.

"You mean, why am I here and not dying in the comfort of my own home surrounded by loved ones, soft lighting, and Norah Jones playing in the background? Why am I here today, so close to the holidays?"

"Right," I say sheepishly, mortified that I asked, but impressed that she could pretty much read my mind.

"My cousin Sarah got married today. I was supposed to be a bridesmaid, but that didn't quite go as planned. After we found out that I was sick again, the wedding was the only happy thing my mom and aunt had to talk about. So I told my family I wanted them to go. Plus, my cousin, she's kind of a bridezilla, so I'm only a tiny bit sorry to miss it. She probably would've insisted I wear a really hideous wig, so I didn't steal all the attention from her, you know, cause I'm such a hottie."

Annie cracks up at her own joke just as Wanda comes in with our dinner trays.

"Girl, you did it! You finally got yourself a roommate. They told me these were private rooms."

"I've got some pull around here, Wanda. You know that."

"Well, enjoy, my love. You deserve a fun Saturday night for a change. I snuck you an extra Jell-O. Don't tell anybody!"

Even though I'm scared to look under the brown plastic dome to see what tonight's meal is, I realize I'm hungry for the first time in a while.

"You're the best!" Annie says, but before Wanda's even out in the hallway she whispers to me, "Don't worry, I've got Domino's on the way."

"What?"

"I hope you like bacon!" she says, eyes twinkling.

"Oh, c'mon, Tess, even pigs would like bacon if they tried it," Izzy always says after she orders a double-decker BLT.

"How did you pull that off?" I ask.

"Tess, I'm dying. Who's going to say 'no' to me?" Annie rolls her eyes.

Minutes later, a large pie arrives. We sit side by side on my bed, pizza box across our laps. I slowly sink my teeth into a slice. It's the best thing I've ever tasted. Greasy, cheesy, salty, delicious. I have to stop myself from moaning. I'm done when I realize Annie's taken only one bite.

"What's up? Let me guess, you had surf and turf delivered for lunch?"

She smiles. "I can't eat like I used to. Sometimes I forget."

I don't tell her I'd give anything to go back to forgetting.

Together, we watch "While You Were Sleeping" on her iPad and agree that Sandra Bullock is pretty flawless even when they try to make her look like a regular person.

Just before it ends, her phone rings, the shrill, fast pulsing of a FaceTime call.

"My parents!" she squeals and leaps toward her bed, fishing her phone out of the blankets. "Dad!"

"There's my girl!" her father says. In the background, a wedding singer does an impressive cover of "Unforgettable." "How are you?"

"Great! I have a new friend. May I present Theresa Annie Porter!" Annie sits back down on my bed and turns the phone toward me. I wave.

"How's the wedding?" she asks.

"It's not the same without you, Ann," her dad says. "You'll love this, Alex has been standing beside the cake for the last hour waiting for a piece, and Sarah keeps telling the staff to chase him away and guard the cake with their lives."

Annie turns to me. "See what I mean? Classic bridezilla!"

"Take a look." Mr. Banks walks over to a boy, who looks about ten, maybe, eleven. I quickly realize this kid, who's inching his finger closer like he's about to swipe a pinch of icing from the bottom of the massive wedding cake, must be Annie's younger brother.

"Oh man! Look at him in that tux! Al! Hey Al! Al!" Annie shouts now.

I watch her face crumple when her brother doesn't turn around. It's the band. They've segued into the Cha-Cha Slide, and the volume triples. She looks so distressed that he can't hear her and doesn't know she's even there, like she's getting a preview of what life will be like without her. She's already watching over him, and he can't sense it. Her dad sees it too and rushes the phone closer to Alex.

"Al!" She tries again.

The boy snatches his finger back as if he's been caught in the act. A huge grin splashes across his face when he sees her.

Oh my God, I love technology, I think, when he yells, "Annie!" so loud I expect a nurse to rush in and check on her. Alex grabs the phone from their dad.

"Al! You look so handsome! How many times did Aunt Patsy ask you to dance tonight?"

"Seven, but then she gave me a $2 bill and some pigs-in-a-blanket that she pulled out of her purse, so it was totally worth it."

He holds up the funny-looking money. Annie's laughter is infectious and I smile non-stop, seeing how happy she is.

"Annie, watch these old people try to dance, it's hilarious. It's like 'America's Funniest Home Videos!'" He spins the phone so we can see a blur of shaking hips and bumping butts straining against tight sequined evening gowns.

"You should be here, Annie, there's gonna be a chocolate fountain in a few minutes. I miss you!" he yells.

"Well, don't worry about me," Annie says, "because I'm having the time of my life with my new best friend, Theresa Annie Porter."

She turns the phone again so I can wave.

"Oh, they're finally going to cut the cake. Annie, I have to go. Love you! Here's Dad."

"Mom and I are going to be there first thing in the morning with a slice for you, and maybe I can smuggle out an extra for your new friend, okay?"

"Sounds good, Dad, thanks," Annie says. "Hey, have Al catch the bouquet for me. That'll drive Sarah crazy."

"Will do. Now get some rest, Annie. We love you."

"Love you, too!" She hangs up and rests her head on my shoulder.

"Your family is amazing," I say and try to push down the sadness and jealousy swelling inside me. I've lost not one family but two. Mom and Dad, Mrs. Potter and Emmett. Three, if you count Izzy and her family.

"I know, right?" she smiles. "Sometimes I think about all the lives I could've had. I might've been a mosquito in the Amazon jungle, a dairy cow in Wisconsin, a house cat right in my own town, and I had the chance to be me, to be a part of this family, to be loved by these people. It was the best."

Hearing her talk in past tense wrecks me, but I refuse to cry in front of her.

"Can I ask you another question? What does it feel like? To know that—"

"To know that I'm going to die really soon?"

I nod.

"I'll tell you what it's like, it's like each day I'm slipping. You know when you're little, and you're in a swimming pool or a lake, and you slide your toes under the lane line? You feel the shallow part sloping toward the deep end, and you're gathering up your courage to duck under and your mom is far behind you screaming, 'Be careful! Don't go! You don't even know how to swim!' And maybe you go under just for a minute to test it out, and then you bob back up on the safe side of the buoys, kind of shaky but okay? That's me. Each day I dip a little bit longer under the lane line. I've done it before, but I've always come back safely on the other side. But not this time. This time, I'm really going. This time feels different."

"Wow," I say. I've never heard anyone describe it like that. "But how can you be so chill about it?"

"I don't dwell on the darkness, Tess, I linger in the light."

"What's that, the Bible? Leonard Cohen?"

"It's me. Annie! Annie Banks!" She punches me lightly in my good arm. "If I'm sharing my wisdom with you, I want full credit. I think of it like this, Tess: There will always be some bad or negative things in your life, and there will always be some good or positive things. Like, for me, I was in remission for a while, and I knew that I should enjoy every single second. But, at first, I couldn't because the fear, the awful fear of it coming back was always with me, haunting me. And then one day I realized I was ruining all my good days by waiting for the bad thing to happen. My point is, the good and the bad? They'll both still be there. Which one you let rule your life—the darkness or the light—well, that's up to you."

"Wow," I say, again dumbfounded by how someone so young could be so wise and so brave at the same time.

"But that doesn't mean I don't want to stay. I do," she says. "So I propose this: If you don't want to live for yourself, Tess, which I totally understand—no judgment, then live for me. Go do everything I want to do. Learn to play the guitar. Kiss a handsome boy under the stars on a hot summer night. Get a dog who can catch a frisbee in his teeth and take him to Central Park. Go to a Chinese restaurant, order a dozen egg rolls, and then eat as many as you can in your car while listening to your favorite podcast."

"Too soon after I gorged myself on pizza, but I like where you're going with that," I say.

"Okay, that last one was just to see if you were listening. You are. Very good. Anyway, get some big old movie star sunglasses, rent a convertible, drive along the ocean, and blast 'When Doves Cry.' Live for me, Tess."

"How did you come up with these?" I'm laughing through tears because all the things on Annie's agenda? They're such sweet, simple things that no one would set out to do, much less savor, until they thought they might never be able to actually do them.

"It's not my bucket list. I'm way more original than that! Think of it as my Tess-To-Do list," she says, yawning. "Think we can finish the movie tomorrow? I just got so tired."

"Of course," I say, and watch as she climbs down off my bed more slowly this time. I wonder if whatever medication they're giving her to make her comfortable is wearing off or kicking in.

I look out the window. It's a polka dot sky, indigo sprinkled with stars. I don't feel as frightened as I have the past few nights.

It occurs to me that Annie is why Lydia had me transferred so suddenly.

"I really think this could be a good spot for you," she'd said. Lydia's gentle smile now seems almost smug. She was clearly pleased with her plan to get me to care about something, someone, again and, at the same time, keep a dying girl from spending a night alone.

Even though I've only known Annie a couple of hours, she's made me look at things differently.

"Well played, Lydia," I think, remembering how initially I was hesitant to accept help from a woman with lipstick on her teeth.

I click off the lights and feel as if I could sleep for weeks.

"Hey, Annie Banks," I whisper. "Thanks for being my new best friend."

I wait for her response, but she's already fast asleep.

Safe Spaces

"Time for PT," says a nurse I don't recognize. She's already taken my temperature and blood pressure even though I'm half-asleep. When it comes to healthcare workers, there are no boundaries. Everything is fair game.

She hustles me into a waiting wheelchair and once I'm in the hall, an attendant arrives to transport me.

"No breakfast?" Not that I enjoy the lumpy oatmeal or runny eggs all that much, but I have that garlicky-pizza aftertaste in my mouth, and I'd love to get rid of it.

"Just following orders. Ask someone about it when we get there. Maybe it'll be waiting in your room when you get back. Believe me, no one else is going to touch it." The attendant laughs as he wheels me in reverse into the elevator.

The realization that James is gone crashes down on me, and I slip into an isolating sadness even as I'm wheeled into the bright and busy therapy room. I'd hoped I might see him again last night in my dreams, or hallucinations, or whatever they might be, but nothing. I had my first uninterrupted, dreamless sleep in days. It must show because Michelle says, "Tess! You look well rested!"

"Thanks," I say.

Seeing her reminds me that I'd told her I hoped to go ice skating with my boyfriend and his brother. No wonder she acted so nervous, babbling about her wedding until she was able to rush out of the room. She must've known about James from the news or my chart and had no clue how to respond. I guess that also explains why she never brought me those pictures of people ice skating that she swore would be motivating. I can't blame her. Who expects a teen with a couple of broken limbs to have my horrifying backstory?

"I'm finishing up with another patient right now. I'll be with you shortly. I can have someone bring up your breakfast. Want coffee or tea while you wait?"

"Tea, please," I say and still feel so disoriented. Maybe it's later than I think, but no, I spot a clock on the wall. It's 8:15 a.m. Why am I up this early? No one usually comes for me until at least ten. I see the date on the whiteboard. It's Christmas Eve. Michelle, wearing her Santa face scrubs shirt, red sweatpants, and jingle bell earrings, must want to wrap up early today.

I can't stop thinking about James. I want to go back to the room and wallow. Michelle is busy with other patients. I wait so long, I have time to pick at breakfast and skim three ancient *People* magazines, trying to distract myself so I don't cry in front of a dozen strangers.

When Michelle finally comes for me, she apologizes, and we get right to work. I practice the usual things. By the end of the forty-minute session, I'm sweating and exhausted.

"Wait right here, okay?" she says before heading over to use the phone.

Like, where else do I have to go, I want to say, but she's already gone.

After waiting another excruciatingly long time, an attendant comes to wheel me back. I'm surprised at how much I'm looking forward to seeing Annie again. While we were eating, she noticed that I'd bitten my nails down to nubs. She said she'd call her mom this morning and ask her to bring nail polish so we could give each other manicures this afternoon.

"Wrong room," I tell the assistant who wheels me back from OT. The first bed where Annie should be is empty. All the wigs that were lined up there yesterday are missing. My wheelchair slows to a halt as she checks the chart.

"Nope, three-twelve. This is it."

"But—" Then I spot the Dominos pizza boxes poking out of the garbage.

"Where's Annie? Where's my roommate?"

"Sorry, don't know about that," she says. "But I can help you get back into bed."

I rest my head against the pillow. Am I going crazy? Was Annie real or, like James' visits, only in my imagination? I close my eyes hoping she'll be there when I open them. She isn't. I'm so confused. I'm about to call the nurse and ask what's going on when Lydia appears in the doorway.

She doesn't look so smug now. She walks over and sits on Annie's vacant bed, stripped of everything but a mattress pad.

"Where's Annie?" I demand.

"I'm sorry, Tess. Annie had a rough night. Her family thought it best to bring her home."

I'm upset that I slept so deeply, I never heard Annie struggling. After all the restless nights, knowing she was there with me was such a comfort, I drifted off almost immediately. When I was whisked out of the room this morning, the curtain was drawn around her bed. I assumed she was sleeping as peacefully as I had. Now I wish I'd been wide awake, staring at the ugly ceiling tiles like every other night, so maybe I could've helped her.

I look out the window and feel betrayed. Lydia tricked me.

"Why? Why would you introduce me to her if she was just going to disappear?" I cry.

I hate Lydia for messing with my soul. She doesn't answer, just looks down at her boots.

"What? Did you think I hadn't lost enough already? You used her. You used both of us. You treated us like some kind of social experiment," my voice rising in disbelief.

"Tess, please don't look at it that way. I think anyone who has the opportunity to meet someone as special as Annie should, don't you? Someone so full of wisdom and positivity. I thought of her more as a gift to you."

Way to make me feel like an asshole, Lydia, is what I'm thinking, but instead I say, "Yes, she's an amazing

262

person, but I wanted more time with her. Now it just feels like one more sucker punch, one more great thing ripped away."

"In introducing you to Annie, I thought it might change your perspective. But beyond that, I thought you could use a friend, someone you could trust. You deserve to feel safe again, Tess. Even though it's not always possible out there in the world, you can cultivate it, and develop it within yourself."

I'm still angry and only half-listening because Lydia has a tendency to go on and on, but a bit, a phrase, sticks in my ear.

"Wait, say that again," I say as a sheen of sweat begins to travel up my body from my feet to my forehead.

"Which part? You deserve to feel safe again and even if—"

I cut her off mid-sentence. "I think I know where Luke Miller is."

Together

"Hey."

I'd know that voice anywhere. I whip my head toward the sound, the one I've been waiting to hear for nearly a week.

"Iz—" I'm crying before I get her name out.

"Tess."

She hugs me fiercely, and for a moment, I forget about everything else and just bask in what has always been Izzy's signature scent a sweet-clean mix of cherry Chapstick and Finesse shampoo. So familiar, it gives me flashbacks of everything I love about her—how, when she was captain in gym class, she'd picked me first to spare me the embarrassment of being chosen last. How she'll sit at the island in my kitchen, cradling Daffy, and pretending my pet could speak. *Tell me all about your day, Tess! I took thirty-two cat naps while you were gone and dreamt of birds and mice every time.* I remember her patience as she tried to help me understand geometry sophomore year. I picture us walking home after school in fourth grade the day she invited me to try my first zeppole. We've been inseparable ever since.

"I'm so sorry, Izzy. You were right, I'm a shitty friend. I wasn't there when you needed me. Thank you for coming. I've missed you more than you could ever know. I wouldn't have blamed you if you never wanted to see me again." I'm babbling and squeezing her so tight with my right arm that I actually hear one of her vertebra crack. "Sorry, again," I say, reluctant to let her go.

I look at my friend. Usually, I think I know her face better than my own after all the time we've spent together, but now it feels like I haven't seen her in a decade. I'd forgotten the crescent moon-shaped scar just above her lip that she got playing field hockey, and the way one of her dark curls always springs loose and hangs in the middle of her forehead, forcing her to sweep it away over and over again.

"Tess, stop. I'm the one who should be apologizing. I would've been here the second you woke up, but your parents asked me not to visit until you knew everything. They figured I wouldn't be able to keep it from you. They were right." She smiles but her lips start to quiver. "I'm so, so sorry about James, Tess."

All I can do is nod between sobs.

"I still can't believe it," she continues. "I can't believe he's gone. He was the best, Tess, and he loved you like crazy. This whole time, I let you think I was this expert matchmaker, but, really, James begged me to set you two up. We had AP French together, and he knew you and I were friends. He said he was too shy to talk to you, which is crazy because he was so, so brave. I saw Samira, and she told me what she saw that night in your house. I was

265

so scared for you, Tess, I was literally shaking for days. I couldn't stop crying when I found out James—"

We hug each other again, my tears soaking the shoulder of her sweater.

"Iz—"

"Wait, I'm not done," she pulls back to look at me. "I'm also sorry I made you feel guilty for missing my birthday dinner. I mean, I'm eighteen. I should be able to stand up to my parents without needing to hold your hand under the table."

"How is everything at home?" I'm scared to hear the answer; the memory of her on my front porch—her begging to come in, me turning her away—will be forever imprinted on my mind. "I mean with your mom and dad and Grams?"

"Better."

"Really? That's incredible. How did you get them to come around?"

"It's because of all this, actually. When my parents heard about everything that happened at your house, and they knew that I'd just been there, they were obviously freaking out. I mean, about James, of course, and about you—you're like their third daughter, Tess. I think knowing that I could've been in there with you guys was enough to make them stop and think about how they'd hurt me and how they could've lost me. They apologized, which never happens with those two. They said it might take them some time to come around to the whole idea of seeing me with a girlfriend, but they promised to try. And they said they'd always love me no matter what. Grams is asking the Holy Spirit for 'wisdom and a heart free of judgment,' so that's a start. Oh, and she said to tell you she's saying the rosary for you every night."

She smiles, recognizing that while that might sound crazy to some people, I get it.

"Wow, Izzy, that's fantastic. So, is Carol coming to visit? When can I meet her?"

Despite everything that's happened to me, I need Izzy to know that I'm as happy for her as she's always been for me.

"She's coming New Year's Eve. I'm excited," she says it in a quiet, casual way, sensitive to the fact that we're now on opposite ends of relationships, hers just beginning, mine ended in the worst possible way.

I'm thrilled for her, but my heart aches because I know what she's experiencing—that fluttering in the pit of your stomach, the giddy, dizzy, breathless sensation that's better than almost anything else in the world. For me, it's gone. Over. I can't imagine ever feel that kind of love again. And if I did, wouldn't I be betraying James?

Izzy's phone buzzes.

"I'm sorry, Tess, I have to go. My mom needs the car. I'll be back first thing tomorrow and every day after, okay?"

"Okay."

She buttons her coat as she walks toward the door.

"Iz, thanks for always being there for me. I couldn't go through life without you."

"Same here," she says, turning around to face me. "I know everything seems unbelievably sad and awful right now, and I wish I could say something funny or stupid to make you crack up, but I think the only thing that will help here is time. And sticking together."

I watch her walk out and am hit with a rush of gratitude that things will be okay with us. I also can't stop thinking about what she said about James, how it wasn't her idea to set us up after all. It was his. Just like he told me when I saw him a few nights ago. My mind flashes to James visiting me, sitting so close I could reach out and trace the dimple in his chin. I can still hear him confessing, "I'm the one who begged Izzy to introduce us."

Was it a dream? A hallucination? It doesn't matter, all I know is it was real to me, and I pray it happens again.

Breaking News

Izzy and I watch game shows, the most entertaining thing we can find on basic cable. I was transferred out of the palliative care unit and into a regular private room while I wait for a spot to open up at the rehab where I'll spend less than a week, Michelle says, since I'm "progressing like a champ!"

I flip around the channels and stop on one of those trashy tabloid journalism programs hosted by an over-the-top former district attorney. Bold white letters across a bright red background at the bottom of the screen catch my eye: Breaking News: Murder Suspect Luke Miller Captured, In Custody.

"Holy shit!" Izzy screams. "Turn it up!"

"Nineteen-year-old Luke Miller, who allegedly shot and killed eighteen-year-old James Potter in a New Jersey home days before Christmas, was found hiding in a treehouse in Tremont, Ohio," explains Sally Sheffield, the host, her voice thick with feigned emotion. "This ends a week-long manhunt for Miller, who's also accused of shooting a sixteen-year-old girl in the shoulder in the same incident."

As soon as Lydia said the words "You deserve to feel safe again," I knew where Luke would be. At first, I couldn't remember the family's name, the ones who took apart the treehouse and reassembled it in their own backyard. It was a man's name—the Petersons, the Robertsons? Finally, it came to me: the Richardsons.

When I told Lydia, she immediately called Detective Warren, who said he had officers combing the Tremont neighborhood. They'd anticipated that Luke might return to his childhood home, but, of course, no one thought to look in a treehouse.

Even though Lydia came by this morning, patted my arm, and said, "They've got him, Tess. Thanks to you," my heart pounds watching the news as if I still don't believe it.

Izzy holds my hand, and we watch in stunned silence as Sally Sheffield interrogates a reporter who's standing knee-deep in snow in what must be the Richardsons' backyard. The reporter fiddles with his earpiece, but I focus on the treehouse, suspended in mid-air like some kind of a magic trick, over his right shoulder. Luke's safe space. It's just a basic brown box, really, with a tiny window. It's nothing fantastic or architecturally-intriguing like the giant ones you see on the Travel channel. But I remember Luke saying he and his dad built it together. That experience, the memory they created, that beats the most innovative design any day.

I think about Lydia's words. Even though I'm still angry with her, I wonder if she's right. Maybe "safe" isn't necessarily a place, but something we create inside ourselves.

"How did the family—the Richardsons—not see him?" Sally shouts in her exaggerated southern drawl. Even with her yelling, it's hard to concentrate on her words because she's wearing an entire cosmetics counter worth of makeup and keeps rolling her eyes beneath daddy-longlegs lashes. "That sketch of his face has been plastered everywhere from Canada to Cancun!"

"Well, Sally, that's a good point," the reporter, Ace Whitaker, says. "The Richardson family left Ohio on the fifteenth to spend the holidays in Japan, where their oldest son is studying this semester. They said they had no idea their former neighbor was using their treehouse as a hideout. Reached by phone this morning, Adam Richardson released a statement, and I quote, 'Our hearts go out to all affected by this tragedy. We had no idea Luke Miller was hiding on our property and are thankful that he's in custody as a result of terrific police work.'"

"No idea? No idea?" Sally shouts, louder this time, and I wonder if she's like this in real life or if it's all an act for ratings. "What's wrong with these people? Do they not read an American newspaper while traveling? This was their former neighbor! No idea my foot!"

They cut back to the reporter, who doesn't seem to know how to respond to Sally. He's getting pelted with snowballs thrown over the Richardsons' fence by kids in the adjacent yard.

They jump to footage of Luke being led away in handcuffs. I'm not ready to see him again. But there he is—same sweat jacket, same creepy grin. I don't realize I've been holding my breath through the whole broadcast and only let it out when I see an officer place a hand on Luke's head and ease him into a police car.

"Speaking of feet, is it true Luke Miller contracted hypothermia and has lost three toes?" Sally barks.

"To the best of my knowledge, that is not the case," Ace, brushing snow from his black wool coat, states.

"What does that mean, 'to the best of your knowledge?'"

"I mean, I haven't given him a pedicure, Sally, what do you think I mean?"

"Knock it off, Ace, you know what I'm asking."

"My sources are telling me he was spending these chilly nights camped out inside the Tremont Walmart."

"Don't Yelp! reviewers refer to that store as 'The Worst Walmart in America?'" No one saw this guy? You've got to be kidding me! Enough about Miller, let's talk about the girl he allegedly planned to murder in her own home."

When they start a montage of photos taken from my Facebook page, I click it off.

"How do you feel?" Izzy asks.

I'm so grateful that she's back, that we're back, that she doesn't assume that seeing James' killer led away in handcuffs changes anything.

"Empty," I tell her. "I just feel empty."

She squeezes my hand. I squeeze back.

Rehab

There must be fifty televisions inside this one-floor rehab center. At least two flat screens hang in every room, more in the common areas. Some are programmed to Food Network. Others are set to ESPN. But a lot—too many—seem to be stuck on news channels, which means as I'm wheeled from my room to the therapy center, I'm blindsided by images of Luke: being led away in handcuffs, his high school yearbook picture, in an orange jumpsuit appearing in court.

As disturbing as those are, it's the photos that come next that totally undo me—the ones of James. There's a shot of him in his cap and gown, taken seconds after receiving his diploma. It had been a perfect June night, no humidity, or mosquitos. His eyes look brighter set against the blue backdrop of the summer sky. Remembering how happy he was that day causes my heart to implode.

Each time I'm caught off-guard by seeing the faces I already can't get out of my mind; I look down at the floor. I hum to myself in an attempt to block the awful statements I can't help but hear: "the grisly murder of a promising journalism student," "an innocent daughter pays for her mother's indiscretions."

"Adultery! Suicide! Murder! This story is one deranged clown away from a Stephen King novel!" Sally Sheffield shouts as she moderates a panel of attorneys who speculate about what Luke's sentence might be.

A prominent defense attorney came forward and offered to represent Luke, believing he's a "victim" who could get off by pleading temporary insanity.

I feel like throwing up each time I hear that piece of news.

Passing a mirror is also pretty unbearable. I'm sickly pale from lack of fresh air and sunshine. I have permanent bedhead. But it's probably all for the best. The staff knows who I am and what's happened to me, but the patients don't, and I'd like to keep it that way. I bear little resemblance to Theresa Porter, the happy girl in the photos they flash on TV, pictured smiling beside her handsome boyfriend licking ice cream cones, going to the prom, sitting behind laptops working on the high school paper together. Even I hardly recognize her anymore.

If anyone asks how I got my injuries, I say I fell down my basement stairs. Not a lie.

My roommate, an older lady named Beverly, who broke her hip after she tripped on an area rug, puts down her soup spoon after the nightly news ends one evening and says, "You look a little bit like that gal, you know. What a waste. Such a handsome young man. And that mother? What a floozy! If you ask me, this world is going to hell in a handbasket."

I'm caught between saying, "No one asked you, Beverly," and "You have no idea how right you are." Instead I say nothing and go back to reading.

I asked Dad to bring me his book, the bestseller he wrote when I was in preschool. He looked genuinely touched when I told him I'd like a copy. I need a new story running through my head, a different voice in my ears, other words in my mind.

I thought maybe it would help me understand the feeling he's been chasing since he published it. Though he was basically a colossal disappointment while I was in the hospital, he's really stepped up over the past few days. He waited until I was settled in here to tell me he rented a condo for us. All our stuff will be moved in by the time I'm discharged, so I don't have to go back to the house. He made sure to pick one that's pet-friendly so Daffy can come with us. It's the reason he's been gone so much of the time, he said, looking at places, signing contracts. It's strange to think about living somewhere new, but it's also a huge relief. I'd been dreading the thought of walking through the front door and remembering every horrific thing that took place inside the walls of our home. I can't help but wonder if Lydia suggested it, or if it was his own idea. It'll just be the two of us. Mom's staying in the house. Dad says they've agreed to sell it, but, of course, it's impossible to imagine anyone wanting to buy it now. I don't ask if this means they're separating, getting a divorce, or trying to figure it out. I have plenty of other problems to worry about without taking on theirs.

Of course, busybody Beverly senses something's off about my family. Yesterday, she made the not-so-subtle statement, "I've only ever see your dad visit. Where's your mom?"

"Oh, you just missed her. She stopped by while you were in your PT session," I told her.

It's a lie, but it's easier than telling her the truth: Mom entered a "treatment facility" a few days ago. I hadn't seen her since that morning in the hospital when she told me about James. I thought she was avoiding me after I hit her with my cast. When Dad said she'd gone to get help, I was surprised that she admitted she had a problem, but not that she's taking better care of herself than she was of me.

"Looks like you're the only one not in rehab," I said to Dad, an attempt at a joke.

"Your mother prefers to call it a treatment facility, Tess. When you see her again, you may want to refer to it that way," he said.

"Of course she does," I said. "But *if* I see her again, I'll call it what it is."

Apparently, neither of them has learned that pretending everything's okay, when clearly it isn't, is exactly what got us all here.

If I had to quantify it, my rage toward Mom might exceed my hatred for Luke, who is pleading guilty to aggravated manslaughter. I see the news on my way to therapy. I'm not sure what that means, but I'm relieved he's not claiming he's innocent. He's not represented by the hotshot attorney either. I sit in stunned silence as I watch a replay of Luke telling the judge, "My father was an attorney, so I'm prepared to act as my own counsel."

Growing up, I'd heard Mom say, "A man who represents himself in court has a fool for a client," so I'm hoping that means Luke will get himself locked up for a long time.

When I return to my room from PT, tired but stronger, I recognize a familiar silhouette looking out the window.

"Samira!" I'm happy but also scared to see her. I have no idea how severe her injuries are—injuries she suffered because of me.

"There she is!" she says and walks toward me, light and graceful as ever, though her right arm is in a sling.

The attendant helps me out of my wheelchair. I put all my weight on my right leg as Samira and I attempt an awkward hug, our damaged arms bumping into each other. I'm afraid I might topple her because she's so slight.

"Come sit down," I say, relieved that my roommate Beverly, a notorious eavesdropper, is having lunch with her grandchildren in the cafeteria.

"I'm so happy to see you. I've been thinking about you non-stop," I say, hopping to my bed.

"Pot meet kettle," she says, pointing from me back to herself. "I've been thinking of you too, Tess. My God, everything you've been through." She makes a sweeping gesture with her free arm as if she, Ms. AP Language Arts, can't summon the right words to address all that has occurred since the last time we locked eyes on what was about to become the worst night of our lives.

We sit for a moment, saying nothing. Most of our exchanges happen over texts after we wave to each other from inside our homes. It almost feels unnatural to have a conversation in person, out from behind our windows and our screens.

My eyes fill up as her fearful face on the other side of my French doors flashes through my mind.

"Samira, I'm so sorry about everything that happened to you because of me and my family. I'm sure you're haunted by it, not to mention the damage to your arm, your shoulder."

"Don't, Tess. Do not say another word. My father is making me wear this sling as a precaution. And, look at it this way, I finally got the break from playing the clarinet that I've dreamt of for...how long? Oh, only about the last eleven years."

She smiles and rolls her big brown eyes, reminding me how funny she can be without even trying.

"I'm so grateful that you were there, that you called the police, that you came over when you did."

"It was James, you know," she says, brushing away any credit. "He saw me and started making all these wild hand motions. I actually thought he was dancing at first. Then I realized he was telling me to call 9-1-1. I was confused, but I knew he would never joke about something like that, so I thought you must be in real danger."

"If you hadn't been there, I'm sure I'd be—" A shiver races up my spine. I can't complete my sentence.

"Yes, I was always there, wasn't I? Practicing my stupid clarinet. But that's not the only reason, Tess. I envied you, your long, curly hair, accent-less voice, successful, pretty mom, novelist dad, and your swimming pool, of course. The list goes on. You were like an American sitcom to me. So much fun, so carefree. I wanted to be you, Tess. That's why I was always watching. I believed, foolishly, that if I studied you like a subject, AP chem or pre-calc, I could discover the formula—how to be cooler, more interesting. People would like me instead of bully me for being a small brown nerd. I thought that if I could just watch and observe, it would work. If I studied long and hard enough, I could somehow learn how to be just like you."

"Bet you don't want to be me anymore," I say and shake my head at the irony. "There were so many times when I wanted to be you. When I saw your name on the high honor roll, your picture in the paper for your perfect SAT score. When I see the love and pride in your parents' faces when you play your clarinet. I've never known that feeling."

"It's odd. Now that I can't play, I do sort of miss it. I know that's massively hypocritical since all I've done is complain about the instrument since it was placed in my hands at age five, but I guess it's a part of me now. Like my bushy eyebrows and knobby knees. I might not always love it, but it makes me me." She pauses and wags a finger at me. "But if you tell my father any of that, I will come back and break your other leg."

I smile. "I'm so sorry you're going to miss the audition for state symphony."

"I was shot, Tess! Screw wind ensemble and state symphony. I'm better than that. I'm like a gangsta rapper. I've taken a bullet, Tess. Who has the balls to mess with me at the bus stop now?"

"Sure as hell not Trey Larkin," I say.

"You're damn right," she says with a laugh. Then she clears her throat, her voice suddenly serious. "I have yet another secret to tell you."

She scoots to the edge of her chair. "I loved James before you did."

I must be frowning because she shakes her head. "Not like that. Okay, here goes: It was my first day freshman year, I was the new girl. But I looked like a boy because my mother insisted I get this incredibly short, horrible haircut to save money, believing this way I wouldn't require another until January. And I'm thinking, 'Hello, we are already at SuperCuts, how much cheaper can you possibly be?' You know my father is a chemical engineer, right? They have plenty of money. But more on that another time.

"I was walking on the path behind the school, near the ballfields, already filled with nerves because it was my first day, when these two sophomores—one of them was, of course, Trey Larkin—they came up behind me and grabbed my new backpack. A Vera Bradley pink and purple floral print. I had seen it in *Seventeen* magazine and spent the entire summer doing odd jobs to earn the money for it and then begging my mother for the rest of the cash. I told her it was absolutely the only way I had a chance at fitting in."

She rolls her eyes again before taking a deep breath.

"I had it hanging off one shoulder, just like the girl in the magazine. When the boys snatched it, one said to the other, 'Dude, what's this little boy doing with a girl's backpack?' Then Trey dumped out the contents, all my new, freshly-sharpened pencils, my notebooks and glue sticks, the enormous maxi pads in their hot pink wrappers that my mother shoved in there so I wouldn't have to spend a quarter in the girls' room.

"Next, they started throwing my beautiful backpack over my head. Like the little fool that I was, I began jumping up in the air, trying to catch it, which only made them laugh harder. 'It's not a boy, it's a little brown monkey. Want to play some monkey in the middle? Too bad you're never going to win.'

"I sat down, blubbering. How could I explain to my mother that I lost this expensive backpack on my very first day? I rubbed my eyes to wipe my tears, and when I opened them again, there he was, riding up the hill on his bicycle. So tall and handsome. He barely had to stretch, he simply reached out and snagged the bag mid-air. Then he handed me my flowery backpack. It was like he'd given me a bouquet. He got off the bike and looked at the boys. 'What's wrong with you?' he asked. He towered over them, Tess. It was like something straight out of one of your Hollywood films. 'What's wrong with you?' he asked again. Still no answer. 'You're in high school, now. Grow up!' He said it so fiercely I saw the one who wasn't Trey flinch. Then he turned to me and said, 'I'm James Potter. If you're new here, I can show you where your homeroom is.' I introduced myself, and he helped me pick up my pencils and glue sticks."

She stops, lost in thought, and suddenly starts laughing.

"What?" I ask.

"We both ignored the giant maxi pads."

Through tears, I laugh too.

"Every time I saw him after that, he said, 'Hi Samira, how are you?' and he waited to hear my answer. Each time, it gave me a warm, good feeling, like one person in that building actually cared."

She stops and dabs at her eyes with her the knuckles of her long, elegant fingers.

"This is what I came here to tell you today, Tess. Not that I am as cool as a rapper. I'm sorry it took me a while to get there. Until now, it is not a moment that I wanted to remember. But I thought you would want to hear it and know that you are not alone in your grief."

I hop down and hug her again. There is no awkwardness this time.

New Year, New You

"James Potter, the New Jersey teen gunned down inside his girlfriend's home two weeks ago, will be laid to rest this morning," Sally Sheffield says, her voice oozing fake sadness.

My already-broken heart shatters inside my chest. Beverly has the volume jacked up so she can hear the TV over her aggressively-loud cereal crunching.

"A private mass was attended by family members who clearly are still reeling from this shocking tragedy."

They cut to footage of Mrs. Potter in a black wool coat and sunglasses. She's holding Emmett's hand as they walk down the front steps of St. Michael's. The sight of them catches my breath. Mrs. Potter looks thinner, paler. Emmett squints up at the sun through the fingers of his free hand.

"Get the f— out of here!" James' dad gets bleeped as he throws punches before launching into a swearing tirade.

I'd only met him once at James' high school graduation, and that was enough. He'd stood at the back of the football field, refusing Mrs. Potter's gracious offer to save him a seat. Every time I snuck a look at him, he was checking his watch.

Now he's kicking the cameraperson, who's on the ground but somehow still filming.

"A father's fury. And can you blame him?" Sally appears onscreen again. "This family is living every parent's worst nightmare. And, Samantha, what's the latest on the girlfriend? Was she there today? Where's she in all of this?"

The screen changes again, this time to a perky blonde who's standing outside the church. "Good morning, Sally. Well, that is the question, isn't it? Sources tell me that she's still recuperating from the extensive injuries she sustained during the incident."

"Too badly injured to attend her boyfriend's funeral? Somethin' doesn't sit right about that with me. Are we absolutely certain that this wasn't a love triangle situation? Could she have been fooling around with Luke Miller on the side? You know what they say, the apple doesn't fall far from the tree, like mother, like daughter… that type of thing."

"Anything's possible," Samantha says.

"Whatever's really going on here, I think it's fair to say that this young woman is going to be reliving these tragic events for the rest of her life," Sally says, shaking her head vigorously for emphasis.

"Can you please turn that off?" I ask Beverly, my insides shaking.

"Huh?" she mumbles, milk trickling down her chin.

"Shut the TV off!" I scream.

Beverly jumps. "Okay, okay, calm down. I haven't put my hearing aids in yet."

I feel like I've been punched in the stomach. Mrs. Potter and Emmett have been on my mind almost constantly, but seeing them exposed like that, as if their sorrow were entertainment for all to watch, guts me. Mrs. Potter must hate me, especially if she knows I asked James to come home a day early and then insisted that he not tell her about it. If he'd stayed in Chicago and had gone straight home Sunday night, he never would've been at my house. Of course, if Mom hadn't started an affair with Mr. Miller, none of this would've happened. I hear Sally Sheffield's voice in my head, "Like mother, like daughter." Mom and I are both deceitful, and now we're paying for it.

I had been feeling slightly better last night after Samira's visit. But I had a major setback the second I opened my eyes this morning. I saw the whiteboard where the nurses write their names, the date, and the day's therapy schedule. Today's date, Dec. 31, stared back at me. Written in red Sharpie, the letters and numbers were surrounded by someone's lame drawing of balloons, champagne glasses, and fireworks.

New Year's Eve. It's the anniversary of the first kiss James and I shared at Fix Kelly's party. It seemed as if my life started that night. Now, one year later, I feel like it's ended.

I have no idea what most of my friends or classmates are doing tonight. Dad offered to bring me my cell phone, but I told him not to bother. I can't bear to think about the outside world. I feel outrageously jealous and angry at all the people who are doing regular things, living ordinary lives, even just walking through their day without broken limbs and a giant boulder of grief weighing down on them at all times.

Watching Sally Sheffield was just another reminder that strangers are saying and writing awful things about me and my family— not that plenty of it isn't deserved. If I think about it all long enough, I know I'll never want to leave the cocoon of this rehab center.

I don't even want to read any well-intentioned "Get well soon!" or "I'm so sorry, Tess!" messages on social media from friends. It's all too much.

I swing my legs off the side of the bed and propel myself toward the whiteboard. I erase until the balloons, champagne glasses, and fireworks disappear, and no traces of today remain.

Izzy and Carol come to visit me around lunchtime. Izzy brings pizza and Yoohoos from Carlo's, our favorite place. I still don't have much appetite, but I appreciate the gesture.

When they sit down, Izzy makes a big deal of introducing me. "This is Tess! My best friend!" like she's a late-night talk show host and I'm her very special guest. Then, she says, "Tess, this is my girlfriend, Carol," beaming. They're official—even Instagram official—she told me during her last visit.

"Wow, that's awesome, Iz. I'm so proud of you. You decided 'new year, new you' at Thanksgiving and look at you now, barely a month later. You did it!" I said when

286

she showed me the Instagram post of her and Carol holding hands at field hockey camp, which had already racked up close to three hundred likes.

"I'm living my most authentic life, Tess," she said with faux sincerity. "Sometimes, when I sit quietly, I think I can hear Oprah clapping."

I like Carol instantly, mainly because she looks at Izzy the way Meghan Markle looks at Prince Harry. She laughs at Izzy's jokes, and she's pretty funny too. Like when I ask her what it was like meeting the Collins family for the first time, her response proves why Izzy is crazy about her.

"Did you see Grams?" I ask. "How did it go? Tell me everything."

"Yes!" she says. "Grams was waiting at the door to bless me with holy water. And I was like all, 'Grams, no! Quit it with that shit! You're fucking up my bronzer.'"

My jaw drops as Izzy holds her stomach laughing.

"No, Tess, I'm totally kidding. But how hilarious would that have been? She did bless me though and she was super sweet and welcoming."

"Score one for the Holy Spirit giving her that heart free of judgment, I guess," I say, almost laughing.

"Totally," Carol says while Izzy shouts, "Amen!"

They're perfect together even though visually they're opposites. With her short blonde hair and brown eyes, Carol looks a bit like actress Michelle Williams. My favorite thing about her is her deep laugh, the way it fills the room. I wonder if I'll ever laugh that easily again.

They talk about the colleges, and where they might end up going. Because they're both smart and play field hockey, they're looking at a couple of the same schools.

"What about you, Tess?" Carol asks. "Where do you think you'll go?"

"Oh, I don't know," I say. "I only just submitted my applications. I'm not the over-achiever that Izzy is."

What I don't tell them is that I'm thinking about not going. Once I leave here, I'm basically starting over. I'll have to adjust to a life without James in it. We talked, texted, or FaceTimed first thing every morning and last thing every night. I don't know if Mrs. Potter will ever want to see me again, or let me hang out with Emmett, and spending time with them had become something I looked forward to each week. I'll be living in a new place—without Mom. If I can ever get used to all that, there's no way I want to have to adapt again in August.

I'm lost in thought when Izzy says, "Tell Tess about the essay you wrote. Carol wants to study bioengineering, and it's so brilliant. Tell her."

Carol smiles at Izzy. "Well, I'm allergic to everything—animals, grass, trees, chlorine—you name it, and it'll make me sneeze. So I wrote this essay about how I'd like to come up with a medication that will erase your allergies. Not a shot, maybe a pill, but you wouldn't have to take it every day, and it wouldn't make you drowsy or insanely thirsty. But all that's kind of a snoozer as an opening, so I started it off like this, 'I want to drink pool water. I want to roll for hours through a freshly-mown lawn. I want to bury my face in my cat's soft coat and breathe in her dander-filled fur.' Then I go on about how I want to find a solid cure so all allergy sufferers can lead wild and carefree lives."

"Genius, right?" Izzy says.

"Wow," I say. "No wonder you got in everywhere!"

"I think it's awfully strange," Beverly blurts out from behind the curtain that divides the room. She closed it before they arrived, telling me she needed a nap if she planned to stay up until midnight "to ring in the new year."

"When you get to be my age, you don't know how many of these you've got left," she said.

I wanted to tell her that was actually true at any age but didn't.

I'd forgotten she was even there.

"Who wants to drink pool water and breathe dander?" she continues.

"I do!" Izzy shouts at the curtain.

"She's like Alexa—always listening," I whisper and roll my eyes, making Carol and Izzy laugh.

I think about the essay I wrote. It was about how life is like a soufflé. You may think you're combining all the right ingredients. You might even follow every step of the recipe correctly, and, still, it can flop. Maybe you misread something. Maybe somebody came along and opened the oven door, or turned it off too soon. No matter what caused it, you're disappointed. You may even feel like a failure. When that happens, the only thing you can do is try again, I wrote.

At the time, I'd been thinking of it as a metaphor for my crappy SAT scores. I'd studied. I'd tried. I'd gotten a tutor. I'd done the work, and it still didn't turn out like I'd hoped. But that didn't mean I should give up on myself. If everything always works out perfectly, where's the room for growth, how will you really know what you're made of?

Now that stupid essay seems like foreshadowing, as if I was subconsciously preparing myself for everything to fall apart. I wish a shitty SAT score and a fallen soufflé were my biggest problems now.

"We're going to go, but I'll come by tomorrow," Izzy says, tossing paper plates in the garbage and plastic bottles in the recycling.

"I'm being discharged tomorrow, hopefully." I cross my fingers.

"Text me your new address, and I'll visit you there," she says.

It occurs to me that I don't even know the street name. I never asked Dad which complex the condo was in, I was just grateful to not have to go home again.

"It was so great to meet you, Tess. I hope I see you again soon." Carol gives me a hug, and I give her bravery points because I know I look about as unappealing and scary as roadkill.

Izzy hugs me and whispers in my ear, "If you're ever up for a Tess-version of new year, new you, I'm here— no matter what time of year it is."

"I know, Iz. Thanks." I squeeze her as tightly as I can with one arm.

I watch them leave. They don't tell me they're on their way to Times Square to watch the ball drop, but I know. Because James and I had planned to be there with them.

Dad comes by after dinner, saving me from having to go to the New Year's Eve ice cream social in one of the common areas with Beverly. He's brought sparkling apple cider and munchkins, which had been our tradition when I was little. Back then, he and Mom usually went out somewhere to celebrate. Before they'd go, Dad would put on his favorite albums, and we'd dance in the living room while Mom finished getting dressed. I'd be in pajamas waiting for the babysitter, and Dad and I would sip our cider out of champagne flutes and pop donut holes into our mouths. Happy. Hopeful for what the new year might bring. When I was eleven, I started going to Izzy's for New Year's Eve sleepovers and our tradition stopped. The fact that he remembered means a lot, especially because those days feel like a lifetime ago.

Dad drops into the chair, exhausted. Even though the lease for the condo doesn't officially start until tomorrow, someone made an exception, and he was able to move most of our stuff in today with the help of students he hired from his community college classes. The whole thing seems to have taken a toll on him.

He reaches over and opens the cider and the donut box.

"Plastic cups okay this year?" he asks.

His head is bent as he pours, and I notice that his hair looks grayer, wrinkles around his eyes seem deeper. For a second, I see him not as my father but as a tired, aging man who has just lost the life he thought he'd built. It makes me want to give him something.

"I finished your book," I say as he hands me a cup of cider.

"Wow, that was fast!"

Part of me wants to point out that I have literally nothing else to do here, but I don't. I loved it actually, but I'm afraid if I say anything too positive that instead of making him feel proud, he'll focus on the fact that more than a decade has passed since he wrote it. But he needs to hear something encouraging.

"It's great," I tell him, meaning it, feeling slightly guilty that it took me this long to read it. It's full of fascinating details about the building of the Brooklyn Bridge, but then there's this fascinating love story involving a young construction worker from Ireland, Francis, and this New York debutante, Catherine, who wants to be an artist. Once a week, she leaves her family's Fifth Avenue mansion and sits along the banks of the East River, sketching the bridge as it comes to life.

One day a strong wind blows off her hat, and it lands in the lap of the young construction worker. It's one of those things that sounds totally far-fetched, but the writing is strong, and you're so into the story that you're willing to believe just about anything. When he returns the hat to her, their eyes meet, an electric current passes between them, and, in that moment, they both see the promise of a better, different future.

She shows him a side of the city he'd heard about but never experienced. She takes him to museums, galleries, nice restaurants. He brings her to meet his colorful countrymen, who all live in a neighborhood called Vinegar Hill. They drink moonshine and dance when his friends put down their whiskey and pick up their fiddles.

But in the end, Catherine's family, who've talked endlessly about the importance of the bridge and the opportunities it will bring for less-fortunate families in Brooklyn, refuse to accept that Francis could be a worthy match for their daughter. When she tells him she can't marry him, he begs her to return to Ireland with him, but she's torn. How can she leave her family and America? Can true love transcend their differences? I'm simplifying, but it's filled with beautiful imagery and all kinds of symbolism. I loved the irony of the bridge. After all that hard work and for all its finished splendor, it should connect people, but, ultimately, it's still not enough.

"I could imagine the whole thing like a movie in my head," I say. "When Francis goes back to Ireland, and Catherine gives up her dream of becoming an illustrator and marries the son of the steel tycoon, I couldn't believe it. It was so sad."

"Yes, my editor and I went back and forth on that. She wanted them to cross the bridge when it finally opens, walk into each other's arms, and live happily ever after. While that's satisfying for the reader, life just doesn't always work out like that. Not everyone gets a happy ending."

If anyone knows that to be true, Dad and I do.

New Year, New Address

Dad pulls up in front of the rehab center in his new, used car. After the police found the station wagon in Pittsburgh, Dad decided to donate it. His current ride is nothing fancy, just a generic sedan. Still, I'm glad it's not the old Volvo. The last image I have of that car involves Luke at the wheel plowing into the half-foot of snow in our driveway.

It's strange to be outdoors. The wintery air shocks my lungs. The sun stings my eyes. Dad comes around and helps me out of the wheelchair and into the warm car.

As we drive along, he fills the silence with offers to stop for food, coffee, anything I might want or need.

"I just feel like going—"

Home isn't the right word.

"Maybe just keep driving," I say and close my eyes to block out all the familiar places we pass that remind me of James.

When we pull into the complex, I'm struck by how gloomy it all is. Every building looks the same. I imagine Izzy's reaction, "Jesus, Tess, it's like a series of side-by-side, two-story turds!"

Yes, it's January, but the landscape seems abnormally depressing. There's not a single mature tree in sight. If an artist were to paint this scene, the top half of the canvas would be a great big nothing.

"Who knew there were this many shades of brown?" I say, then realize how rude and ungrateful I sound remembering how hard Dad worked to make this happen so I wouldn't have to go back to the house. "I'm sorry, I didn't mean—"

"Don't be sorry. I didn't design it," Dad says, pulling into a short driveway. "Well, this is it."

Not knowing how long I'll be in the wheelchair, Dad requested a ground floor unit. He rolls me up to the front door and turns the key in the lock. A chill runs down my spine as I try not to think about Luke letting himself into our house who-knows-how-many times.

Daffy runs to greet us, probably struggling to adjust to the new surroundings too.

"Daffy!" I'm so happy to see her, I could cry. I want so badly to reach down, scoop her up, and let her soothing purr work its magic, but I can't with one hand.

I look around. It's disorienting to see all our familiar things—our couch, framed photos, plants, lamps—assembled in a new setting. It's as if someone is putting on a stage play of our lives.

Sliding glass doors look out on our backyard, a narrow rectangle the size of a child's sandbox. Beyond that is a parking lot. No more view of Samira at her stand. No more music. Just mounds of snow piled against light poles and a handful of dirty cars.

Dad wheels me into the kitchen. It's tiny and an outdated mustard-y yellow. He opens the fridge. It's nearly empty except for fruit, cut and shaped like a floral arrangement, on the middle shelf.

"Mrs. Walters sent it for you," Dad says. "She wanted me to tell you Evie's been asking for you every day."

"That's nice," I say, trying to shake the numbness that's spreading over me like a rash. This is it. My new normal. Life in this small, sad space. Everything feels fake. I wish it were.

"Let me show you your room," Dad says, sensing I'm freaking out.

My bed and desk look enormous in the tiny white room.

"We can paint it if you like," he volunteers. "I asked, and it's not a problem. I've got a cable guy coming tomorrow. So we'll have TV and wifi before you know it."

"It's okay. I don't miss them," I say, wondering if he's trying to avoid the news just like I am. "I think I'd like to rest for a bit."

"Of course, let me help you."

I hold out my right hand, and he pulls me up, to balance on my right foot. It's a slow, awkward dance every time.

"Tess, about school—"

"I'll go tomorrow," I tell him, lowering myself carefully onto my bed.

"Tess, you don't have to. Before she left, your mom and I talked about it, and if you want to take more time, that's—"

"No, I'd rather just get it over with."

"The ripping-off-a-Band-Aid approach. I get it," Dad says.

I'm lying on my back, staring up at the ceiling, hoping he'll just leave. Instead, he sits down in the oversized pink bean bag chair I've had forever. He leans forward, forearms on his knees.

"I meant what I said when you were in the hospital, Tess. I know I haven't always been there, and I'm going to try to make it up to you—especially in the short time we have left before you go off to college. I'd like to start over, if you'll let me. I've got an interview lined up later this week for a copywriting gig at a PR agency. I figure maybe that's a more lucrative way to channel what's left of my creativity."

"Sounds good," I say, wanting to believe him, but wondering if, after all this time, he'll give up on his dream of writing another bestseller, and choose his real family over his fictional ones. I'm inclined to doubt it, but then I think about how he remembered our sparkling cider and donuts tradition. I have to give him points for trying.

"I'll get out of here so you can take that nap." He walks toward the door but then turns back to face me. "Ravioli okay for dinner?"

"Sure," I say, knowing it's one of only five things he makes.

He's still standing there. So many things remain unspoken between us. How have we not talked about what happened between Mom and Mr. Miller, when Mom's coming back, or how I'm barely holding it together after being terrorized by a madman and losing the first boy I ever loved? The person who meant absolutely everything to me? And why are we not at least discussing that this condo feels like we're living at the corner of Depressing Drive and East We're-Completely-Fucked Street?

People talk about having an "elephant in the room," well, I'd say we've got a whole damn circus-full.

Dad leans against the doorframe and takes a deep breath. I steel myself for whatever comes next.

"I'm not going to lie to you and say that things will get easier, Tess. But I hope that in time they hurt a little less."

"Me too," I say, relieved that he's opening a door but not forcing us through it. "Thanks, Dad," I add, but he's already gone.

After dinner, I decide to go to bed early to rest up for tomorrow. I couldn't fall asleep earlier because someone kept coughing on the other side of the wall. It's probably for the best that I didn't nap, or I'm sure I'd have awakened with my heart racing and no idea where I was. Like when you wake up in the middle of the night at a sleepover and panic, thinking, "What the hell? This isn't my house!"

I'm scared I'll have trouble falling asleep here tonight. It's nice to be back in my own bed, but when I think that this is my new home—where I live with just Dad—I have a hard time not losing it. When it's quiet, and I have too much time to think, memories of that awful day flood my mind, and I'm overwhelmed with fear and sadness. I'm dreading going back to school, but I can't spend any more hours alone with my thoughts, and I can't hide forever.

I pull on a giant t-shirt with oversized armholes that allow my cast to slide through.

"'Night, Dad," I call out knowing he can hear me from any room.

"Hey," he says, appearing in the doorway seconds later. "I forgot. This came for you." He walks over and hands me an envelope. "There's no return address. Could be junk mail, but I figured I'd let you decide."

He kisses me on the top of my head.

"Goodnight, Tess. I love you."

"Love you, too," I say, but I'm preoccupied with the envelope. The handwriting doesn't look familiar. Dad's right, it's probably junk mail, like yet another offer from a tutoring company. Or worse, what if it's from a crazed Sally Sheffield viewer writing to tell me I deserve everything that's happened to me? A dozen weird thoughts cycle through my head as I open it.

Nothing could prepare me for what's inside.

Dear Tess,

If you're reading this, that means I've slipped beneath the lane line into the deep end for good. Sorry I didn't get a chance to say good-bye in person. Turns out I'm much better at hellos, so I'll keep this short.

I'm glad I had a chance to be your best friend, even if it was just for a night. And I know you didn't want to make this promise, but I'm still counting on you to go out and live a big, fancy, fabulous life.

Or don't. It's your life. I just want you to be happy.

I hope you'll think of me from time to time. If you do, I want you to remember this: Don't dwell in the darkness. Linger in the light.

XO

Annie Banks

P.S. I'm leaving you my Elsa wig. (You're welcome!) My mom will mail it to you. Wear it and know you are a queen!

She's gone. Just like that. How can someone like Annie or James die and the whole world not jolt to a sudden stop? How can people with so much goodness, so much light and love, leave the planet and the entire earth not quake with loss?

My tears dot the page. I quickly blow them dry before the ink smudges and I lose another piece of Annie.

I stare at her words, and they give me an idea. I lurch toward my desk and dig through the school supplies Dad boxed up for me. I pull out a pad of yellow Post-its and red, orange, green, blue, and purple highlighters.

"Don't dwell in the darkness. Linger in the light." I scrawl Annie's words over and over again until I fill the pad and my right hand cramps.

Next, I hop around the small room, and stick them everywhere I can reach. Annie Banks-inspired wallpaper. She'd like that, I think. Yellow flags of hope, fluttering gently when warm air flows up from the floor's heating vent.

I sit down on the bed and look at them again before turning off the light. Then I fall right to sleep.

Back to School

I'm prepared for the whispers and stares. What I'm not ready for are the news vans parked outside the high school. As Dad pulls up, he puts a hand on my knee, and says, "Wait here. Unless you want to turn around and go back home?"

I shrug. "I'll have to do this eventually Might as well be now."

Reporters swarm as soon as they see him remove the wheelchair from the trunk.

"Mr. Porter! How is your daughter? Where is your wife? How do you feel about Luke Miller's guilty plea?" Dad ignores them as he opens the chair.

People and cameras are pressed to the windshield of the car. I stare down at my broken leg and wish I could run as far from here as possible. It might be all in my head, but whenever I'm anxious, the skin under my casts itches more than usual, which only makes me more stressed. Going back to school after winter break is typically awful. But to return like this—a physical and emotional mess *and* part of a story that's still getting local and national attention—makes it a million times worse.

The car rocks from the weight of reporters who elbow each other for a chance to gawk at me through the windows. Over the noise and chaos, a shrill whistle blows. Principal Vance parts the crowd and begins instructing everyone to step aside. She's called the police, she says, and wants the news teams and vans away from the entrance asap.

Dad helps me out and into the chair while Principal Vance and the school security guard do their best to shield us from the mob. But it isn't enough to block out the voices screaming my name.

A chorus of "Tess! Tess! Over here, Tess!" erupts as Dad places my backpack in my lap and starts rolling me toward the building. Some reporters, the ones who probably realize I'm not going to talk to them, waste no time finding parents who'll answer questions, grabbing their fifteen minutes of fame. I overhear soundbites from moms I don't know eagerly gossiping about my family as Dad attempts to push me through the crowd.

"Carolyn Winslow? Nope, I rarely ever saw her. She was never involved, never volunteered. Sure, she'd send in checks for fundraisers, but that's not the same as chairing a PTA committee or chaperoning an event like the prom or project graduation. But I guess now we know she was busy doing other things."

"The dad? He's kind of cute, actually. They were an attractive couple. So, yeah, I was kind of surprised. But you know what they say, 'You never know what goes on behind closed doors.'"

"My daughter is traumatized. For this to happen in our sleepy little town, it's devastating. She's a freshman, so she didn't know James Potter or Tess Porter. Or is it James Porter and Tess Potter? I can never get that straight. Anyway, it's been really hard on my Miranda."

Before we reach the front doors, Izzy appears, breaking through the herd by swinging her backpack overhead to clear the way. I'm more glad than usual to see her because I was beginning to lose my nerve.

"I've got her from here, Mr. P.," she says, leaning down to give me a quick hug.

"Thanks, Izzy," Dad says. He looks at me, knowing "Have a good day!" would sound pretty ridiculous right now, so he squeezes my shoulder. I try to smile and pray the days passes quickly.

Everyone is nice—to my face, at least. The Key Club checked out my schedule and recruited volunteers to wheel me to and from my classes. Of course, Izzy offered, but then she'd be late for each of her subjects. Still, she picks me up for lunch at my locker, and even though it's only 10:50 a.m. and all I've done is sit, I'm still exhausted.

As I expected, tons of people stare at me—especially in the cafeteria. The bruises on my cheeks are down to just small scabs now. The black-and-blues across my forehead and cheekbones have faded to a pale yellow that I can cover with concealer. My hair, well, that's still a mess. Anyone who's ever tried to recreate their usual hairstyle using their non-dominant hand knows it's nearly impossible. With a little help from Dad, I'm able to sweep it into a messy bun. Still, I'm thinking about cutting it to just above my shoulders.

"It could be the first step in my 'new year, new you,'" I tell Izzy.

"Okay, just promise me you won't try to do it yourself—at least not until you can use both hands," she says and reminds me of the time she gave herself bangs and ended up looking like Frankenstein for at least a month.

Every day feels pretty much the same. I go to school, sometimes PT or OT or both. Dad and I eat dinner, then I do my homework, pet Daffy, and go to sleep. At the same time, everything feels different. Cold. Hollow. Less.

I've heard people say that when their dog dies, they find themselves looking for him in every room. They think they see his tail wag just around the corner. They'll save his favorite table scraps, and then whistle for him seconds before they remember: He's gone. I understand it now. Somedays, I'll be going along okay, maybe not great, but something will happen—a teacher will mention a book, there'll be a typo on the homepage of the school paper, I'll get an email that prom tickets are about to go on sale—I'll think of James, and then I'll remember: He's gone. And then the rest of the day is a slow, sad stretch until I can go back to sleep.

Dad got the job at the PR place. "So far, so good," is how he describes it. After so many years of writing isolated in his home office, he says it's "interesting and probably healthy" to be out of the house and with other people for most of the day. "Even if they're all half my age," he adds.

Mom's called about a dozen times since she got out of rehab. My voicemail box is full, and I can't bear to listen to any of the messages—from her or anyone else. Well, except for the two from James that I'd never deleted.

The first one's just a quick "Hey! It's me. Hope your Spanish test went well. Call me when you have a chance." The second was from early December. He'd gone to a holiday party hosted by the media company where he interned. The message begins with him singing, "I'm dreaming of a white Christmas," then he clears his throat and says, "Actually, let me try that again... I'm dreaming of Tess Porter...Okay, I hope you haven't deleted this already, I know I'm no 'American Idol' contestant."

Horns blare in the background, bells that I imagine belong to street corner Santas ring.

"Anyway, Tess, I'm calling because I miss you. Madly. And I don't know if I've told you that enough since I've been here. You are the best. The care packages you've been sending me—you totally nailed that chocolate chip cookie dough fudge, girl—and all you've done for Emmett, my mom says you've been a lifesaver."

He cuts out for a second but comes right back.

"...if my voice hasn't given it away, I've maybe had more than my share of egg nog, but in my defense, I had no idea it was spiked until the second, maybe the third glass. It tasted like the best milkshake ever, Tess. You'd have loved this stuff. I'm walking back to my dorm now, and I just really wanted to hear your voice. I cannot wait to see you, Tess. This is going to be the best... um, the robot just told me to wrap it up so if I only have twenty seconds left, I just want to say this: I love you, Tess, more than you'll probably ever know."

The message ends. I hate myself for deleting all the others. How could I know that there would never be more?

I listen to that one first thing in the morning and the last thing at night, before I cry myself to sleep, Daffy curled up beside me, no doubt wondering when the hell we're going home.

When Mom finally gets the hint that I don't want to talk to her, she calls Dad's phone. Fortunately, he doesn't put me on the spot by handing it off to me. He simply tells her he'll pass along the message.

I'd done a project about Alcoholics Anonymous for health class freshman year. One of the twelve steps of recovery is getting in touch with everyone you've wronged and attempting to make amends.

"She must really be flying through those twelve steps, huh?" I say, pushing around pieces of the chicken cutlet and microwaved broccoli Dad made. He cuts up everything that I can't slice with a fork into bite-size chunks, making me feel like a preschooler again. "What is forgiveness? Step number eight? And what's she been out? A week. Wow. I'm sure that's gonna last."

"I don't know, Tess, you might want to give her a break. She sounds like she's really trying. And remember

308

when I told you you didn't have to go back to school right away and you decided you'd rather go with the ripping-off-a-Band-Aid approach? Don't you think maybe it's better to just meet with her rather than drag this out? You can't ignore her forever."

"I'm not ready. And, honestly, I don't know if I ever will be," I tell him.

I know I sound like a drama queen, but it's how I feel, and after all I've been through, I should be able to take as much time I need.

"Well, your mom and I have been talking, and we'd like you to see a grief counselor, Tess, someone who can help you move forward in a positive way," he says, refilling our water glasses, trying to make eye contact.

"I don't really think that's necessary," I tell him, staring down at my lap. My attempt to sound firm fails as tears spring to my eyes.

"Tess, c'mon. The walls in this dump are thinner than potato chips. I can hear you crying most nights. It's time."

"I'll consider it," I say, wishing Daffy ate broccoli so I could give it all to her and leave the table.

My casts come off in early February, revealing my pasty white, withered skin. The saw they use to remove them is terrifying, but I forget all about it when I see that my left leg is so hairy, it looks like it belongs to a Yeti. There's a funky smell too. I thought I'd be so relieved to be rid of them, but it's bittersweet. The casts tied me to that night, what they symbolized—the broken bones, the devastating loss—they allowed me to wallow. Without them, I'm free. If only I'll let myself be.

One night I dream that I'm at the beach, sitting on the boardwalk, staring at the ocean. I'm wearing shorts, and my legs—which look normal and not super-pale and hairy—dangle over the dunes. All of a sudden, I feel a hand covering mine. I look to my right. James. He smiles as if it's an ordinary day. The wind ruffles his hair. His eyes are the same intoxicating blue.

"Why did we only go to the beach together once?" I ask.

"Because we thought we'd have more time," he says.

Brightly colored kites fly past us, their simple white strings fluttering, held by no one.

"Emmett's birthday is coming up," he says.

I'm watching the water as the waves build then break.

"I miss you every single second of every day," I say.

When I turn to look at him, he's gone, replaced by a seagull.

I wake up and miss him more than ever—something I didn't know was possible.

Signs line the hallways at school, encouraging everyone to send each other a flower (red for love, pink for like, and white for friendship) for Valentine's Day. Each stem costs five dollars and supports the American Heart Association.

When Izzy goes up to get a second plate of curly fries one day, I unlock her phone, get Carol's number, and text her to ask if she'd like me to order some for Izzy. It's the kind of thing I know Izzy would do for me.

Carol texts right back, "How about twenty red? I'll Venmo you! Thank you!!" followed by heart and flower emojis.

I'm especially glad I did it when a couple days later Izzy says, "So, Valentine's Day is a Wednesday this year, so I'm thinking you and I make it a Galentine's celebration. Wanna go for pizza and Yoo-hoos like we used to?"

"Galentine's? Iz, that is exactly the kind of shit I'd expect you to make fun of," I say.

"Tess, I'm at the point where I'm willing to do or say anything if it makes you smile again. Duh."

Tears spring to my eyes.

"Well, that backfired," Izzy says.

"No. Yes. I mean, thank you. I'd love to be your Galentine. But there is actually somewhere else I'd like to go if you don't mind taking me?"

"Sure, as long as you don't mind riding in a car that perpetually smells like feet mixed with wet dog?"

Izzy's family got a puppy for Christmas. Freddy, a black lab. He's adorable, but her brothers keep taking him sledding with them. Now their SUV reeks like damp wool coated in doggy slobber.

"Sounds perfect," I say.

When I get to my locker Valentine's Day morning, I have three white roses from Izzy and one from Samira. Next to them are three pinks with a note: "Hey Tess,

Good to have you back in gym class. V. dull without you. — Rob (Wallace)."

I bite my lip and feel my face turning as pink as the flowers. I'm a complete spaz when it comes to any type of athletics. It doesn't matter if we're taking foul shots or in one of those sections where we're supposed to learn simple line dances, count on me to screw it up, and possibly even fall down. Rob and I have known each other since kindergarten. He's nice, but we don't have any classes together—except for gym. And we don't really have any friends in common, so I hardly ever see him—except when he's there helping me up after we've been forced to do fifty sit-ups for some fitness test and I'm writhing in agony.

"No pain, no gain, Porter! Let's go!" Rob, who looks like he's spent plenty of time in the weight room, will say.

Because of my broken bones, I'd been going to study hall instead of gym until last week. With our rotating schedule, I drop it today, so I'll have to track Rob down and thank him for the flowers. It's a nice gesture, but awkward too.

I see Izzy just before the bell rings for the start of last period. "Meet me at my locker, and we'll walk to my house and get the car," she says. She's been smiling continuously since finding the veritable rose garden Carol sent her in front of her locker this morning.

"Okay. I just have to do one thing first," I tell her.

She raises her eyebrows mysteriously, and I wonder if she asked Rob to send me the pink roses. On the one hand, I hope so because that would make it less random, and I could just apologize for my crazy friend and not think about it again. On the other, I hope not, because that would mean Izzy pities me to the point of involving third parties.

I catch him on his way out to the senior parking lot after the last class.

"Rob! Wait!" I yell. He stops and turns around.

"Tess," he smiles.

He's just a couple of inches taller than I am, maybe 5'11" so I'm looking right into his eyes. They're a warm shade of brown, like chocolate. I hadn't ever noticed that before.

"What's up?" he asks.

"I just wanted to thank you, you know, for the flowers. That was a, um, really nice surprise." I shift from foot to foot, feeling self-conscious, and hoping I don't have any poppy seeds left in my teeth from the bagel I ate for lunch.

"I'm just glad you're back. Without you, gym class is so—I don't know—serious. Everybody knows the rules, nobody trips over the bleachers, or shoots out a light bulb during archery. No one nails Mr. Tempesto in the nuts with a tennis ball and then spends the rest of the period apologizing."

I start to laugh. "Oh my God, I'd forgotten about that."

Rob smiles and shakes his head. "I hadn't."

"Rob, you coming?" Chip Brearly claps him on the shoulder before pushing open the door that leads to the parking lot, letting in a blast of cold air.

"Yeah, be right out," Rob says. "Tess, listen, I gotta go, but there's something I wanted to ask you, and I hardly ever see you, so here goes: Would you be my prom date?"

My stomach drops. All the blood rushes to my face. Time stands still, and I suddenly remember Izzy is waiting at her locker for me.

"Did Izzy put you up to this?" I ask.

"Huh?"

"Did my friend Izzy make you ask me?"

"Um, no." He looks so genuinely confused; he can't be lying.

I take a deep breath and try to figure out how to say "no, thanks" without coming off like a jerk.

"I'm flattered, Rob, but I'm not really great company lately."

"Why don't you let me be the judge of that?"

When I say nothing, he looks right, then left, and whispers. "I was there when you wet your pants on the playground in kindergarten, Tess. If I can get past that I think you should at least give me a chance."

"Wow, Rob, you really know how to sweet-talk a gal." It feels like I'm flirting with him, against my will, but I can't seem to stop. "Look, you're smart, you're cute, you're funny, why don't you ask some star athlete with better bladder control?"

"Because I'd like to go with you, Tess. Even just as friends. I like that you don't take yourself too seriously. And, remember freshman year, that bake sale you organized for the kid who got hit by a car while riding his bike home from middle school? That was my cousin."

"Wow, how is he?" I ask.

"Great, full recovery," he says. "He actually taught me these dance moves that I was only going to show you as a last resort." He breaks into one of the ridiculous Fortnite dances Izzy's brothers always do.

"Jesus, Rob, what the hell? Are you coming or not?" Chip is back, holding the door open again.

"Seriously, Tess. What's it gonna take to get you to say yes?"

When I don't answer, he says, "Okay, I've got to get to hockey practice, but just think about it."

"Wait, you're on the ice hockey team?"

"No, Tess. I am the ice hockey team." He squares his shoulders, which are pretty impressive, then returns to his usual posture and laughs at his mock cockiness before heading toward the door.

An idea pops into my head. "I'll be your date if you'll help me with something!" I blurt.

"Name it, and I'm in," he says with a wink. Then he opens the door and disappears into the frosty February afternoon.

As we walk back to her house, Izzy buries her face in her roses, taking deep long sniffs, while I tell her about Rob.

"Tess, I know you're going to think it's too soon, but I think it's fantastic," she says. "I didn't know how or when to bring it up, but I'm going to ask Carol to be my date, and I was really hoping you'd consider going."

"I said 'yes' but I have ulterior motives," I reveal.

"Oh man, you're not going to treat him like a sex doll, are you?" Izzy doubles over laughing, and I attempt to punch her in the stomach.

"I'll explain at dinner," I say as we drop our backpacks in her foyer, say hi to her family, and then grab the car keys.

When we get to the cemetery, I go into the office and ask where James is buried. I practiced the sentence one thousand times in my head, but my tongue froze whenever I tried to say it out loud. I can't believe I got it out now. I can't believe any of this is real. The woman working behind the desk also looks stunned when I say his name. Of course, she's seen the news coverage and clears her throat to try to get her colleague's attention. She wants confirmation that it's really me. "The girlfriend." Luckily, the co-worker is too busy playing Candy Crush on her phone to notice.

She offers me a map and draws a line with a pen, directing me to the plot.

"No headstone yet," she says, then lowers her voice. "The mom's havin' a real hard time, and the dad? Yikes. Bad situation. How are you doin', hon?"

"Not great." I thank her for her help and rush back to the car.

Most of the signs that would point us in the right direction are buried under snow, so Izzy and I circle around for ages before locating it. The whole time we're lost, I say silent prayers that we don't see Mrs. Potter and Emmett there. I picture them on TV, on the steps of St. Michael's, and I'm not prepared to see them in person.

But I know they've been here because on top of the frozen ground is a Valentine card with a rock pinning it to the earth. Lightning McQueen. Emmett. I start to cry and feel like I might never stop. Izzy puts her arm around me, and we stand there together until the sky grows dark, and I feel like I have no more tears left.

"Is it weird to talk to him?" I ask her.

"I don't think there are any rules for this." She shrugs. "Say whatever's in your heart. I'll give you some privacy."

I wait for the car door to close and look around to make sure I'm alone before I say, "James, if you can hear me, I'm so, so sorry. This is all my fault. Mine and my family's. I don't know how, or if, I'll ever be able to make it up to your mom or Emmett.

"You saved me, and because of that, I know I should do something, make my life count somehow, but I just don't know how to do that without you. Nothing means anything now that you're gone."

Just when I think I'm all cried out, I start sobbing again thinking about last year's Valentine's Day. Mom was working, Dad had a class, so James came over. I made dinner for us—penne with vodka sauce—then we kissed on the couch until Dad got back from teaching.

"I wish we had more time, James," I whisper now. "It wasn't enough. You were everything to me. And I'll always love you."

When I get back in the car, I feel empty, and my feet sting from the cold.

Izzy jacks the heat up to full blast.

"Thanks for driving me, Iz," I say. "I know this isn't exactly a fun way to spend the afternoon."

"I wish I could make it better, Tess. These last few months have been the worst."

I nod and stare out the window. The cold wind lifts the edge of the Lightning McQueen card. It flutters like it's waving good-bye.

After more wrong turns, we find the exit, and Izzy drives to our regular pizza place.

"Still want to be my Galentine?" she asks, parallel parking like a pro.

"Of course!" I don't tell her that I'm dreading seeing any happy couples inside.

Carlo, the owner, greets us the way he always does. "Izzy! Tess! Have a seat, have a seat!" He ushers us toward a table in the back.

We're so cold, we stay bundled in our coats and scarves.

"Look at you, ladies, all grown up! I remember when you'd come in here when you were this big!" He holds his hand even with the tabletop. "I know, I know, you don't need menus. You'll have the usual?"

We nod in unison.

"Just tell me one thing: Why aren't you two beauties out on dates tonight? I've got some nice nephews I'd be happy to fix you up with."

"You know what we need instead, Carlo? Garlic knots! Right away!" Izzy says without missing a beat. Then, as if she can read my mind, adds, "Actually, you know what? Can we get everything to go?"

We take the food back to Izzy's house. When we're finished eating, we sit on the basement floor and let Freddy, the puppy, lick our faces. For a few minutes, everything feels slightly less terrible.

Spring Break

When I first woke up after I dreamt of James at the beach, I felt sad. He hadn't really said anything about us, not even a simple "I miss you," or "I love you." It's weird and lame to be mad at someone for not saying the right thing in *your* dream. But that's the thing about emotions, they don't always make sense, and yet that doesn't make them any less real.

But then I realized it wasn't about me. It was about Emmett.

"Emmett's birthday is coming up," was one of only two sentences James spoke in my dream. I couldn't ignore it.

For his last birthday, I made a non-dairy ice cream cake using coconut milk, bananas, and frozen berries. It couldn't compete with Carvel, but it was pretty good, and Emmett was thrilled with the toy car cake-toppers I found online. He jumped up and down as we sang softly to him. When he blew out the candles—something he'd struggled to do only a year before—I made a wish: that I would be there, beside James, feeling like part of that family, for many more celebrations.

There's no chance of that now. But still, I wanted to do something. So I sent Emmett a box of things I thought he'd like. A bright yellow taxi, a coloring book, crayons, and some of his favorite snack bars—ones that fit the guidelines of his diet but don't taste like cardboard. I wrapped everything and mailed it but didn't enclose a note. I wouldn't want to confuse him since I haven't seen him in months and don't know when or if I will again.

I hoped my present made him smile. But the real gift I wanted to give Emmett was a new friend. As soon as Rob told me he was on his way to ice hockey practice that afternoon on Valentine's Day, it gave me an idea. Even though agreeing to go to the prom with him felt like I was betraying James, connecting Rob and Emmett made it seem okay. I like to think James would've approved.

I found Rob the day after Valentine's and explained that Emmett loved to skate. One good thing about all the awful news coverage, Rob knew everything and understood why Mrs. Potter might not want to see me again, which saved me from repeating every terrible detail.

I gave Rob their address and asked him to introduce himself as a classmate of James' who hoped Emmett might want to skate with him sometime. I told him about the pond behind their condo complex. I taught him Emmett's secret signals—how he squeals when he's happy, presses his fists to his face when he's frustrated, and licks his gloves when he's thirsty. I told him how he likes to make playlists and skate to music, but only if it isn't too loud.

"It's cool, Tess," Rob said. "My neighbor has autism. I get it."

He and Emmett have skated together a handful of times already. Rob said Mrs. Potter was surprised but glad to meet him. He told me she stood by the pond and almost smiled while he taught Emmett a couple of hockey moves. Now that it's milder outside, they meet at an indoor rink. Rob texted me a photo from their last outing, the grin on Emmett's face made me feel something close to happiness for the first time in months.

"Thanks, Rob," I wrote. "You have no idea how much this means to him. And to me."

"Happy to do it," he texted back. "When we're finished, this kid will be the next Henrik Lundqvist."

I had no idea who that was, but it sounded promising.

With Izzy's help, I sent a note to Mrs. Potter. For weeks, I'd been composing a letter in my head, but it never sounded right. I wanted to tell her how sorry I was, how much I loved James, how I missed hanging out with Emmett and spending time with her, how, if she'd ever forgive me, I'd like to start over. I needed her to know that I would give anything to go back in time and change everything if I could.

"I think it's best to keep it short," Izzy said.

As usual, she was right. So this is what I wrote:

Dear Mrs. Potter,

Words can't express how truly sorry I am. James was the best person I've ever met. Not a second goes by that I don't think of him.

I know that he was smart, kind, compassionate, and courageous because of you and Emmett. I miss you both, too — more than you can imagine. If you can ever find a way to forgive me and my family, I'd like to be a part of your lives again.

But if I don't hear back from you, I understand. I'll respect your wishes and not contact you again.

Thinking of you,

Tess

She hasn't responded. I don't know if she will. And I suppose I don't blame her if she never does. But I had to send it. The thought of running into her at the cemetery or in town without having told her how I feel... Well, that would destroy me.

Not that I go out much these days. It's mid-March, and the mountains of snow in the parking lot behind our unit have dwindled down to softballs. It's spring break, but I'm not going anywhere. Dad doesn't get any time off from his new job yet. I'm still avoiding Mom, but Dad said she's gone back to work too. This time for herself. He said she's not ready to deal with the stress that comes with a big firm. I tried not to roll my eyes because it seemed like she ate that stress for breakfast, lunch, and dinner for years.

Izzy's gone to Carol's house in Connecticut for the break. Carol's mom is taking them for a second look at a few colleges they both like. Izzy invited me to join them, but I'm still undecided about the whole idea of college, though I haven't told that to anyone but Daffy.

Last night, I went to Home Depot and bought some tulips. I'm rushing the season. Spring only just began, but I want time to speed up. I need years to fly by, even though I know there's no guarantee that will make things hurt any less. I'm going to plant some in pots to place around our makeshift porch, which is really just a cement rectangle. I'll put some under my bedroom window, which faces the street. Anything to break up the endless shit brown of this complex.

I shovel potting soil into a bright blue planter when I hear a man's voice I don't recognize. "Tess?"

I'm scared to look up. Once Luke's trial got underway, reporters started popping up everywhere— not just at school, but outside the condo, at physical therapy, in Izzy's driveway. I never know if some asshole might leap out of the bushes and ask if I'm following the trial, if Mom's out of rehab, how I plan to honor James' memory, and a whole bunch of other questions that are no one else's business. At first, it seemed like something I'd never get used to, and each time it happened, it took me a while to recover. I can only imagine how awful it is for Mrs. Potter. But now I just accept it, ignore it, and move on with my day.

"Tess? Tess Porter?" he says again.

I squint up at the tall figure, the sun in my eyes momentarily blinding me. I stick my small shovel in the planter, stand up too quickly, and immediately feel dizzy. A headrush made worse by the fact that he looks so familiar, but like a thinner version of someone I've seen before. Just as I'm putting it together, he says, "I'm Nick. Nick Lawrence."

The ground shifts. My hands start to shake. For a second, I think I misheard him. But no. I have a flash of Lydia pulling his photo out of her folder. The perfect teeth, the freckles sprinkled across his nose. They're right there in front of me.

"Sorry," he continues. "I didn't mean to catch you off-guard. I wanted to talk to you. I don't know if now is a good time."

"No, I'm—it's okay," I stammer. I don't say that there's never a good time, that there'll probably never be a good time again.

Staring at him, my knees buckle. I wave my hand, motioning for us to sit in the red plastic Adirondack chairs Dad and I picked up at the grocery store last week. As we slide into the seats, I grip the armrest to steady my trembling fingers.

"I didn't mean to startle you —"

"No, it's fine. I'm fine," I lie, both curious and terrified about why he's here.

"I don't really know where to begin, so I'm just going to start if that's okay?" he says. I nod, and he takes a deep breath.

"That night at the airport, Tess—you leaving with that maniac—it's my fault. I'm tortured by it. I can't sleep. I don't eat. My grades suck."

I think he means because he asked James for a ride, but he seems so agitated, there has to be more to it.

"What do you mean?" I ask, still unsure I want to hear the answer.

"So, you know how I fell asleep at the gate at O'Hare and didn't realize my wallet and phone had been stolen until I landed in Newark? Well, I started freaking out. I thought, 'Who do I know who lives close and is nice enough to pick me up?' Right away, I thought of James because we'd talked about possibly getting together over the break.

"So I go up to this girl—woman, really—who's checking her phone. I asked if I could borrow it to make a call. I explained the whole thing to her, and while we were talking, her flight got delayed again. So she asked if I wanted to get a drink with her. Since I had no wallet, she said she'd buy. One beer turned to four, maybe five. I was hungover from the night before, so it was like a hair-of-the-dog thing, and I felt like celebrating because finals were over, and I thought I'd done pretty well. The airport was decked out for the holidays, and everything felt kind of festive, like the perfect homecoming."

I don't want to interrupt, but I feel like he's stalling, and I wish he'd fast forward to what he came to tell me.

"So I'm hanging out with Jess, that's her name. She's twenty-three, an art teacher, and we're talking about our crazy families and our new year's plans. She's making me laugh, and she's buying one round after another, and suddenly I say, 'Wait, what time is it?' And she looks at her phone and says '6:15' and I'm like 'Holy shit, James' girlfriend is going to be looking for me.' So I chug the last bit of beer, give her my number, even though I don't have a phone, and start running. The whole airport's packed with stranded travelers. You saw it."

He's drumming his fingers nervously on the arm of the chair. I don't know what he usually sounds like, but his voice cracks every few words. I should offer him a glass of water, but I just want him to get to the part that brought him here.

"I'm stumbling down the escalator on my way to baggage claim, and I think I see you. Even in my drunken haze, I recognized you from pictures in James' dorm room. You were wearing this big black coat, but your hair caught my eye. I was about to yell your name when I see this guy walk up to you and start talking, so I think, 'Oh, wait that can't be Tess,' but then you turned, and I saw your face. I knew it was you."

He puts his face in his palms and takes a breath so big it's like he's been underwater for minutes. Then he looks directly at me.

"I watched you shake his hand and then I just stood there like a selfish idiot saying to myself: 'Why's she leaving with him? That can't be Tess.' Of course, I knew it was you, but I didn't want it to be because I wanted to go back to the bar, to keep talking to Jess. I watched you shake that guy's hand and walk out of the airport. I knew you were leaving with the wrong guy, and I did nothing to stop you.

"When I first saw the news, I knew I had to go to the police. But I did it more to clear myself. My name was in your phone. You were there because of me. I didn't tell them that I saw you, that I just watched you go…"

As his words settle over me, he looks down at his shoes. His feet bounce involuntarily, it seems. He's waiting for me to say something, but I have no words.

Of course, I'm upset that Nick saw the whole thing and did nothing to stop it, yet it probably wouldn't have mattered. Luke would've followed us home. Would James, Nick, and I have been able to overpower Luke and his gun? Possibly. Or, maybe Nick would be dead, too. We'll never know. I think of something Luke said as he stood in my living room, gun pointed at my head, words I only remembered a few weeks ago.

"You're probably wondering why I went all the way to the airport, why I didn't just sneak in and hide, wait for the right moment to make myself known," he'd growled, that smirk lurking in the corner of his mouth. "Sure, I could've hung out here until you and the actual Nick Lawrence showed up. But then I thought, 'If I can pull this off, pretend to be this other guy, what a mindfuck that would be, wouldn't it?' And didn't you and your family deserve that, Tess? I wanted you to feel the way I did when the cops showed up at my door at the crack of dawn and asked me to 'come on down to the station,'—like I'm on fucking 'The Price Is Right!'—and collect my dead father's personal belongings."

I can picture him if I close my eyes, smell the sweat pouring off him, feel the spit on my cheek as he hissed, "I wanted you to feel shock, confusion, fear. And you made it so easy, Tess. I should thank you, actually. Seeing the terror on your faces, it was like an early Christmas gift. Probably the only one I'll get this year."

I shake my head to clear it of that horrible memory. Nick looks up, cued by my sudden movement, and braces for me to speak.

"It wouldn't have mattered," I say. "Nothing could've stopped it. Him. Luke. He was determined to hurt my family, and he had nothing to lose. Don't blame yourself. Plus, nothing can change what's happened."

Tears spill down my cheeks, and I say the thing that I keep telling myself. The phrase that I hope will help me let go of at least some of the rage that bubbles up inside me when I least expect it. "Nothing's going to bring James back. No amount of guilt or sadness. No matter how long you beat yourself up, it doesn't fix anything."

"I tried to call Mrs. Potter a hundred times, but she hasn't returned my messages."

"I've written, but I haven't heard back either," I say.

We sit in silence for a few more moments. The sun is directly overhead. It should be warming us yet I'm ice cold. Power walkers stride past us, talking about a reality show. They wave—neither of us waves back.

"I don't know why, but I felt like I had to tell you. I had to tell someone. I know it doesn't change anything. But I just couldn't be alone with it anymore."

I nod as Nick stands up.

"Thank you for listening, Tess. I hope someday you can forgive me."

There's a lump in my throat, I can't bring myself to say his name or anything at all, so I lift my hand in a half-hearted wave and watch him walk away.

If Nick had come to see me a few months ago, I'd probably have screamed in his face. I'd have wanted to gouge his eyes with my garden shovel, call him every swear word I know, tell him I hate him and that everything is all his fault. Add to his guilt. Make him carry some of mine for a while.

But I don't do any of those things. I just sit and breathe. I've been seeing that grief counselor Dad suggested. I didn't want to at first. It was actually Grams, Izzy's grandmother, who talked me into it. On Valentine's Day, she'd called me into the kitchen while everyone else was watching TV.

"Ah, Tess, c'mere and have a seat for a moment, love," she said. Because of her Irish brogue, Grams can get me to do just about anything.

I was reluctant, fearing she was going to suggest we say some prayers to St. Valentine together. But instead of her usual rosary beads, she pulled out a box of Russell Stover chocolates.

"Don't tell the others, but there's a man at the senior center—Ralph is his name—he's sweet on me. Gave me these this morning right after Bingo. He included a little note complimenting my sparkly eyes." Grams smiled and batted her eyes, bright blue just like Izzy's, at me. "Lovely man, hair as white as an arctic fox. I don't have the heart to tell him he hasn't got a chance in the world with me. Anyway, dear, I thought you could use a caramel."

I took one and she told me how after her husband, Izzy's beloved Grampy, died, she couldn't get out of bed.

She didn't put on lipstick or even go to the beauty parlor for her standing Saturday appointment. After several months of floating around in a fog, Izzy's mom dragged her to see a grief counselor, "kicking and screaming," Grams said.

"Okay, not really kicking and screaming, more like limping and wailing. And it actually helped—the talking about it. I'd put so much energy into keeping my feelings buried, being proud and strong. But that makes you weary, love. And my insides were turning to stone from trying to act so brave all the time. And I wasn't even foolin' anyone!

"You see, Tess, what I learned is that there's no quick remedy—one day you're grieving, the next you're not. Believe me, if there were, I'd have found it!" She threw back her tiny white head and laughed. "But the talking about it, it made it easier for me to put one foot in front of the other, to look ahead a little more, and behind me a little less. And if a stubborn old bird like me can be helped, I'm sure a bright young woman such as yourself can find her way to feeling better."

"Thanks, Grams," I said.

"Have another caramel, dear, you could use it. Just don't tell anyone where you got it." She smiled and batted her eyes again.

When I went home that night, I asked Dad to make an appointment for me. Grams was right. It did help, with the sadness, and the guilt, and the anger. Monica—the grief counselor—she explains it like this: I could go on hating Luke forever. But that hate is like a rock that's stuck in my shoe. It starts out like a boulder, and my foot feels uncomfortable, pinched all the time. If I keep walking around with it, I might wear it down 'til maybe it becomes the size of gravel, and, later, a pebble. But I'll always feel it. I'll still know it's there, and while it is, it's wearing me down too, piercing, puncturing, roughing up my skin. And just generally making me miserable.

"But you have the power to stop at any time, Tess, and empty your shoe. Whether it's a boulder or a pebble, you don't need to carry that stone with you. Let go of what doesn't serve you. When you choose not to forgive someone, you're hurting yourself as much or more than you're hurting them," she told me.

It made sense.

And what about Mom? Have I forgiven her? I'm working on it.

That night, I try to get Nick Lawrence out of my head. I text Izzy to ask how her trip's going. They're on their way back home, but they stopped at some fancy spa and got facials.

"The lady who gave me mine asked if I'm a landscaper, that's how gross my pores are! Do not tell Becca!" she writes back.

I scroll through social media before going to sleep. The ice hockey team won the state finals. I didn't go to the game, but I see the score on Instagram beside a photo of Rob and his teammates hugging as best they can with all that padding, sticks raised high in the air.

I text Rob.

Congratulations!

We've become good friends. Since I asked for his help with Emmett, they've skated together once, sometimes twice a week. Seeing how committed he is and hearing him talk about Emmett's progress, makes me like him more than I ever expected to, which is good but also kind of weird.

"You totally have a crush on him, Tess. Just admit it," Izzy said when I showed her the video he sent me of Emmett skating backwards.

"Stop! He's a really nice guy who's doing something that makes me feel a tiny bit less awful about life," I tell her.

"And that right there makes him completely lovable—not to mention, he's totally ripped."

"I hadn't noticed," I lied. Everyone who's ever seen Rob has noticed.

"James would want you to be happy, Tess," Izzy said.

When Izzy says "James," it feels like ripping off a scab, opening a wound. It's crazy to think that the name that once made my heart beat faster is the same one that now shatters it.

"It's okay to like Rob, Tess, that's all I'm saying. Hell, James would love him for what he's done for Emmett."

I push Izzy out of my mind too, put my phone down, and turn off the light. Daffy circles around, trying to find just the right spot, settling firmly against my back.

I'm drifting off to sleep when I hear a noise outside. It comes again—a knock at the window.

My heart stops. Some nights when I can't fall asleep, I think about Luke, about him letting himself into our home, about him getting out of prison, finding me, finishing what he started.

I creep to the window, Daffy follows me, my furry bodyguard. At this moment, I wish she were a Rottweiler instead of a house cat. I pull the blinds back slightly, my heart in my throat.

It's Rob.

I raise the blinds a few inches and open the window.

"Hey, sorry to startle you. You weren't asleep, were you?" he asks.

"It's 1 a.m. so, no, my cat and I were just doing a little yoga followed by some light bookkeeping."

"You have a cat? That's cool. Some people don't like cats. But I think cats are dy-no-mite!"

I can smell the beer on his breath as it mixes with the cool night air. He sways a bit and holds the windowsill to steady himself.

"Congratulations on your win. Looks like you've been celebrating?"

"Thanks! What a game! I wish you'd been there. And, yeah, Chip's older brother got us a couple of cases. Their dad lives over that way." He waves his arm toward another block of mud-colored condos then spins around. "Or maybe it's over that way. Anyway, he's a cool guy, doesn't really care what we do, so the whole team's staying there tonight."

"Sounds fun," I say, trying to act like I don't notice the way the moonlight shines in his soft brown eyes.

"You know, I came here to tell you that I used to think of you as a goofy girl with great hair, but you're a really good person, Tess Porter. I know you've been through a shit-ton of bad stuff lately, and I just wanted to say that with Emmett, and with you, I'm not trying to take his place. I just remember that before everything happened, you had a really great smile, and I'd like to see it again."

He leans in to kiss me. For a second, I panic. Do I shut the window, close the blinds, grab Daffy, jump back in bed, and hide under the covers? Or, do I stop fighting everything and let it happen? I choose that, and it's amazing.

When I eventually pull away, he looks down, and then looks up at me guiltily.

"What? What's the matter?"

"I'm sorry," he says. "I think I just crushed all your tulips."

"It's okay," I say. "It was worth it."

This Is How It Ends

We're at The Cheesecake Factory when it happens. Izzy and I have spent most of the afternoon at the mall prom dress shopping with her older sister Becca, who's declared herself our personal stylist. As we were leaving Izzy's house, she announced she'd be joining us to offer her "fashion insight" on everything from dresses and hairstyles to shoes and clutch purses — essential for carrying makeup and phones, she insisted.

"I can sort of trust you, Tess," Becca said. "But without me, Izzy will try to wear Birkenstocks and her field hockey costume."

"It's a uniform, and I like to be comfortable, what can I say?" Izzy snorted, pretending to be offended.

We're taking a break from trying on dresses only Taylor Swift can afford—gowns that make us feel like we should be headed to the Golden Globes instead of our local Hilton—when I see it.

The restaurant's packed, so we're sitting at a hightop table in the bar area, waiting for our strawberry lemonades, avocado egg rolls, and chicken potstickers when Sally Sheffield appears on the TV in the corner. The screen is so big, her head looks like a Thanksgiving parade float.

"Jesus Christ, doesn't that bitch ever take a day off?" Becca says.

Over the past few months, I've realized that there are very few places left where you're not bombarded by televisions.

The scene jumps to a courtroom. Luke stands beside the lawyer the judge appointed for him after he was found unfit to represent himself. His head is shaved, and he's wearing a baggy black suit. Both make him look thinner and older. Though he barely resembles the lunatic who played Scrabble with me before he murdered my boyfriend, the stoop of his shoulders and his sideways glance bring it all back. I'd run to the ladies' room to throw up if I weren't frozen in place, paralyzed, waiting to see what comes next.

We can't hear Sally's voice, which is fine with me, but we can read the words that appear in bold letters at the bottom of the screen: Luke Miller to Serve 25-Year Prison Term.

I read the captions as they pop up. "Under New Jersey's No Early Release Act, Miller has no chance for release on parole before he serves eighty-five percent of the twenty-five-year term. Is that all James Potter's life was worth?" The screen jumps back to Sally. Her mouth hangs open in a scream directed at the panel of attorneys, each poised to interject.

I can do this simple equation. He'll be in prison for twenty-one-and-a-quarter years. Nothing compared to what was taken from us. A blink.

Dad told me last night that the sentencing was scheduled for today, but it had already been postponed once, so I tried to put it out of my mind. Izzy didn't say anything, but now I wonder if it's the reason she suddenly decided to skip lacrosse practice and insisted we go shopping.

The camera pans to the back of the small courtroom where Mrs. Potter is consoled by a man who hands her fresh tissues and looks so much like her, he must be her brother.

Mr. Potter, seated several rows behind them, hangs his head. In sorrow? Relief that one small portion of this hell is over? Or, regret that he was rarely there for his son the way he should've been?

Words spool out beneath Sally's fast-moving mouth. "Again, where's the girlfriend? This disturbed young man might be going up the river for more than two decades, but the question remains: Where was Theresa Porter today? Why wouldn't the young woman whose life was spared when her boyfriend took the bullet for her show up today to see this bit of lukewarm justice served? Can anyone answer me that?"

I can, Sally. I'm a coward. I couldn't bear to be in the same room with Luke Miller again. I still have nightmares about him. In some, he's in the kitchen with a corkscrew in his hand. But instead of wine, blood flows from the bottle, thick and smelling of copper. In others, he's in the living room, wildly swinging the fireplace poker, hacking off branches of our Christmas tree. They fly into the fireplace as gray-black smoke surrounds us, and I can't see where he's going next. I wake up choking and screaming.

I'm afraid to see Mrs. Potter in person, too. I know it's pre-recorded footage, that she isn't live there now on the other side of the monitor, but her sorrow is so intense, it spills out of the screen and through me 'til I nearly slide off the barstool. She never responded to my note, and I didn't want mine to be one more face that adds to her misery today.

The picture cuts back to the courtroom where the camera zooms in on Danielle, Luke's older sister. Alone in the row behind him, she's crying into her palm, grieving the loss of the last member of her immediate family. She extends her hand to touch her brother's shoulder. He shrugs it off.

I've tried to ignore the media coverage of everything related to this. I've closed my eyes and scrolled past all the pseudo-journalists' clickbait headlines: *Holiday Horror: 3 Teens Terrorized, 2 Shot, 1 Murdered by Revenge Killer; Possible Ménage à Trois Ends With Bullet Through Boyfriend; Mistletoe & Murder: Is Mom's Infidelity to Blame in Death of Innocent Teen?*

I've hated the random people from our town who turned their tears on and off for the camera, pretending to be James' best friends, eulogizing him on social media.

I've looked away in disgust at all the celebrity psychiatrists who talk over each other on tabloid-style shows, so excited to share their theories about the conditions they believe Mr. Miller and Luke likely shared—depression, bipolar disorder, suicidal ideation, impulsivity— ticking them off like items on a grocery list.

It all makes me sick.

But the one person I can't take my eyes off is Danielle. She looks like a grown-up version of the girl in the Christmas cards. When Mr. Miller said she'd gone to art school, my brain defaulted to stereotypes. I imagined her with blue hair and a dozen holes in her face. In reality, her shoulder-length hair is the same deep brown as Luke's. Unlike Luke's dark, evasive eyes, Danielle's are a light hazel. But now, just like his were as he stood in my kitchen howling, "This is how it ends!" they're full of pain. She's lost everything too.

One night, when I couldn't sleep, I put in my earbuds and watched the single interview Danielle has granted.

Even though I was sitting on my bed, my limbs went weak as I waited for the video to load. I was afraid of the answers, but a couple of questions haunted me: Did she hate my mother for being what I consider that very first domino—the piece that caused everything to collapse? Did she have any idea my father had started a novel based on her father's tragic end? And, did she, like her brother, think we got what we deserved? I needed to know.

Before it began, the interviewer, Julianne Sanders, anchor of a long-running nighttime news program, introduced the segment by noting that Danielle only agreed to speak as a way to "shine a spotlight on the importance of recognizing the warning signs of depression and suicide."

Though it was clear from the start that Julianne wanted Danielle to say she hated my family, she didn't come right out and ask. Instead, she tiptoed around it by asking, "You've experienced devastating losses in the past year, Danielle. Is there a moment that you can point to that served as the catalyst, the thing that set this tragedy in motion? Is there one person you blame for all of this?"

Danielle inhaled sharply, then exhaled. A trick I recognized. She was trying her best to keep it together. I waited, my heart pounding as I gnawed at what was left of my cuticles, expecting to hear Danielle trash my family.

"I blame myself, Julianne," she said. "When our mom was first diagnosed with cancer, I was in my late teens. I was totally focused on getting into art school. I don't want to say that I didn't grasp the severity of her condition, but I think it was more that I went into a state of shock, or maybe it was denial. I sort of adopted a this-isn't-really-happening attitude, almost for self-preservation. After she passed, I was offered my dream job, and I moved to the West Coast. Selfishly, I wanted to get away. Make a fresh start."

Julianne sat perfectly still, reminding me of Daffy right before she pounces on an unsuspecting spider. The silence was too much. Danielle's shoulders began to shake as she cried. "I should've been there for them—my dad and my brother. I knew when I talked to them that they seemed so down, so sad, but I was, too. How could we not be, you know? We'd all just lost this amazing woman."

Danielle took another deep breath, smiled sadly, and dabbed her eyes with her fingertips.

"When we were little, my mom would write us these funny poems on the napkins she stuck in our lunchboxes. She was always volunteering at our schools, at our church, too. She'd do anything for anyone, that's the kind of person she was."

"You say your father and brother were sad when you talked to them, but then you began to notice a change in your dad. Tell me about that," Julianne said, attempting to frown with concern, an impossibility thanks to extensive cosmetic work.

"Over the summer, my dad started to sound happier. He told me he was seeing someone. I thought it felt fast, too soon, but I didn't say anything because I was relieved that he was doing better. He was trying to convince my brother to enroll in a technical school since he's always been really good with computers. I thought things were improving."

"Little did you know, things were about to get a lot worse." Julianne shook her head and turned down the corners of her mouth, attempting to appear sympathetic.

"After my dad's accident, I knew my brother was in a bad place. We'd Skype once, sometimes twice a week. I tried to encourage him to get help. Maybe find a support group, or go talk to someone, but he always told me he was doing fine. Then one day, I noticed he seemed different. More confident. Maybe determined is a better word. He told me he'd come up with a plan. I thought he was talking about going back to school, following up on what our dad wanted for him. I didn't ask what he meant. I never pushed for details. I chose to believe he would be okay even though I think, deep down, I knew he wasn't. I was having a hard time with our dad's death, and I used that as an excuse not to deal. My brother needed me, and I wasn't there for him."

She paused before looking directly into the camera. "The reason I'm talking about this is because I wish I'd done something to help my father and my brother when I had the chance. If you or someone you love is depressed, or struggling with terrible, dark thoughts, please encourage them to get help. Don't wait until it's too late."

Julianne shuddered and closed the segment by reading hotline numbers viewers could call for assistance.

I couldn't sleep after I watched it. I kept thinking about how we were pieces of the same ugly puzzle, Mom, Dad, Nick, Danielle, and I, forever connected through guilt and shame brought on by our own selfishness. Mom wanted to feel good about herself again, so she encouraged a man she knew was vulnerable. Dad wanted to believe he could still write the great American novel, so he stole Mr. Miller's heartbreaking story, not realizing his wife's role in it. Nick wanted to talk to a woman in a bar, so he watched me leave with the wrong guy. Danielle wanted to start a new life, so she overlooked her brother's pain. I wanted one night alone with my boyfriend, so I ditched my best friend and encouraged James to not tell his mom he was arriving home a day early. If we'd all done something differently, James might still be here.

"Tess?" Izzy squeezes my arm. I don't know how long she's been saying my name, the white noise inside The Cheesecake Factory creating a steady hum.

Sally Sheffield has been replaced by a truck commercial. Our smiling waiter arrives and places drinks, appetizers, and plates in front of us.

"Hope you ladies are hungry!"

Emptying my shoe

Dad's right, I can't dodge Mom forever. It's been almost four months since I've seen her.

"She'd really like to do something with you, especially this weekend, Tess," he told me at dinner on Tuesday. "Your eighteenth birthday is a big deal."

"How can you still talk to her?" I didn't look at him when I asked, just kept pushing mushy peas around my plate. "I don't get it."

Dad hasn't told me what's up with their relationship, and normally, I wouldn't ask, but I'm sick of him trying to guilt me into seeing her.

"I know it may be hard to understand, but I have to own my part in this, Tess," he said, resting his fork on his plate and trying to get me to meet his eyes. "For so long, it was all about me—my success, my failure, my desperate need to feel good about myself again. Your mom backed me one thousand percent, but it wasn't supposed to go on like that indefinitely. I lost sight of her feelings, her needs. I'm a huge part of what went wrong. If I don't learn from that, then nothing will ever get any better."

I thought about his words. He had a point. If I continued to ignore Mom, pretend she didn't exist, where was that getting me? I certainly didn't feel any less bitter when I thought about her. I was still walking around with that rock in my shoe, as Monica, my grief counselor, would say. Maybe it was time to stop and empty it?

I agree to meet Mom on my birthday. It's a Saturday this year, so I suggest breakfast, easily the fastest meal you can have while dining out. We meet at a café that's a ten-minute drive away. Everything in our town still reminds me of James.

My nerves jangle, and I'm gripping the steering wheel so tightly my knuckles turn white as I parallel park. It feels unnatural to not want to see the person who gave you life—especially on your birthday—the first guest at your tea parties, the woman who taught you how to French braid your hair, the one who kept calling you "sweet potato" even after you begged her to stop five thousand times. Yet how can I make those memories blend in with the most recent one, the one in which she said, "James is dead, Tess. I thought you knew."

It's unusually warm for mid-April, and as I walk up to the restaurant, Mom is already there, sitting under an umbrella. I fight the urge to bite my nails. She stands when she sees me. She looks better than she has in ages, healthy. She opens her arms to hug me, and instinctively, I back up, pretending to swat away a bee. She takes the hint and doesn't try again.

We sit and, mercifully, a chipper waitress takes our coffee order immediately. I'm grateful when she sticks around to run through a long list of specials because it kills time.

On the drive, I decided I'd let Mom do all the heavy lifting here. During those months after Mr. Miller died when she'd be home sitting on the couch, her glass of wine always within reach, it was up to me to try to keep every conversation going. I'm done with that.

"So! Happy birthday!" she says, smiling nervously, fiddling with her napkin, almost dropping her fork.

"Thanks," I say. To make this any easier for her would feel like I'm betraying James.

We sit in awkward silence, pretending to read our menus and watching robins flit in and out of a nearby tree. The waitress returns to take our order: avocado toast for Mom, brioche French toast with berries for me. With that out of the way, Mom leans in.

"I've missed you, Tess." She smiles at me again, but I refuse to return it. I keep my arms folded across my chest, even though I know it makes me appear as hostile as I am.

"Tess, I don't expect you to forgive me, but I hope you know how sorry I am about everything that's happened. Every bit of it, Tess. I behaved like a—"

I wait for her to insult me by saying, "teenager."

"—I behaved in a way that is completely inexcusable for an adult, for a married, adult woman. I got swept up in something." She looks down at her full cup of coffee and then back up at me. "No, that's not accurate. 'Swept

347

up' makes it sound like I bear no responsibility, and that's not true. I knew what I was doing, I just didn't know how to stop it.

"I was at a point where I'd begun to feel invisible. Your father had spent years holed up in a room obsessing about his writing. You had your own friends, your own life, you didn't need me as much. My career had hit a plateau. Then, Ned came back, and he was in such a bad place, Tess. I wanted to help him. I wanted someone to see me as a whole person again. And he did. And then I ended up hurting him even more, making things worse. For everyone."

My leg bounces beneath the table. I cross and uncross my legs to make it stop.

A tear slips down her cheek. She wipes it away with her napkin and takes a sip of coffee. Seeing that I'm still not talking, she continues, "I'm so sorry, Tess. I know James meant everything to you. And I know I wasn't there for you the way I should've been when you were in the hospital. I completely understand why you wouldn't want to talk to me. I know we have a very long way to go before we can ever get back to the way things were before, but I'd like to try."

I bite my lip, determined not to cry as the waitress brings our breakfast.

"Extra syrup?" she asks.

"I'd like that," I say.

"Be right back with some!"

"Oh, sorry, I was talking to my mom." I look at Mom. "I'd like to try to get back to the way things were before, too."

She smiles. We eat in a not-uncomfortable silence. When we're almost done, she leans forward and places an envelope next to my plate. My birthday card.

"Thanks," I say, "and thanks for breakfast, too. Dad's idea of French toast is, well, you know, basically toast with him saying, 'For you, mademoiselle!'"

Mom grins and then looks more serious. "He mentioned that you haven't done much cooking lately. Or any baking, either."

"Yeah, I haven't felt too inspired."

"Maybe this will help." She points toward the card.

I open it, and wish I'd taken AP French like James and Izzy. The words "On Rue Tatin" stare back at me, looking vaguely familiar.

"You're going to a five-day cooking class in France in July, Tess. It's a birthday and graduation gift. Oh, and it's from Dad, too," she says.

"But how?" I ask, stunned as I look at the brochure: *Cook with the finest local and seasonal ingredients, enjoy sumptuous meals, each accompanied by artisanal cheeses.*

"Well, I remembered you read about it last summer on that food website and you were so excited about it. We thought you could use a vacation doing something you love, something you're great at. Some of my happiest memories are of the times you made teacakes for me in your Easy-Bake oven. I should've known then you were destined to be a chef."

349

"But how did Dad afford—"

"You don't know? He sold his records. He's moved into the twenty-first century and gotten himself a Spotify account."

It hits me that I never even realized the albums didn't make the move to the condo.

"We love you, Tess. We want you to follow your dream, and even if that means standing over a hot stove, wearing a hairnet, we fully support you."

When we leave the restaurant, we hug goodbye and the whole drive back, I remember the smell of those teacakes and how Mom would take bite after bite and say, "Mmmm! That's so yummy, Tess!" even when I'd burned them beyond recognition.

Days later, I walk in from watching Izzy's final lacrosse game and see Dad working at his laptop at the table. Daffy comes to greet me like she always does. I squat down and scratch her velvety ears.

"Hey, Tess!" He stands and walks over to me. "How was your day?"

"Okay. Izzy's team lost, so they don't advance, but she scored a goal. I think she's just glad to be done with it. How was your day?"

"This came for you." Dad hands me a letter. We both recognize the return address, which explains why he's frowning.

I walk toward my bedroom, scooping up Daffy for moral support.

"I'm just on the other side of the door if you need me," he says.

"Thanks," is all I can manage. I sink into the beanbag chair and rub Daffy's chin so she won't leave me as I open the envelope slowly with one hand.

Tess,

Thank you for the package for Emmett. You know him so well. Those are all his favorites.

It took me a little while to put it together, but now I'm certain you were the one who sent Rob Wallace to us. Thank you for that. He's made Emmett laugh again, and that has brought me some comfort during this unbearably difficult time.

We are struggling to get through every day, as I'm sure you are as well.

I wish the best for you, Tess. I really do. But I'm not ready to see you. I'm sorry if that sounds harsh. I hope that, in time, I will feel differently.

Forgive yourself and your family, Tess. None of this is your fault. No one could've anticipated this tragedy.

Move on and be happy. I know that's what James would want.

Emily Potter

My mouth feels like it's packed with cotton. My legs have turned to jelly. I don't know what I expected. She was never going to write, "Hey, Tess, thanks for reaching out! Don't worry, we're cool now. Why don't you come over Saturday?"

Still. It hurts. More than I'd expected.

I lean back and rest my head against the wall. I stop rubbing Daffy, but she stays in my lap anyway.

I think about Monica, about how at the end of every counseling session, she says, "You don't have to be so brave all the time, Tess. You're not alone. You're surrounded by people who love and care about you."

It makes me do something I normally wouldn't.

"Dad?" I yell, my voice cracking.

He pushes the door open gently a second later like he's been on the other side the whole time. Waiting. He sees my face, kneels beside me, and lets me sob into the shoulder of his soft, worn flannel, the one he wears when he's feeling inspired. Daffy dozes on my lap.

The three of us stay like that until I have no tears left.

If you saw the photos on Dad's phone or Izzy's Instagram, you'd have seen me smiling, looking happy and carefree. A young woman in a fancy dress on her way to the prom. You'd never know that with each pose, I was remembering a similar one from the year before. So much is the same. Everything is different.

Rob is undeniably cute in a tux, and, more importantly, he's funny and kind. Izzy and Carol look amazing together. A few guys, the ones I always suspected had a crush on Izzy, stare as they put together why she never flirted back with them. Then, they move on with their night. After two pre-parties filled with hovering parents and spiked punches, we arrive. The ballroom is beautiful, the band is impressive, and we dance. For maybe fifteen or twenty minutes—not in a row, but one at a time—I remember what it feels like. My life before. That unabashed, under-appreciated happiness.

Samira is here too, the date of a senior boy, a saxophonist in the wind ensemble. When the band plays "In the Mood," Rob lifts her in the air and swings her around while we stand back clapping and cheering. It's like they've spent months rehearsing a routine, and this is their "Dancing With the Stars" moment. I'm not surprised about Rob because I believe anyone who can ice skate backwards is probably full of secret talents, but when Samira lands gracefully, beaming, I ask her, "How did you learn to dance like that?"

"Honestly, Tess, did you forget that I am a musician?" she says with a sly smile. "I was born with natural rhythm."

She's gone back to playing the clarinet. "I'm doubling down on my practice time. Next year's state symphony? That first chair is all mine," she vows.

We leave early like most of our classmates and go to the beach. It's a hot June night, and no one can wait to dive into the chilly, dark water. After we swim beneath the light of the moon, we unpack our tents and camp on the sand in front of Rob's aunt and uncle's house.

In the morning, the sun beats down. I grab my towel and sit, watching the water as the waves build then break.

"Tess." I look around. No one else is up yet.

When I turn back, a seagull has joined me. He sits at the corner of my towel. Our eyes meet for a moment.

Then he spread his wings and soars into the cloudless blue sky.

In those moments when I feel guilty for returning Rob's smile, or laughing at something crazy that Izzy said, I think about Annie's words. "If you don't want to live for yourself, then live for me, Tess," and I realize she was right. Each second is too precious to waste.

Graduation is tomorrow. Mom and Dad will be there. Together, but not together, and that's okay.

I got into three of the six colleges I applied to but decided to take a gap year. I was never much of a student. After I come back from France, I'm hoping to work in a restaurant or café and decide what feels right from there.

I got a new journal, and now that my left hand is free from the cast, I'm really writing in it. Monica said it might help me process everything—find meaning again. Like the diary Lydia gave me, just knowing I have it and can stare at the unlined pages and get lost in my mind when I need to, is a comfort.

And maybe, after so many years of avoiding it, writing isn't so bad after all. Maybe thinking things through as if I were going to put them on paper is what brought me this far.

Dad, James, and every Language Arts teacher I ever had told me, "Write what you know," so maybe I'll write about this:

Maybe I'll write about how people keep secrets, dark ones—ones you'd never want to know, and that can be their undoing.

Maybe I'll write about how love can blindside you at any age and make you do things you'll regret, possibly for the rest of your life.

Maybe I'll write about how grief can drive you mad if you sit alone with it for too long.

Maybe I'll write about how friendship, old or new, can save your life if you let it.

Maybe I'll write about how to claw your way back into the light when darkness threatens to pull you under.

Maybe I'll write about how to keep moving forward when all you want to do is go back.

Maybe I'll write about how a true safe space is something you create deep in your soul. And once it's built, you must guard it fiercely.

Of course, I'll need to figure all that out first.

But I've got time.

Acknowledgements:

Attending The Leopardi Writing Conference spurred me to move this idea out of my head and onto the page. Thank you to Lain Hart and Thomas Cooney for organizing such a magical experience. Special thanks to Michael Gardner for reading early pages and a synopsis and having the vision to guide me toward a more graceful ending.

I would be lost without the thoughtful feedback of my writing group. Bonnie Taggart, Rose Casanova, and Deb McCoy, thank you for listening and for all your support along the way.

Thank you to my friends Alice and Jeff Ralston, Kris Pfeifer, and Celeste Romano for the kind words and endless encouragement. I'm indebted to Kiri Blakeley for serving as my cyber-therapist, commiserating about the challenges of the writing life.

I'm forever grateful to the team at Between the Lines. Cherie, Siân, Jace, Suzanne, thank you for helping to make this dream a reality and being an absolute pleasure to work with.

Finally, thanks to my parents for telling me to "go read a book," and my husband, Rich, and sons, Sam, Ben, and Charlie, who put up with me while I wrote one.

Liz Alterman is a writer who lives in New Jersey with her husband and three sons. This is her first young adult novel.

Follow her on Twitter at @LizAlterman

CPSIA information can be obtained
at www.ICGtesting.com
Printed in the USA
BVHW081554050821
613736BV00008B/311